OUT OF
JERUSALEM

OF GOODLY PARENTS

OUT OF JERUSALEM

VOLUME ONE

OF GOODLY PARENTS

a novel by

H. B. MOORE

Covenant Communications, Inc.

Cover image *My Father's House* © Al Rounds

Cover design copyrighted 2004 by Covenant Communications, Inc.

Published by Covenant Communications, Inc.
American Fork, Utah

This is a work of fiction. The characters, names, incidents, places, and dialogue are products of the author's imagination, and are not to be construed as real.

Printed in The United States of America
First Printing: August 2004

10 09 08 07 06 05 04   10 9 8 7 6 5 4 3 2 1

ISBN 1-59156-549-9

2004303619

I too, like Nephi, have been born of goodly parents.
Dedicated to my parents, Kent and Gayle Brown

ACKNOWLEDGMENTS

First and foremost, I would like to thank my husband, Chris, who has supported me from the beginning. His continual love and faith helped me believe in my writing. And thanks to my children, Kaelin, Kara, Dana, and Rose, who are my infinite sources of happiness.

Tremendous credit goes to my parents, who diligently read the sparse beginnings and answered many questions. Because of them, I was able to live and travel throughout the Middle East during my childhood. At the age of seventeen, I lived in Jerusalem for a year, sparking my interest in an ancient time and culture.

Appreciation extends to the staff at Covenant, namely Shauna Humphreys for her genuine kindness and support and Christian Sorensen for his insightful editing and assistance.

Through the League of Utah Writers, I met some wonderful authors who invited me into their writer's critique group. Special thanks to my critique group for their honest evaluations and encouragement—LuAnn Staheli, Stephanni Hicken, Annette Lyon, Jeff Savage, Lynda Keith, and Michelle Holmes—I couldn't have done it without you! And thanks to Amy Finnegan, whose review helped fine-tune the manuscript.

Lastly, my gratitude extends to the Book of Mormon scholars, including my father, who have spent their lives studying and sharing their insights for the benefit of others.

PREFACE

The sole purpose of the Book of Mormon is to convince Jews and Gentiles that Jesus is the Christ.

Through my personal love for the scriptures, namely the Book of Mormon, and respect for Lehi, Sariah, Nephi, Sam, and those who faithfully followed the Lord during this era, I have chosen to illustrate the historical and sacred events of First Nephi 1–16 in fictional form. This interpretation of Nephi and his family is in no way meant to replace or supersede the Book of Mormon itself or the scholars who have dedicated their lives to studying its doctrine.

I have read many noble works of those who have studied the scriptural accounts of Lehi and his family. Every moment of research has been enjoyable, but because of the scale of my project, I have not read all available sources. I have selected scholars who are well respected in the Mormon community. I regret if I have overlooked pertinent information. It has been my purpose to present the material in a manner that is generally credible. Very rarely have I taken the road less traveled. The majority of the time I have backed my own intuition with that of well-supported points of view.

I chose to give names to the female characters in the story. All of the women existed, however we only know the name of Lehi's wife, Sariah. Even though much of the experience of women in scriptural accounts is left unsaid, their contributions were indispensable to the society, particularly nomad society. Not only did they bear and raise children, they prepared meals, spun and wove clothing, braided mats, collected water, and gathered firewood. They also disassembled tents, loaded them onto camels, and set them up when the next camp was reached (Charles Doughty, *Travels in Arabia Deserta*, 1:257, 262).

Overall, this book is meant to illuminate the events that took place in First Nephi and perhaps add to the knowledge and possibilities that we as students of the scriptures entertain. It is my hope you will enjoy the easy narrative and fast-paced nature of this story, and in the end, the next time you open the Book of Mormon, vivid colors, sights, and sounds will reach into your heart, drawing you into the fascinating events.

Enjoy!

⊹—❧ CHAPTER 1 ❧—⊹

I, Nephi, having been born of goodly parents . . .
(1 NEPHI 1:1)

Orange fingers of light stretched across the Valley of Jehoshaphat, illuminating the bent backs of the Israelites who worked furiously against the setting sun. Harvest season was upon the city of Jerusalem once again. The Feast of the Tabernacles drew closer each day, and there was not a moment to spare.

Yet even the sinking sun didn't decrease the merciless heat in the eastern vineyards. Perspiration trickled between Nephi's tanned shoulder blades, settling at his waist. His muscles ached, and his throat was parched. Because of the recent plague spreading through Jerusalem, even wealthy sons had to work the fields. Though Nephi was no stranger to hard work, there was something different when one had to labor from dawn until dusk with little food or water.

Nephi stood and mopped his brow with the flaps of his turban, which draped loosely over his head. His hands and feet were stained with the rich purple juices from the grapes. Laman and Lemuel, his older brothers, still hadn't returned from their "water break." He should have guessed they'd tarry when he had seen the two unveiled girls approach his brothers just as they drank their fill. An hour had passed since he'd left them at the well, and now they would fall behind the others in their work.

Usually Nephi was composed, but today his patience was weak. He grabbed his basket of ripe fruit. With the fading light, some of the workers were beginning to leave. He strode down the narrow dirt aisle that was flanked by bursting vines, then pulled his dangling robe from a vine and put it onto his shoulders, absorbing the day's sweat into the linen fabric. Without looking behind him, he felt questioning eyes follow his strong frame. People were curious about his family, who were often the targets of public ridicule—his father, Lehi, was not afraid to share his religious beliefs.

This sometimes led to awkward moments for Nephi and his siblings. Last Friday morning, Lehi had stepped into the middle of an argument in the market square. A man had accused his neighbor of letting a donkey graze in his field. Lehi put his sun-browned hands on each of the men's shoulders and declared, in front of everyone, "The great prophet Moses said, 'Thou shalt love the Lord your God, to walk in all his ways, and to cleave unto him.'" Sariah, Nephi's mother, a few stalls away, simply smiled. Nephi, who was carrying the market basket laden with fresh produce, felt his neck and face grow crimson as people around him scoffed. Others just shook their heads. But despite all of the unwanted attention he received from his father's bold declarations, Nephi couldn't help but admire him for his unwavering faith in God.

A snapping sound interrupted his thoughts. He looked to his right where a tight group of olive trees stood, their silvery brown branches gnarled and twisted with age. A swatch of yellow clothing peeked through a split trunk. Laman. He wouldn't be surprised to find Lemuel hidden in the grove too, probably sleeping.

Feeling suddenly younger and weaker than his sixteen years, Nephi decided to retrace his steps. The wrath of his brothers was not something any sane person would desire—and the wrath of his brothers aroused from sleep was even worse.

Nephi turned his back to the slumbering men and started to leave. Then he heard a voice call his name in a falsetto.

"You found us, little brother. Are you here to whip us?" Laughter erupted from behind the sage-colored leaves.

Nephi spun around with a ready answer, but his jaw locked when he saw two girls emerge from the trees, the same girls from the well. He was so shocked to find his brothers breaking the Mosaic law of respect for unmarried women that he did not even react. Instead, he stood like a forbidden idol while the girls, with downcast faces, walked past him. He didn't dare meet their eyes for fear of the shame he would see in them.

A lump formed in his throat as he tried to tame the bile rising from his stomach. His hands trembled as he clenched them into tight balls. If his brothers had shamed those girls, the consequences would be great.

A slap on his back startled him to his senses. "Don't worry, Nephi. They won't be stoned." Laman's breath was hot and sour on his face. His unshaven whiskers stood out like ore spikes. "We were just enjoying their company."

"Hey, little brother," Lemuel hissed from behind, gripping Nephi's neck fiercely. "Why aren't you in the fields like a good boy?"

"I—" Nephi choked back his mortification.

"Now, you're not going to say anything to Father about this, are you?"

Nephi squeezed his eyes shut against the anger burning in his chest. If his brothers pressed any further . . .

"Good. We'll see you later."

When the footsteps and laughter receded, Nephi sank to his knees, his sweat mingling with dust, and finally let the salty tears fall. Slowly, he whispered the words, "Lord, please forgive me for my weaknesses and soften my heart. Help me love my brothers. I need Thy strength, O Lord. I need Thy guidance . . ."

The skies had turned violet by the time Nephi rose to his feet. He knew questions would be asked about his absence from the vineyard, although none would be asked about the recent desertion by his brothers.

He fell into line behind the departing laborers. The tired faces and moist bodies silently filed along the dusty road the evening breeze had stirred to life. A few of the wealthier workers rode donkeys. The workday had ended.

By the time Nephi skirted the western base of the Mount of Olives and reached the Hinnom Valley, it had been dark for over an hour. His donkey plodded the familiar way unbidden, leaving Nephi to his own thoughts. Confrontations had been escalating between him and his brothers over the past year. He could trace it back to last year's harvest time when his father had given each son his annual blessing.

The words of Nephi's blessing echoed those of his brothers' blessings: "If thou art faithful, thou wilt be blessed . . ." But Nephi's blessing took an unusual turn—Nephi was promised by the Lord, through his father, that he would be the leader of many nations and that his words would be known throughout the generations.

After the blessing, Nephi saw surprise on his father's face. The room was silent for several moments. Since that time, Laman and Lemuel were aloof toward him. Gone were the carefree games and jesting over Egyptian and Hebrew lessons. Laman and Lemuel became inseparable, even more so than before. Nephi was always the brunt of their jokes, and nothing he did to get along with them made a difference. Sam, his brother just older than he, was the only one he could talk to.

As Nephi continued home, his heart grew heavy with anticipation. He suspected that his brothers had already complained to his parents about their difficult labor in the vineyards, but as always, his father's pure heart would see through the lies.

Nephi heard another donkey approach but didn't turn until a deep voice spoke behind him.

"Coming from the vineyards, lad?"

Pulling his donkey to a stop, he turned. It was his father's cousin Ishmael. Nephi waited for the broad-shouldered man to reach him. They rode side by side. "Yes, sir. It's time to bring in the harvest," Nephi said.

The man chuckled. "You must be a great help, son."

"Thank you. And how is your family?" Nephi asked.

Ishmael raised an eyebrow. "Ah, interesting that you should inquire."

Nephi looked away, not daring to hope.

"A certain daughter of mine asked me just this morning how your family was faring," Ishmael said.

Grateful that the cloak of darkness masked his flaming face, Nephi said, "You may tell her that all is well."

Ishmael nodded knowingly and grinned. "You are a good lad. Give your father my best wishes." They had arrived at Ishmael's settlement, and Nephi bowed his head in respect and bid him safe passage.

* * *

Isaabel heard the clopping of hoofed feet signaling the approach of her father's donkey. She ran into the courtyard to embrace him.

"Let me get off the donkey first," Ishmael said with a hearty chuckle. "Why are you in such a hurry to greet me?"

Isaabel's deep eyes danced with joy. "I've missed you, Father."

"I've only been gone half a day." He leaned down and kissed his daughter's copper cheek. But something else lay beneath the girl's welcoming expression—her real purpose in greeting her father alone. Ishmael stepped back from the young girl. "Ah, I think I know why you have come in such a rush, Isa."

She turned her face upward and met her father's eyes with a steady gaze. "Did you find out how Lehi's family is doing?"

Ishmael could hardly contain his laughter. His youngest daughter was not demure by any means. He just hoped she would stay out of trouble long enough for him to find her a proper husband. "Ah, you come right to the point. That's my Isa. As a matter of fact, I ran into one of Lehi's sons on the way home tonight."

"Which one?" Isaabel blurted, confirming her father's suspicions.

"You can probably still see him from the gate," he said.

Isaabel flew past her father and ran down the lane. She came to a stumbling halt just outside the gate. The night held a growing moon in the sky, and the stars twinkled merrily above as if they were laughing at her.

Even from the distance of several dozen yards, Isaabel recognized Nephi's form sitting astride a donkey. She bit her lip to keep from calling out to him. She would not allow herself to act like a fool. In the quiet night, she was sure that he must have heard her stumbling footsteps and definitely her labored breathing, if not the thudding of her heart. But he did not turn around, eventually disappearing from sight. Isaabel sighed and leaned on the open gate. She heard her father calling her name.

"I'm coming," she called in reply. The cooling wind picked up around her and she drew her gamma mantle tightly against her body. Lost in thought, she did not hear the approaching travelers until it was too late.

"Greetings, miss," one disheveled man called in a slurred voice. His face was boyish but his eyes lazy and mouth slack. The men's fine cloaks exuded an obvious wealth.

Isaabel turned away.

"Where are you going on such a fine night?" The taller man climbed off his donkey and veered toward her. He grabbed her arm. He was quite handsome, but his manner was repulsive.

Her heart lurched as she pried off his sloppy fingers. She shut the gate between them, but not before she smelled the sour wine on his breath.

"Aren't you going to invite us to your home?" he asked slowly.

Isaabel was through holding her tongue. "This is my father's home, and drunken men are not invited."

Laughter echoed around her. The taller man draped his arms over the gate, his hands fumbling for her again. "You must be Ishmael's daughter. Your beauty needs to be tamed."

The other man joined his partner at the gate and opened the latch, his watery mouth smiling. "Tell your father to come meet us," he said, moving toward her.

Isaabel's eyes began to sting. She clutched her hands over her chest and took a step backward.

"Who goes there?" said a loud voice from behind.

She had never been so relieved to see her father. She would have flown into his arms sobbing if the two strangers hadn't been present. For now, she swallowed her rising dread and told her father that the men wished to speak with him.

Ishmael turned to the drunken men. "Ah, Laman and Lemuel. You've been celebrating."

Isaabel froze. Nephi's brothers were Laman and Lemuel. She hadn't recognized them in the dark.

"Daughter, your mother's expecting you in the cooking room," Ishmael said.

Isaabel's eyes focused once more on the three men standing before her. She bowed her head and turned.

She walked back to the dwelling, even though her head told her to run. When she reached the courtyard, she realized that she wasn't ready to face her sisters and mother yet. Her mother, Bashemath, was too keen and would notice Isaabel's troubled face immediately. So she walked into the stable to pet Curly, the first donkey she had ever ridden. Her brothers had laughed at her when she picked Curly's name, but it had seemed simple to her—the donkey's mane curled when it rained.

Footsteps approached, and Isaabel heard her father talking to Nephi's brothers. *Please don't come in the stable,* she thought. But it was worse than she feared. Her father led the men through the courtyard into the house. "You are in no condition to travel. I insist you eat with us," she heard her father's receding voice say. Now she would have to enter the house after them, which was sure to create a stir. She would have to find some excuse to get out of serving them supper.

When the men's voices faded, Isaabel crept out of the stable. Gales of laughter floated from her home. Her mother called her name, and Isaabel took a deep breath.

"I'm here, Mother," she said, entering the courtyard.

Her mother stared at her with curiosity. She motioned with her hand for Isaabel to come into the house. Isaabel hung her head and stepped through the doorway, knowing who was waiting to greet her.

"Ah," her father said. "Here is my wife, Bashemath, and you have already met my youngest daughter, Isaabel."

Laman and Lemuel both nodded. Isaabel looked down at her hands, waiting to be dismissed.

"Yes," Laman said. "She is beautiful like her mother."

Isaabel felt the heat rise in her face—a compliment from these men was like being slapped. She heard a movement behind her. Her two older sisters had entered the room to be introduced.

"Yes. And here are my first and second daughters, Rebeka, the eldest, and Anah, the next," Ishmael said. "My other daughters, Tamar and Puah, have been ill. They are sleeping."

The visitors murmured something incoherent that passed for concern.

"Let's serve supper, daughters," Isaabel's mother said. Isaabel followed the women into the cooking room.

"Laman is so tall," Rebeka said, her eyes shining. "Is he the oldest?"

"I think so, but he's not as handsome as Lemuel," Anah said.

Rebeka snorted. "That's your opinion."

Isaabel remained silent, filling the silver bowls with steamed barley and placing the newly baked bread onto a platter.

"Oh, poor Isa. Don't worry, I know they have younger brothers," Rebeka said.

For a moment Isaabel thought her sister was being serious until she heard Anah snicker. "You'll have to wait your turn, little sister."

"Silence, daughters," Bashemath said. "I will not have that talk. Isaabel, fill the dishes. Rebeka and Anah, you will serve them."

The two sisters gathered the first bowls and headed triumphantly out of the warm room. Isaabel wiped a stray tear when her mother's back was turned. She was glad to stay in the cooking room but felt humiliated by her sisters' comments. She was always fifth in line—and actually even farther down than that. Her brothers and their families came first, then her older sisters. She outranked only the donkeys in the stable.

Isaabel glanced at her sister-in-law, Zillah, who sat on a stool in the corner cutting vegetables. Zillah offered a sympathetic smile, but Isaabel looked away. Her sister-in-law was carrying her second child and would not be expected to serve.

Just a few moments ago, Isaabel was planning how to get out of serving, but now she was being disgraced in front of members of Nephi's family—loathsome as they might be. She was nearly fifteen years old, plenty old enough to be betrothed, yet her older sisters had to be married first. With four sisters ahead of her, Isaabel had a long wait. It was not an easy task for her father, a modest farmer, to provide dowries for five daughters. And in this time of unrest in Jerusalem, not many marriages were being planned.

Many prophets had risen up in the past year, Nephi's father among them, condemning the sinners and predicting the city's destruction. It all seemed unimaginable to her. The city of Jerusalem was one of the greatest in the world. How could it be destroyed in the manner the prophets foretold? Her father respected Lehi as a great spiritual teacher, but she doubted he believed all Lehi said. If so, wouldn't they be packing their camels like some of the more devout families?

Isaabel heard her mother whispering to Zillah. She strained to understand the words without stopping the arranging of sweet cakes on a tray.

"The daughter of Tiras is with child," Bashemath said.

Zillah covered her mouth in shock. "What will happen to her?" she whispered fiercely.

"The family bribed the officials so she would not be punished publicly. The world must be coming to an end if girls are allowed to have babies in such a manner," she hissed. Then she moved away and busied herself shelling pinenuts.

Before long, the guests prepared to leave, and Ishmael requested the presence of his daughters. Isaabel stood behind her mother to avoid eye contact, but that did not deter the men.

"We look forward to seeing you again," Laman said, looking at her, his grin revealing a broken tooth.

Isaabel stared at the floor. Soon they were gone, and she fled back into the cooking room to eat her share of the leftovers. The crisp browned fish was the only main dish that was left. Hungry as she was, Isaabel found that she could only pick at the meat. Finally, she made herself eat a fig.

Her mother looked at her sharply during the women's supper. "Are you all right, child?"

Gulping down the last morsel of the fig, Isaabel managed to say, "Yes. I'm just tired."

Rebeka and Anah giggled, and Isaabel thought she heard one of them whisper, "She is jealous."

✦ CHAPTER 2 ✦

For mine eyes have seen the King, the Lord of hosts.
(ISAIAH 6:5)

"Good boy," Nephi crooned to the donkey that was already past its prime. He scratched the animal's head and offered him a fistful of barsim. Empty stalls indicated that Nephi's brothers hadn't yet returned. *Just as well,* he thought. *It will give me more time to speak with Father alone about some of his latest prophecies.* Nephi wished that he had the same strength and conviction that his father did. He closed his eyes briefly, praying for understanding.

The sound of a shuffle interrupted his prayer.

A familiar stocky figure stood there, his head covered in unruly black curls that framed his round face.

"Sam—"

"Shhh. I'm not supposed to be out here. But I thought I'd better let you know what's happened," Sam whispered.

"Happened with what?" Nephi asked, stepping closer.

"It's Father. He's had a vision—"

"A vision from God?" Nephi interrupted.

Sam nodded, his eyes wide. "He was on his way to Jericho to meet with an olive merchant this morning. But he came home hours ago and went to bed. He's been restless and calling out strange things. Mother thinks he's gone mad."

Nephi placed his hand on Sam's shoulder. "What sort of things?"

"He says he's seen God sitting on His throne, with angels surrounding Him." Sam's voice grew louder. "A Man descended out of the heavens with twelve others following Him, and there's something about a book." Sam stopped and stared at Nephi. "Your eyes, they look like fire."

But Nephi didn't hear him. He walked out of the stable and into the house. His mother rushed to him, clinging, sobbing. When she saw his eyes, she released her grip and fell into silence.

Beyond the indigo curtain that separated his parents' bedroom from the main house, Nephi heard moaning. Without hesitation, he parted the curtain and saw his father trembling upon the bed.

He crossed the room and knelt beside the writhing man, clasping his father's hands. "Father, it is I, Nephi."

"Great and marvelous are Thy works, O Lord God Almighty! Thy throne is high in the heavens, and Thy power and goodness and mercy are over all the inhabitants of the earth. And because Thou art merciful, Thou wilt not suffer those who come unto Thee that they shall perish," Lehi said in a throaty, quivering voice. The words reverberated off the clay walls, bouncing back and forth into each other.

Nephi bent his head and squeezed his eyes shut, feeling his father's words pierce his heart. His father had *seen* the Lord. Nephi felt his eyes begin to burn, and just as he thought he would burst, a terrific sensation of heat spread from his face down to his toes. Nephi's throat constricted, making him feel faint. Then the pressure eased and an utter peace passed through his entire being.

And he knew.

His father was all he claimed to be, and God was real! Nephi's heart pumped furiously as he tried to comprehend the words his father spoke. He opened his eyes and looked at his father's reddened face, mapped with age. Perspiration soaked Lehi's clothing.

"Mother," Nephi called over his shoulder. "Bring me water."

Moments later his mother entered, spilling some water as she handed it over. Tears cascaded down her cheeks. "His burden in so heavy. I am afraid."

"He'll be fine. I just want to make him comfortable," Nephi said quietly.

Sariah nodded and backed out of the room, her unsteady hands clasped against her chest.

Nephi knelt beside his father again and placed a damp cloth against his forehead. A few moments later, Lehi's ragged breathing quieted and his body calmed. "Father," Nephi whispered, "are you all right?"

Lehi's eyes opened slightly, and he turned his head toward Nephi. Nephi looked into his clouded gaze, knowing that his father didn't see him. Words formed on his lips, and Nephi leaned closer to hear them.

"Bring . . . the . . . records."

"Father, you need rest," Nephi protested.

Lehi rose and propped himself up on his elbows. The cloudiness in his eyes began to disappear, and he now stared hard at Nephi. "No. I must make a record of my visions."

Nephi hesitated, then crossed to the other side of the room. He removed a rug from the floor and lifted a loose stone. Beneath the ground was a small cavity containing sheaves of papyrus on which Lehi wrote his prophecies. But Nephi had never been permitted to remove them from their hiding place before. He reached into the hollowed earth and lifted a flaxen cloth. Below it was a metal box containing the records. After carefully picking up the container, he carried it to his father's bedside.

"Now open the box and remove the top scroll. I want you to write my words," Lehi instructed.

Nephi bit his lip. His hands trembled as he carefully removed the fine papyrus and writing stylus. This was an honor that none of his older brothers had ever received.

Suddenly Lehi gripped Nephi's shoulder. "I stopped and prayed on my way to Jericho—praying for our people to come unto repentance. I felt a searing heat, and when I opened my eyes, a great pillar of fire was before me. I heard the voice of the Lord." Lehi released his grasp and relaxed onto the bed. "He told me many things, some of which I am forbidden to repeat.

"When I returned home," Lehi spoke slowly, as though he were seeing the vision for a second time, "I fell upon my bed. I saw One descending out of the midst of heaven, and I beheld that His brilliance was greater than that of the noonday sun." His voice was raspy, sounding like he had been preaching for many hours.

The house remained silent as Nephi wrote Lehi's words— as if the clay walls were holding their breath. Nephi wrote carefully, trying to match his father's neat penmanship. He now understood why his father had so often asked to see his Egyptian writing lessons. Lehi must have known this day would come.

"I saw twelve others following him, their brightness exceeding the stars in the firmament."

The hairs on Nephi's arms stood up. His father's voice was powerful, yet reverent. Nephi could almost visualize for himself what Lehi had seen.

"The first came and stood before me and gave me a book, bidding me that I should read." Lehi began speaking more rapidly, his eyes shining. "As I read, I was filled with the Spirit of the Lord. Jerusalem will be destroyed. Many will perish by the sword, and many will be carried away captive into Babylon."

Nephi felt a burning begin in his chest and spread throughout his body. It radiated from his fingertips as he wrote the words effortlessly.

Lehi stopped speaking. Nephi pulled his eyes away from the papyrus and saw that his father had risen from the bed. "I must warn our people," Lehi cried. "If they don't repent, they will be destroyed."

Leaping to his feet, Nephi said, "Wait! You must rest and gather your strength. Tomorrow you may warn them."

Lehi's eyes weighed the proposition. Finally, he nodded. Nephi helped his father back into the bed, and soon the prophet fell into a fitful sleep.

Nephi gathered the writing materials and placed them back in the hiding place. His heart still hammered from his father's words. It was true that the wickedness in the city of Jerusalem was increasing. The Mosaic laws were not being adhered to in the temple, common people bribed priests to overlook their sins, and those who disagreed with King Zedekiah were imprisoned.

He felt a pair of eyes watching him. Glancing up, he saw Laman standing in the doorway. A look of confusion and hurt played across his eldest brother's face.

Nephi replaced the stone covering and rose to greet him, but Laman had disappeared.

* * *

"The king is coming! Make way for King Zedekiah!" the royal herald shouted.

Isaabel was shoved into the stone wall, a rough protrusion scraping her arm. "Ouch," she cried out. But the assailant was gone. She could see a great flurry of activity down the market road. Suddenly she remembered Tamar, who had recovered from her illness that morning and insisted on accompanying Isaabel. She looked around frantically but couldn't see her sister.

The crowd of people pressed closer to the wall, locking Isaabel into an alcove. The herald's voice grew louder and, above the dark heads, Isaabel soon saw the man whose presence was creating the stir. King Zedekiah sat in an open chariot pulled by four magnificent steeds. The crimson turban on his head twinkled as jewels reflected the sunlight. The king's tunic was white, signifying the beginning of Sukkoth. His outer garment was of rich purple, woven with gold threads, and the girdle surrounding his waist was fine silk. Isaabel wondered how many thousands of shellfish had been used to dye the king's clothing.

After the chariot passed, the crowds thinned. Isaabel rushed in the opposite direction of the procession. When she arrived at the central marketplace, she asked the meat seller, Japeth, if he had seen Tamar. The burly man shook his head and grinned, exposing rotted teeth. "I will help you find her," he said.

Looking at his bloodstained hands, Isaabel felt her stomach churn. "No, thank you," she said. She moved past him and hurried through the throng.

Isaabel stopped when she reached a tightly clustered group of people. A voice spoke over the murmuring.

"Wo, wo, unto Jerusalem, for I have seen your abominations!" *Another preacher among the streets,* she thought. Then Isaabel glimpsed Tamar standing at the front of the crowd. Isaabel pushed her way through the people until she reached her sister.

"Tamar! I have been looking—"

"Shhh. Listen," Tamar said.

Turning from her sister, Isaabel looked at the man who was speaking. He was tall, yet his shoulders stooped. Streaks of gray and white ran through his dark beard. His voice trembled with emotion, and Isaabel felt its strength. It was Lehi, she realized. The man who—then she froze. Nephi stood behind Lehi, supporting his father's elbow.

Isaabel had never dared to look at Nephi from such a close distance. He stood taller than his father, his head raised, jaw firm. His dark curly hair spilled just past his shoulders. He wore a white tunic with an outer garment of blue wool and long *sisith* at the hem. She knew his family was wealthy in land, but his coat made him look almost regal. Her eyes trailed farther down, and she caught herself looking at his brown feet, strapped in good leather sandals.

Lehi's voice rose as he told the crowd that Jerusalem would be destroyed. A hiss of disapproval erupted around her. Isaabel had heard these ravings before—prophets were plenty in the great city. But seeing Nephi supporting his father caused her to listen to the powerful words. She found herself wondering if Jerusalem really would be destroyed.

"Many will perish by the sword, and many will be carried away captive into Babylon," Lehi said.

The crowds jostled, and Isaabel clung to Tamar, who smirked.

Isaabel jabbed her in the ribs.

"The old man looks like he's going to collapse," Tamar said.

"He's not *that* old. And besides, he's our father's cousin," Isaabel said, drawing looks from those nearby.

"Everyone is Father's cousin—"

"Shhh!" Isaabel interrupted.

The crowd grew restless around them, and a few people threw vegetables, which splattered at the prophet's feet.

Lehi stretched his arms outward and gazed up to heaven. Two men next to Isaabel started to laugh. "You had better go home and rest, *prophet*. Your days are numbered," one called loudly.

"I have seen your wickedness." Lehi stared at the stranger. "Repent or Jerusalem will be destroyed."

The man's eyes narrowed and his face twisted in anger. "Are you calling me wicked?"

Lehi's voice grew louder, "I have seen your abominations. If you do not repent, you will perish."

"We'd better go, Tamar, before this gets too dangerous," Isaabel whispered. She pulled her sister's sleeve, and they moved through the people. As they left the crowd, gasps spread among the onlookers. Isaabel turned to see the prophet disappear from view. A dull thud echoed as Lehi's head hit the ground.

Nephi yanked the attacker off his father and pushed him aside. "You will have to fight me instead of my father," he said.

The man glared at Nephi. "My issue is with your father. He will pay for what he has said." He turned to the gathered crowd and shouted, "Jerusalem will not be destroyed. This man who claims to be a prophet is a liar. It is time we rise up and defend our names. I say we stone him!"

Shouts erupted from the crowd. But Nephi stood before them, his eyes blazing. "There will be no violence here today. Go about your business!"

Several in the crowd jeered, but others shrugged and moved away.

Standing with his arms crossed over his chest, Nephi's gaze dared anyone to contend with him. They eventually lost interest and dispersed. Only the man and his friend remained. "Watch yourself, lad. Next time, your father won't be so lucky," he warned.

Nephi didn't flinch. "It is you who must watch yourself. My father is a man of God. God is the one you must fear."

The man spat at Nephi's feet and walked away.

Nephi stared after the man, his jaw working. Then he turned around to see his father trying to sit up.

Before Isaabel realized what she was doing, she pushed through the diffusing onlookers. She reached Nephi, who was kneeling next to his father. Lehi moaned in pain.

"Lie back," Isaabel ordered. She gently touched Lehi's head and pressed her mantle on his bleeding wound. Isaabel looked at Nephi. "He needs water."

Nephi's eyes met hers, and Isaabel felt her face ignite, but she didn't have time to be embarrassed by her boldness. Nephi rose and left.

The minutes dragged while Isaabel waited for Nephi's return. The prophet took deep breaths and groaned. She heard laughter behind her. "So much for the destruction of Jerusalem. It looks like the only things falling are prophets," someone said.

When Nephi returned, relief flooded through Isaabel. She held Lehi's head while Nephi poured water into his mouth, causing Lehi to sputter.

"Drink slowly, Father," Nephi said. He put one arm around his father's shoulders, touching Isaabel in the process.

At Nephi's touch, Isaabel withdrew her arm. Nephi looked at her, a faint smile on his lips. She was about to return the smile when Lehi groaned, breaking their gaze. He began to mumble and wave his hands.

Isaabel swallowed the lump in her throat and stood slowly. While Nephi continued to speak reassuringly to his father, she slipped away.

* * *

"Thank you," Nephi said, looking up. But Ishmael's youngest daughter was gone. He knew her name was Isaabel, yet, somehow, it didn't seem proper to think of her by her first name. Her copper skin had shimmered like the desert at sunset. Though he'd never seen her hair, he imagined it long, wavy, and black, like her mantle. The dark color of her clothing couldn't conceal her inner brightness—

"H-Help me stand."

Nephi looked at his father, whose face was still pale. "You must rest. I'll borrow a cart to take you home."

But Lehi pushed his son aside and grabbed his staff. "I'm not finished."

Nephi spoke with firmness. "The crowds have lost interest. We'll return tomorrow if you wish."

Lehi frowned and looked around. Finally he nodded, and Nephi helped him to his feet and led him to their waiting donkeys.

CHAPTER 3

*The Spirit of the Lord
spake by me, and his word was in my tongue.*
(2 SAMUEL 23:2)

When Lehi and Nephi reached the courtyard of their home, Sariah ran to meet them. "Jonas is dead!" she cried.

"Jonas the prophet?" Nephi asked.

Sariah nodded through her tears.

A cold wave of fear swept through Lehi. Jonas had been preaching the same doctrine in the Phoenician markets as he had preached today. Lehi climbed off his donkey and reached for his wife. "Are you sure?"

Sariah gripped Lehi's robe. "He was preaching in Bethlehem this morning, and the crowd grew angry. They chased him and beat him to death." She buried her face in his tunic, sobbing. "What if the crowds come after you?"

Lehi held her close, his eyes rimmed in red. After his experience this morning, he knew the danger was real, but to kill Jonas for preaching the word of God? His body felt numb with disbelief.

"What about Jonas's family? What about *us*, Lehi?"

He turned his face upward as if reading the sky. "The destruction of Jerusalem is surely at hand. The death of the prophet Jonas is a precursor of what is to come."

Nephi had heard of such events happening before, but never to someone they knew. He stared at his parents clinging to each other. Jonas had been a close friend to his father. Now Jonas was dead.

His parents walked into the house together. Fear grew in Nephi's heart. The episode at the market today was much more serious than he'd first thought. He knew if he told his mother what had happened to them, she would be terrified. He led the donkeys into the stable and gave them water.

When Nephi entered the front room, his parents were sitting together with their heads bowed, praying. Nephi paused and listened to his father's supplicating words. Lehi prayed for Jonas's family to be protected. Then he prayed for the people of Jerusalem and pled for their deliverance. Nephi bowed his head and felt his chest burn. It was impossible to believe that the people in Jerusalem would repent. The hatred in their hearts was too strong.

"Amen," Lehi said. His eyes full of sorrow and determination, he looked up to meet Nephi's gaze.

Suddenly Nephi understood. His father loved his people so much that he was willing to perish because of their wickedness. Lehi would not hide in his house away from angry crowds. He would preach the word of God, even if it meant that he too was put to death.

* * *

Lehi lay awake in the dark next to his sleeping wife. Her rhythmic breathing usually lulled him to sleep, but not tonight. Not on the night of the prophet Jonas's death. Why he hadn't told Sariah about the incident in the marketplace, he didn't know. Perhaps he was afraid she would insist on leaving their home and taking refuge in another city. That would only mean one thing—he would no longer be able to preach the word of God to his people.

Tears stung his eyes as he thought about the people of Jerusalem, his people. Since God had called him to be a prophet, his heart seemed to expand with love for all of them. It was similar to loving his own children. Even when his older sons disobeyed him, his love for them didn't lessen. He couldn't ignore his knowledge. He knew that Jerusalem would be destroyed if his people didn't repent. Even with Jonas's death, he knew he couldn't stop preaching. There might be someone out there who was willing to repent.

Sariah stirred next to him. Lehi slid out of bed, trying not to disturb her. He knelt on the rug and clasped his hands together.

"O Lord," he began in prayer. "What is Thy will? My people have grown so wicked that they have killed their own prophet." Lehi felt a lump form in his throat. He continued in earnestness, "I need strength, Lord, to continue my preaching. The fear in my heart has multiplied, and the worry for my family's safety increases. But I will do Thy will. I will take Thy word to Thy people, even if my life is taken."

He buried his face in his hands. His life was in the Lord's hands.

* * *

On the other side of the house, Nephi lay awake, restlessly listening to his brothers snore. After what seemed like hours, he finally rose and went outside. The moon reflected in the sky, and the stars appeared numberless. He propped himself against the inner wall of the courtyard and pondered in the quiet night. His heart ached as he thought about his father's willingness to sacrifice his life for the Lord.

Nephi thought of his mother and her devotion to her husband. If anything should happen to his father, he knew his mother would want to die with him.

He wondered why his older brothers were so different from the rest of the family. They spent their time looking for immediate pleasures. They had stopped taking lessons several months ago and spent most of their time in idleness. In contrast, his brother Sam was serious about his studies and worked hard with the flocks. His two younger sisters were quiet and obedient, much like Sam.

Nephi arranged his coat on the ground and lay down. He stared at the night sky, then thought about one last person before drifting off to sleep—a girl with dark eyes whose gaze penetrated his very soul.

* * *

Nephi awoke with a start. Something was burning. He jumped to his feet and ran through the courtyard toward the smell. Footsteps sounded behind him. Nephi spun around in time to see a figure in gray robes running away. He would have chased after him, but smoke was billowing from the stable, choking the early morning air. Sprinting toward it, he shouted, "Sam! Laman! Lemuel! Bring water!"

He entered the smoke-filled stable. The donkeys were jittery, watching the orange flames lick the north wall. Nephi untied the ropes and swatted the animals to hurry them out of the burning shelter. His brothers arrived with jugs of water and soon doused the fire.

"What happened?" Laman demanded.

"The fire was deliberately set. I saw a man running down the road just after I smelled the smoke," Nephi said.

"You were outside?" Lemuel asked.

"I slept in the courtyard," Nephi said.

"Thank the Lord for your restlessness," Sam said, clapping him on the back.

Lehi, Sariah, and their two sleepy daughters appeared. "Is everyone all right?" Lehi asked.

The brothers nodded, and Sariah's eyes filled with tears.

"Father," Nephi said, "I think this has something to do with what happened in the market."

Lehi's jaw tightened.

"What are you talking about?" Sariah asked, glancing from husband to son. Nephi looked away.

Ignoring the question, Lehi turned to his family. "Let us go inside and prepare the morning meal. After we eat, I must tell you about the dream I had last night."

Sariah studied Nephi for a moment and then went into the house to begin cooking, her daughters following her.

The brothers knocked down the burned section of the stable, and Nephi stacked the ashen boards in a pile. By the time they finished, the meal was ready.

The men sat at the table, and Sariah served boiled barley with buttermilk and fresh cucumbers and tomatoes. The family ate in glum silence.

After they finished eating, everyone gathered in the front room. Nephi's sisters, Elisheba and Dinah, nestled on each side of Sariah. Laman sat with his arms folded, his heavy beard concealing his frown, while Lemuel hunched over and stared at the ground.

"I'm not afraid of who set the fire or of the men who killed Jonas," Lehi began. "What happened to him will become more commonplace. The people are hard-hearted and refuse to repent. Yesterday . . ." Nephi clenched his jaw in frustration, knowing what his father would say next. ". . . I was fortunate to have Nephi with me in the marketplace. One man nearly brought an entire mob against me. And this morning . . . even with the stable on fire and my life in danger, I will not stop preaching."

Laman stood. "Father, we cannot protect you against a whole city."

"I know." Lehi held up his hand. "But you will not have to."

Everyone stared at him in surprise. Sariah held her daughters closer.

"I have had a dream."

Nephi detected a sigh coming from Laman as he settled onto a cushion. Lemuel shifted where he sat, his face a mask of stone. Sam looked at Nephi with questioning eyes, but Nephi shrugged, not knowing what his father meant. "Last night, the Lord spoke to me in a dream," Lehi said. "He said, 'Blessed art thou Lehi, because of the things which thou hast done; and because thou hast been faithful and declared unto this people the things which I commanded thee, behold, they seek to take away thy life.'"

The hairs on Nephi's arms stood as his father spoke. The Lord had specifically spoken to Lehi about their dilemma.

Lehi paused and looked gravely at each family member. "The Lord commanded me to take my family and leave Jerusalem."

Gasps echoed throughout the room. Sariah brought a hand to her mouth, her eyes wide with shock. Laman lurched forward in protest. "Leave Jerusalem?"

"We will protect you, Father," Lemuel interjected.

Laman rose, his fists clenched. "This is madness. You would leave our home because of a dream? If you would stop telling people how to live, maybe your life wouldn't be in danger."

Lehi remained calm and spoke with firmness. "We will gather only the provisions that we absolutely need and depart into the wilderness the day after tomorrow."

Nobody moved or made a sound. Then Laman started laughing and soon Lemuel joined him. Nephi shook his head at his brothers' disrespect. His mother's face drained of color, and his sisters remained quiet.

Sam, whose face had paled, stood and crossed toward Lehi. "Father, is there no other way?"

Nephi rose, his heart pounding. The burning of his soul diffused the knot of fear in his stomach. "Father has spoken. We must prepare to leave."

Sam moved toward Nephi in support.

Lemuel jumped to his feet, the smile disappearing from his face. "We can't leave our home and our inheritance," he declared.

Laman nodded in agreement. "We'll stay behind and protect our land," he offered.

Sariah turned to her husband, tears streaking her face. "Lehi, this is so sudden. We need more time."

Lehi grasped her hand and squeezed. "We will forge a new life for ourselves, Sariah. The Lord will take care of us," he said, his own eyes moist.

Then he turned to the others. "The Lord has commanded us to flee into the wilderness." His voice remained firm. "No one will stay behind." Lehi lowered his voice and spoke to his wife. "Take our daughters and gather clothing, bedding, and cooking utensils. We will need enough food to last several weeks." He looked at Laman and Lemuel. "You must visit our neighbors and purchase extra panels and ropes for tents. Sam and Nephi, go to the market

and see if you can sell any of our flocks. Then prepare the
donkeys and camels for the journey."

Nephi let out a long breath and nodded at Sam. Laman's
eyes narrowed as he turned to follow Lemuel. As the
brothers slowly filed out of the room, Lehi took Sariah into
his arms and held her trembling body close.

* * *

Nephi and Sam mounted their donkeys and began the
journey to the market. Nephi was dazed at his father's
news. But in his heart he believed that his father was a
prophet of God.

It took most of the day to find buyers to come and look
at the sheep and goats. When the brothers returned home,
Sam carried sacks of grain from the storehouse to the courtyard. He then began to arrange baskets with olives, dates,
and figs.

Laman and Lemuel had already returned home with
camels piled high with provisions. Lehi was going through
each purchase when Nephi approached him.

"Father, the flocks have been gathered and the buyers are
on their way."

"Thank you. Now see if your mother needs help with her
preparations," Lehi said.

Nephi entered the house and was surprised to find it
quiet. Clay vessels of olive and sesame oil covered the table.
Baskets filled with figs and dates lined the wall. Sacks of
wheat, flour, barley, and dried sour milk were propped next
to the entryway. A cold meal sat waiting for the men. Then
Nephi heard a hushed voice. He stepped through the
hallway and found his mother kneeling in her room,
praying. A white mantle covered her head and trailed down

her back. Nephi was about to leave when he heard her whisper, "Bless my sons Laman and Lemuel that they may obey their father and soften their hearts toward Nephi."

Nephi's eyebrows rose. So his mother had noticed the recent tension between them.

"Give me the strength to travel into the wilderness with my family, and bless us with health," she said.

Backing out of the hallway, Nephi stood in the front room and surveyed the surroundings. He wondered how long it would be before he returned to his childhood home. His father had provided them with a comfortable life. The rooms were decorated with pottery, metal art, faience vases, fine carpets, and carved ivory plaques. He knew that these precious things would all be left behind. There was no room for them in the reality of desert living.

Nephi's heart sank when he thought of the hardships his mother and sisters would face. He felt the need to pray growing within him. The day had passed in a blur, so he hadn't absorbed the magnitude of what was happening. He made his way to his room and knelt in the quiet darkness next to his reed bed frame.

Hearing footsteps behind him, he turned and saw Sam in the doorway.

"A group of men are approaching the house. Father wants everyone to arm themselves and gather in the courtyard," Sam said.

Nephi leapt to his feet and followed Sam out of the bedroom, grabbing a knife from the cooking table. He ran into the courtyard with Sam and stood with his brothers. They heard loud voices coming from the road, and soon a group of men approached. It was obvious they had been drinking wine. Many carried knives.

Lehi spoke first. "Greetings, men. What has brought you to my home tonight?"

"We're looking for the man who calls himself a prophet," one wild-eyed man said.

Laman stepped forward, his knife drawn. "You're trespassing on my father's land."

The group of scowling men moved closer together. "We only want to question him," another man said.

Laman's eyes narrowed, and in a gruff voice he said, "Do you have a mandate from the sarim?"

"We don't need permission from the counselors to ask questions," a man yelled from the back of the mob. The men jostled toward the brothers.

Lemuel moved next to Laman, shoulder to shoulder. Sam and Nephi closed in behind, guarding Lehi from the crowd.

"Which one of you set our stable on fire this morning?" Lemuel asked, glaring at the men.

They looked at each other and shook their heads.

"A crime has been committed here, and if you don't leave our property now, you'll become suspects," Lemuel shouted.

One man stepped forward, his knife pointed outward. "We know nothing of your stable. Show us the prophet."

In a flash, Laman grabbed the man's wrist and twisted his arm behind his back. The man cried out.

Laman brought his own knife to the man's throat and glared at the mob. "Leave our property now, or your friend will die."

With wide eyes, the captured man nodded for his friends to obey.

Slowly the group backed away and turned from the four stoic brothers. After they had reached the main road, Laman released his prisoner.

"Don't ever step on our property again," he said, shoving him to the ground.

The man clamored to his feet and dashed to meet his associates.

Lehi clapped Laman and Lemuel on their backs. "Thank you, sons. You've granted us more time."

Nephi grimaced. He hoped the family would be left in peace until they could depart.

↦ CHAPTER 4 ↤

*Choose you this day whom ye will serve; . . . as for me and my house,
we will serve the Lord.*

(JOSHUA 24:15)

Isaabel stretched her aching fingers and closed her eyes.
The flax she had spun into thread was nearly gone. She would
have to buy another bundle tomorrow before she could start
weaving. In the dim glow of the candle, she squinted at the
finely spun thread. Though her handiwork was finer than her
sisters', her mother rarely praised her. Isabel tried not to let it
bother her, consoling herself that someday perhaps her own
daughters would appreciate her craft.

Wrapping a fresh piece of flax around the clay whorl,
Isabel stretched the thread along the notched stick. She
began to twist the spindle, which created momentum as it
whirled. The steady rhythm soon caused her to yawn, but
she decided to continue working until her father came
home. He had been away all day, trying to find the best offer
for their wheat crop. Though her mother told her not to
expect him until late, Isabel wanted to wait up for him. She
wanted to tell him what had happened to Lehi at the market
the day before.

As she worked, she thought about seeing Nephi in the marketplace. She recalled the moment when the angry man struck Lehi. Without realizing what she was doing, she had rushed to his side. She remembered the warmth of Nephi's breath on her cheek and how his arm had brushed hers—he had been so close. Even now, a shiver ran through her as she thought about it.

Nephi had looked at her. Was he pleased with what he saw? Isaabel inhaled deeply and pretended that she could still smell his scent mixed with herbs. Her left hand tingled as she thought about his brief touch.

A slight jerk from the whorl brought her back to the present. A lump of flax was caught in the spindle. Isaabel removed the offending piece and began the meticulous process again.

Noises erupted from the courtyard—her father was home. She put the bundle aside and rose to meet him. When she arrived at the outer door, she heard her mother's voice full of distress. She slipped outside and hid in the shadowed corner, listening.

"I was so worried about your safety," her mother said.

"So you've heard the news about Jonas, then?" Ishmael asked.

"Only that he was killed yesterday, nothing else," her mother said.

"Yes," Ishmael said quietly. "They found him beaten not far from his home. He was trying to escape an angry mob."

Bashemath let out a choked cry. "What will happen to his family?"

"They may be in danger too. With the prophet Jeremiah in prison and Jonas dead, preachers of the Lord are no longer safe," he said.

"What about your cousin Lehi?"

From a shadowed corner, Isaabel drew her breath in sharply.

Ishmael spoke slowly. "That's the reason I'm so late. As I traveled home tonight, I passed a group of drunken men coming from Lehi's home. They spoke of bringing charges against him."

Isaabel bit her lip to keep from making noise. If Lehi was in danger, so was his family.

Her father lowered his voice. "Then it occurred to me that I had seen something unusual when I passed by Lehi's home."

Isaabel strained to hear what he said next.

"Lehi's flocks had been gathered together and men were inspecting them," he said.

"Do you think he is selling them?" Bashemath asked. "Maybe he needs the money?"

Ishmael replied, "It could mean that Lehi is moving into the city. But due to the danger within the walls, I doubt it. I think Lehi is leaving Jerusalem."

Isaabel gasped, then covered her mouth. *It couldn't be true,* she thought. *But what if it was?* She would rather have Nephi safe than in danger, but . . .

"You look ill, Ishmael."

Isaabel heard her father grunt.

"I'm fine. Let's go inside. It's late," Ishmael said.

Backing out from her hiding place, Isaabel rushed to the chair.

Soon her father entered the room, beads of perspiration at his brow. "Ah, my little night bird is still awake."

She turned and smiled, trying not to betray the knowledge in her eyes. "Hello, Father."

"No anxious greeting for me tonight?" he asked, teasing.

Isaabel lowered her eyes.

"You're tired. Go to bed and finish your work in the morning," Ishmael said.

She consented and kissed her father on his cheek, smelling the night air on his clothes.

Once in the darkened bedroom, Isaabel climbed into the bed she shared with Tamar and Puah. She lay stiffly, not wanting to touch Tamar's outstretched arm. Her mind jumped around thinking of other reasons for Lehi to gather his flocks. Shearing season had ended, and lambs wouldn't be born until spring. That left only one explanation. Lehi must be selling them and preparing for a journey—a long journey.

Tears stung her eyes. Undoubtedly Nephi and his family would go with their father. Isaabel shook her head and blinked her tears away. She was acting like a foolish child. A *woman* would have the best intentions at heart for the man she loved.

Isaabel sat up. Did she really love Nephi? Or did she have these strong feelings because she was last in line to be married and dreaming was her only hope?

"Isa, why are you awake?" Tamar asked, stretching.

She turned to her sister with shining eyes. "The prophet Jonas was killed, and Lehi's family is in danger."

Tamar blinked. "Am I dreaming?"

"No, it's true. I heard Father tell Mother," Isaabel said.

"That's awful." Tamar grew serious. "What will happen to his family?"

"Jonas's or Lehi's?" Isaabel asked.

"Jonas's, of course," Tamar said.

"I don't know. But Lehi is leaving Jerusalem . . . and taking his family."

Tamar smiled gently. She sat up and put her arm around her sister. "Isa, I know you've been watching Nephi."

Isaabel started to protest, but Tamar said, "Shhh. Don't try to tell me otherwise. I saw what happened in the marketplace. But you must be careful. You do not have a choice of whom you will marry."

Isaabel's face flamed in the darkness.

Tamar continued, "Don't be embarrassed. I won't tell the others. It might be a good thing that Nephi's family is leaving. You'll be betrothed last in our family, and by then, Nephi will already be married."

"I don't—"

"Please trust me. You'll understand when you are older. It's better to have your heart broken now than later," Tamar said.

Isaabel looked away, feeling her eyes sting.

"Try to get some sleep. Everything will seem better in the morning. I promise." Tamar gave her a squeeze, turned over, and quickly fell asleep.

Listening to her sisters' quiet breathing, Isaabel angrily wiped away her tears. She was a fool to let Tamar see how she felt about Nephi. She lay down and pulled the blanket over her shoulders. Tomorrow, she decided, she would find out the truth about Lehi's family, even if it meant telling her father that she had eavesdropped.

* * *

The persistent braying of a donkey awoke Nephi. He climbed out of bed and threw on his cloak, glancing at Laman and Lemuel, who slept through the angry noises. Then he paused. Today the family would leave Jerusalem. Nephi closed his eyes and offered a silent prayer.

Entering the courtyard, Nephi saw Sam loading goatskin bags onto a donkey's back in the early morning darkness. The donkey let out a grunt and kicked Sam's leg. His face went red as he gritted his teeth in pain. Nephi smiled at the sight.

"Don't laugh. Help me," Sam said with a grimace.

Nephi grabbed the donkey's bridle and patted its head. "Calm down, boy. Sam won't hurt you."

Sam rolled his eyes. "Are Laman and Lemuel still asleep?"

"Yes. Why didn't you wake us?" Nephi's forehead creased. "Everyone should be out here. I'll go and rouse them."

"I will. You finish loading this beast." Sam nudged Nephi in the ribs and grinned.

Nephi hoisted another goatskin bag filled with water onto the animal and lashed it to the saddle.

It wasn't long before his sleepy-eyed brothers appeared, their tempers as unruly as their hair.

"It's not even light," grumbled Laman.

"I hope Father's changed his mind," Lemuel added with a loud yawn.

"He hasn't," Nephi said. "You and Laman start with the camels. Sam and I will finish with the donkeys."

"Who put you in charge?" Laman asked, glowering at Nephi.

"Do as he says." Lehi appeared behind the brothers. "We're running out of time. Dawn arrives in less than an hour. I'll wake Mother and the girls."

Laman and Lemuel shuffled off, heading around the back of the house to load the tent panels and bags of grain.

When Nephi heard the stubborn grunting coming from the camels, he chuckled. "It looks like no one is happy this morning."

Sam stared at him. "What about you, Nephi? Aren't you worried about leaving our home?"

Nephi set down the bundle of clothing he held. "Yes, I'm worried. Mother and the girls are used to an easy life compared to what we'll encounter in the wilderness. And I don't relish the thought of contending with Laman and

Lemuel during the journey. But Father's safety is more important than any of my concerns."

"I know." Sam sighed. "I feel the same way. It's just that we have a good life here. Education, family, inheritance—"

"None of that will matter when Jerusalem is destroyed," Nephi said quietly.

Sam's shoulders slumped. "You're right. I don't know what we'll encounter in the wilderness, but I believe in Father."

"Let's finish loading. We're in God's hands now, brother." Nephi lifted a basket of olives and hefted it onto a donkey.

* * *

Lehi stepped into the sleeping room that he'd shared with his wife for twenty-three years. He had established a home of prosperity, love, and devotion to God. Now they would be leaving it. Would they ever return? If they did, would the house still be standing?

He crossed the room and removed a metal box from a hole in the floor. Running his hands over the lid, he thought about the many instructions he'd received from the Lord. Always, he obeyed without hesitation. Although he'd been firm and unwavering with his family, his heart ached at the thought of leaving his homeland.

Opening the lid, he placed sheaves of papyrus in the box. The last written page contained Nephi's handwriting. Oh, how blessed he was to have such a son. Lehi felt his eyes brim with tears. Despite his prosperity, the only things that mattered were the word of God and his family. The only other things he would take into the wilderness were those necessary for survival.

* * *

As the sun spilled over the eastern horizon, ribbons of light reached Lehi's homestead. Lehi and Sariah led the procession, each astride a camel. The metal box containing Lehi's prophecies was tightly lashed onto the prophet's camel. Behind them rode Elisheba, thirteen years of age, and Dinah, only eleven. Laman and Lemuel rode in the middle of the procession, followed by Nephi and Sam on the donkeys that were tied together one behind the other.

Sariah held her head high, adorned in her finest jewels. The gold earrings that Lehi had given her on their wedding day weighed on her earlobes. Rings sparkled on her hands, and bracelets tinkled on her arms. But the finery was not worn for celebration. Sariah was now a desert woman and would travel like one. As they rode farther away from her beloved home, she covered her face and began to moan.

Lehi reined his camel to a stop. Animal by animal, the group came to a halt. "What is it, Sariah?" he asked tenderly.

"My mother's box—I forgot it."

Lehi hesitated for a moment. "I didn't know you were going to bring it."

Sariah looked at him, eyes moist. "I want to keep the things she gave me, for our own daughters. I don't want looters to uncover it."

Lehi nodded. "So be it. Nephi!" he called behind him. "Mother forgot her trinket box. You know where it's buried, right?"

Nephi untied his donkey, turned the animal around, and spurred it into a trot.

The family continued while Nephi made his way back to the house. He was surprised that his father allowed him to return for his mother's jewelry. His father had brought a bag of money in order to buy things along the way, but the family was instructed not to bring any valuables. Lehi had checked all of the loaded provisions to make sure nothing was hidden.

Nephi arrived at the empty house. Everything was still except for a few chickens that pecked in the yard. He knew they would soon be claimed by surrounding neighbors. He moved through the silent rooms. The spirit of the house was gone. He exited through a back entrance and walked into the grazing field. Ten paces from the fourth olive tree, he began to dig. Two feet below the surface, he found the trinket box wrapped in layers of linen. He removed a corner of the covering and ran his fingers over the wood, delicately painted with vermilion from Tayima. He knew his mother carried the key to the lock with her, as he had seen it hanging from her veil.

A shout from the courtyard startled him. *The mob must be back,* he thought. After covering the hole, he hurried to the house. He would have to find a way to keep them from following him to his father. Nephi slid into the back entrance of the house—no one was within. He walked quietly to the main hall, fingering the knife at his waist, then stepped into the courtyard.

A single figure stood before him. Shielding his eyes from the sunlight, he realized it was only Ishmael. Nephi held the box behind his back with one hand.

"Ah, someone is home. Good morning," Ishmael said.

Nephi sighed with relief and moved forward to greet his father's cousin. "Good morning, sir."

Ishmael scanned the empty courtyard and settled his hooded gaze on Nephi. "Your father is well?"

"Yes."

"Where is the rest of your family?"

Nephi hesitated. "We are going on a trip."

"Just as I thought. A long one, I gather?" Ishmael asked.

Nephi glanced around, even though he knew no one else was there to overhear. "I don't know."

"Son, I'm your father's cousin. I can protect the property, if you wish. My family wants to help," Ishmael said, taking a step closer. "Two of my daughters even came with me. They are waiting down the path."

Heart racing, Nephi wondered which daughters Ishmael had brought and why. He decided to be honest with Ishmael. "My father has been commanded by the Lord to take his family into the wilderness. We don't know if we'll return to our property."

A look of astonishment crossed Ishmael's face. He suppressed the many questions that came to his mind. "I see you are a faithful son." He bowed and stepped aside. "I'm keeping you from your journey. May God be with you."

Nephi mounted his donkey and tucked the trinket box into his sash.

He rode down the lane and slowed as he approached the two female figures. It was Isaabel and her sister who had been in the marketplace two days before. He wanted to stop and speak with them, but he was afraid of their questions.

Nephi glanced at the girls, and for a brief moment he locked eyes with Isaabel. Her expression was steady, although he detected both curiosity and sadness behind her gaze. This was the second time in a matter of days that he had stared into her eyes. Though he would probably never see her again, he ached to say good-bye. But he clenched his jaw and ignored his inclination, continuing past the girls.

Once Nephi reached the road, he urged the donkey into a trot. His family was waiting.

CHAPTER 5

Surely the Lord God will do nothing,
but he revealeth his secret unto his servants the prophets.
(Amos 3:7)

Sam spotted Nephi first. "I see him."

The family had reached the Mount of Olives by the time Nephi caught up with them. Lehi frowned with concern as he watched his youngest son approach. "Were you followed?"

Nephi shook his head as he rode to his mother's side and handed her the bundled trinket box.

She tucked it into the pack behind her and kissed Nephi. "Bless you, son," she said, smiling.

He turned to his father. "Are we going over the Mount to Jericho?"

"No, we'll travel southward around the Mount, then head southeast," Lehi said.

Involuntarily, Nephi gazed in that direction. Nothing was eastward—except for Arabia, a vast desert. He had thought they would head southwest toward Egypt, a journey his father had made many times. Then his heart lifted. Maybe his father would take them to Hebron, a beautiful town with plenty of oases. The animals pressed forward, and Nephi moved into his place. He decided to tell his father about Ishmael's visit when they were alone.

Laman moved his camel next to Nephi. "It's your turn to ride in the center with our sisters," he said.

Lemuel laughed. "We'll follow the donkeys."

Nephi sighed as he watched his brothers take up the rear of the formation. They spoke in low tones, and every few minutes, loud laughter erupted from them.

Sam sidled up to Nephi. "What took you so long?"

"Donkeys aren't very fast," Nephi said, not sure if his brother was teasing.

"What was it like—seeing the empty house?"

Nephi looked at Sam, who usually kept his feelings to himself. Now he realized Sam was already homesick. "It wasn't the same without the family there. The life was gone out of the rooms."

Sam nodded, deep in thought. They rode in silence for a few more minutes.

"Why do you suppose Father let Mother bring her trinket box?" Sam asked.

"Maybe Mother knows the needs of our family best, and Father understood that today," Nephi said.

Sam tilted his head with consideration. "Perhaps you're right."

By midday, Laman and Lemuel trailed far behind. More than once, Lehi had to slow the group and wait. The brothers were quick to apologize, but Nephi knew they were not sincere. The family was disappointed when Lehi turned his camel east just before reaching Bethlehem. They would not be stopping in Hebron.

The afternoon sun beat upon the laden animals and tired travelers. The group passed Tekoa and continued toward the

Ascent of Ziz. Nephi stared in wonder at the caves and immense cliffs of the changing landscape. A few years ago, he would have wished to explore each cave.

Dusk fell upon the exhausted family. Nephi was grateful when his father stopped his camel and drove his staff into the ground. The procession had been called to a halt. Lehi helped Sariah climb off her camel, and they stood quietly talking for a few minutes. Then Sariah and her daughters unloaded cooking utensils and began to search for firewood.

"Laman," Lehi called. "Help your mother set up the tent. We'll erect only one for the women tonight. The men will sleep in the open to keep watch."

Obliging, Laman spread out a tent cloth. He found a stone and hammered the pegs into the ground. Then he grabbed a stake and placed it under the tent cloth, stretching the tent upward until it was standing.

Sariah smiled at her eldest son. "Thank you, Laman."

But Laman greeted her with a scowl. "Maybe you can convince Father to turn around tonight."

Sariah bit her lip as he turned and walked away. Though Sariah felt weak with hunger, she had to prepare the men's meal first. Dinah, her youngest daughter, tugged on her garment and dumped an armful of firewood at her feet.

"Mother, I'm hungry," she said.

"I know," Sariah said. "Bring me the dough, and I'll start the fire."

Dinah brought the dough, which was tied in a cloth. She helped her mother make it into flat cakes that they covered with burning embers in order to bake them.

Several yards away, Nephi clenched his jaw. He had heard the exchange between his mother and Laman. He worried about her health and wished he could relieve her burdens.

When the meal was prepared, Lehi gathered the family around the fire. "Let us pray and thank God for our safe journey out of Jerusalem."

Laman tossed a rock into the fire, and the flames surrounded it, trying to find its fuel. He reluctantly bowed his head.

After the prayer, the men ate quickly. The hot bread and boiled barley in sour milk was gone within minutes. Each took a handful of olives and left so that their mother and sisters could eat.

Nephi followed his father a short distance. "Father," he called.

Lehi lowered himself onto his haunches and indicated for Nephi to do the same.

He settled next to his father and said, "When I left to retrieve Mother's trinket box, I ran into Ishmael at our house."

"My cousin?" Lehi asked, turning to look at him.

Nephi nodded. "He asked so many questions that I finally told him we were commanded to leave Jerusalem." Nephi watched his father closely, but he didn't seem upset.

"Ishmael is a good man. He will not betray us," Lehi said, moving his gaze to the sky.

"He had two of his daughters with him," Nephi said.

Lehi stroked his beard. "I wonder why none of Ishmael's daughters are married yet."

"Not many marriages are being planned." When Lehi didn't respond, Nephi looked at his father, but he was still staring at the heavens. "What are you thinking about?"

Lehi was silent for a moment before he shifted his position. "I'm worried about Laman and Lemuel. I think they might be planning to desert us. It could be tempting if we run into caravans heading toward Jerusalem," Lehi said, his voice carrying a tinge of anguish.

Startled, Nephi stared at his father. Did he really think his own sons would leave the family? "But you saw how they defended you against the mob of men last night."

Lehi continued as if he hadn't heard Nephi, "It is a curious thing to raise children. What makes one believe and another falter? Your mother has wept many hours over your brothers' rebellious hearts." He fell quiet.

Nephi noticed the moisture in his father's eyes. After a few moments of silence, he asked, "Where are we going?"

"We'll continue on the Wadi al 'Araba to Eloth," Lehi said.

Nephi furrowed his eyebrows, realizing they were traveling farther than he thought. "Why are we going to Eloth?"

"Because beyond that is nothing but rock and sand."

He understood his father's implication immediately, but another concern rose in Nephi's mind. "The donkeys will never make it in the Arabian desert."

"There will be camel merchants in Eloth with whom we can trade the donkeys," Lehi said, stifling a yawn. "We'll rest a few hours, then leave before dawn."

Stretching his aching muscles, Nephi said, "Mother and the girls will be exhausted."

Lehi scanned the stars above. "But the Lord will provide a way. If we travel at night until we reach Eloth, there will be less chance we'll be recognized. And," he said, rising to his feet, "we'll avoid the desert heat."

* * *

"Wake up."

Nephi mumbled and turned over. It was still dark. Then he remembered—they were leaving before dawn. He sat and rubbed his eyes, the past few days coming into focus.

"Let's go," Sam said, nudging him.

After rolling his bedding into a tight ball, Nephi strapped it to his donkey. His mother's tent had already been loaded onto a camel. Laman was kicking sand over the remnants of the dying fire. His sisters climbed sleepily onto their animals, and Lemuel appeared, leading the donkeys behind him.

Sam handed Nephi a metal cup filled with steamy tea. "Drink the rest of mine. Everything else is packed."

"Why did you let me sleep?" Nephi asked.

"You were still talking with Father when I went to bed, so I thought you could use the rest," Sam explained.

Nephi nodded, but his expression was grave. "Please don't let me oversleep again."

When the family had assembled and loaded all the provisions, Lehi tapped his driver's stick against the flank of his camel. The journey had begun. Again.

Soon a cool wind picked up, and Nephi drew his outer garment around him. The moon and stars shone brightly in the cloudless sky. Before long, his sisters fell asleep in their riding positions. Even Laman and Lemuel were quiet.

An hour had passed when Lehi halted the group. "A caravan is heading toward us."

Nephi heard strain in his father's voice. He hoped the travelers would be friendly. Encountering a caravan in the middle of the night could mean danger. As the caravan grew closer, they heard a shout.

"Who approaches?"

Laman and Lemuel accompanied Lehi to the waiting group. Sam and Nephi followed, remaining a few yards behind. A camel stepped forward, carrying a man dressed in a striped tunic. Its fine weave shone with luster in the moonlight.

Lehi bowed and said, "We are a single family traveling south."

The man assessed the family and grinned. "I am Ahmad Hamin," he said with a thick accent.

The desert Arab tapped his camel, and it dropped to its knees, bellowing. "How far are you traveling?" he asked, climbing off the groaning beast.

"Into Arabia."

Ahmad squinted at the family's donkeys. "You're not well prepared, I see."

"We'll trade for more camels along the way."

The Arab rubbed his pointed beard, chuckling. "It is your lucky night, my friend. I'm a camel merchant."

Nephi saw his father stiffen.

"We can make the journey to Eloth with what we have," Lehi said.

The merchant bowed. "Ahmad Hamin has the best camels in Arabia. Traders in Eloth will take advantage of you."

Nephi held his tongue. The merchants in Eloth would compete against each other for his father's business. This man could easily take advantage of them.

Ahmad looked at Lehi's sons. "I will give you my best price, and if it does not suit you, we'll depart in peace."

Lehi agreed. Ahmad walked slowly through the donkeys. Lehi followed close behind. When they approached the sleeping girls, Ahmad whispered, "Beautiful daughters. Are they betrothed?"

"They are too young to be married," Lehi said sharply.

Ahmad winked. "Not in my country."

Steering Ahmad away from the sleeping girls, Lehi said, "How many camels do you have for sale?"

"I have four strong adults. They have at least fifteen years of service left."

Lehi hesitated then asked, "What is the price?"

"All of them for one of your daughters."

Lehi's face went red. "You insult me."

Ahmad's laugh echoed through the caravan. "I meant no harm. Your daughters are worth many camels." He put his arm around Lehi. "Let us make a deal. I'll give you camels for three donkeys each. That is more than fair. Camels carry more, drink less, live longer. The camels of Ahmad Hamin have many strong years left."

Lehi folded his arms, considering the proposition. He only had three camels and six donkeys. He would need at least three more camels, but he didn't want to lose all of the donkeys just yet. "Will you trade for grain?"

"No," Ahmad said. "We have enough food. It would be an unwanted burden." He paused. "Where you are going, the donkeys will slow the group."

Lehi gave in. "Let me see what you have."

Ahmad grinned, exposing yellow teeth. "Follow me."

Lehi passed through the center of the caravan and to the rear where the unburdened camels stood.

The Arab merchant gripped a rope to hold one animal steady as Lehi circled, looking for wounds or malnutrition.

"He is young and strong," Ahmad said.

Lehi patted the camel's side. "Do you have a nursing female camel?"

"You want fresh milk?"

"It would be a luxury." Lehi's gaze was steady.

Ahmad offered a lopsided grin. "Indeed, we have one, but it isn't for sale."

"How much?" Lehi pressed.

Ahmad's grin faded. "I cannot give you a deal."

With a sigh, Lehi circled the camel once again. Then he stopped resolutely. "I'll trade four donkeys for two camels."

Ahmad chuckled. "You are a man who likes a bargain. Because I like you, I will comply." He clasped Lehi's shoulders and kissed each cheek. "Chocran. Thank you. Thank you. What may I call you, good friend?"

Lehi hesitated. "My name is not important."

"I understand." Ahmad winked. "Would you like to wear my scarf? The Hebrews will mistake you for an Arab." He began to remove his head covering, but Lehi held up his hand and shook his head.

Ahmad bowed. "Very well. I'll have my men unload your donkeys."

When the supplies had been repacked onto the two camels, Lehi thanked the camel merchant.

"Al-hamdu-l-illah," Ahmad said, kissing Lehi on each cheek.

Lehi's family watched the caravan pass slowly. The swarthy men wore checkered scarves wrapped around their heads, concealing their mouths and noses. Dark, glittering eyes appraised Lehi's group. The procession was silent except for an occasional grunt of a camel and the faint tinkling of bells.

By traveling through the night, the family was able to reach Ein Gedi before dawn. Palm trees dotted the landscape, a welcoming sight to the desert travelers. Bedouin tents were pitched at many of the wells. Lehi spotted a deserted one and led the others to it. They loaded goatskin bags into the shallow well, and the animals drank their fill. As the sun rose, illuminating the silvery shores of the Dead Sea, Sariah and her daughters soaked dates in sour milk for the morning meal.

CHAPTER 6

*And let them sacrifice the sacrifices of thanksgiving,
and declare his works with rejoicing.*
(PSALM 107:22)

Laman and Lemuel lounged under a palm tree, eating dates.

"How long do you think we'll stay out here?" Laman asked.

Lemuel spat date seeds into the sand. "I don't know. Father is determined to reach Eloth, which will take at least ten more days. Maybe once we arrive, he'll feel the danger is over."

"I'm glad your friend Gomer is watching the house. How much did you pay him?" Laman asked.

"Enough for two months, with the promise of more when we return. He'll spread the word that we're returning in several weeks. He's probably sleeping in one of our beds right now."

Laman snickered. "Gomer's living in luxury at our expense. Do you think there will be anything left when we return?"

"Don't worry, I counted all of the valuables and made a record of them," Lemuel said, grinning. He withdrew a folded piece of parchment from under his turban. "Look at this."

Laman snatched the list. "Six beds, four tables, seven vases, seventy-two ropes of glass beads . . ." He looked at his brother and scoffed. "You counted the glass beads?"

Lemuel's eyes narrowed. "No one steals from us."

"I'm happy to be in your favor," Laman teased. "What about the animals?"

"They'll be stolen before Gomer claims them."

"You made the right choice," Laman said, nodding thoughtfully. "When Father realizes his mistake, we'll surprise him with his lands and inheritance intact."

Lemuel leaned against the tree. "What do you think happened to those girls?"

"Which ones?"

"Maybe you were too drunk to remember." Lemuel laughed.

Laman threw a date at his brother. "I wouldn't forget a woman."

"In the olive grove, by the vineyards," Lemuel said.

"Oh. I was thinking about a different set of girls."

Lemuel eyes widened. "Who?"

"Ishmael's daughters," Laman said in a low voice. "I would not mind seeing the youngest again."

"You mean Isaabel?"

"Isaabel . . ." Laman repeated gently. "Too bad her older sisters aren't married."

Lemuel jabbed him in the ribs. "You're actually thinking of courting a woman properly?"

Standing, Laman stretched. "Maybe. But until then, there must be attractive women in Ein Gedi, right?"

Lemuel rose next to his brother. "Let's find out."

"Shhh, here comes Father."

When Lehi approached them, he asked, "Have the animals been watered and fed? Come and eat the supper your mother prepared."

* * *

"Eloth," Lehi said, halting his camel and scanning the horizon. It was as beautiful as ever. But he never thought he would travel past Eloth into the barren Arabian desert with his family. In his heart, he offered a prayer asking for continued protection.

Nephi squinted into the dissipating darkness and saw the faint outline of palms. They had been traveling by night for nearly two weeks. With Eloth in sight, an excited murmur spread throughout the family.

"Now we may have fresh fruits and vegetables," Sariah said. Her eyes no longer drooped, but carried a new sparkle.

Elisheba squealed from her perch. "Is there a market? Can we buy a trinket?"

Dinah clapped her hands together. "Can we play with the Bedouin children?"

"Wait and see. We can learn a lot from the desert dwellers." Sariah smiled at her daughters.

Lehi clicked his tongue, and his camel started its loping steps toward the oasis. A shadow crossed his face as he thought about the bustling town they were approaching. The King's Highway funneled to Eloth from the north. Travelers and merchants would be plenty in the town. He hoped his family would not be recognized.

Without provocation, the camels lengthened their stride. Laughter floated through the family as the camels' pace increased.

"Father," called Dinah, "the camels can't wait to get to Eloth."

He looked at his youngest child with affection. "They can smell it."

Lehi and Sariah were the first to crest the next rise. Sariah gasped at the sight. The blue waters of the gulf, encircled by golden sand, shimmered in the early light. Stately palms stood erect, surrounded by flowering oleanders. They had reached the borders of the Red Sea.

Pulling alongside his father, Nephi asked, "What is that smoke?"

"Since King David's capture of the kingdom of Edom, Eloth has become the center for smelting copper and iron ore. King Solomon once stationed his ship fleet here and turned it into a shipbuilding center," he said.

Nephi waited for his father to continue.

Lehi glanced at his youngest son's serious demeanor. "We'll spend the day replenishing our water. Laman and Lemuel will come with me to barter for camels. Your mother will purchase seeds and grain. Take Sam and watch the building of the ships."

Several questions arose in Nephi's mind, but he decided not to ask them yet.

The morning passed quickly as Nephi and Sam walked through the town. Men's bare backs bent over fires as they pounded metal into shape. The sharp sounds rang in Nephi's ears as he paused to watch. Sam kept walking until he reached a low, open building. Inside, men were carving wood planks by hand.

A man dressed in a bright tunic looked up and smiled. "Looking for work?"

Sam shook his head. Nephi arrived and stood next to him.

"What are you shaping?" Nephi asked.

The man grinned and ran his calloused hand along the wood. "The keel. That man over there is shaping the bow and ribs."

Nephi and Sam watched in fascination.

"Would you like to try to work the adze?" the man asked, rising.

Nephi took the sharp, iron blade, squatting in the same fashion the man had. He slid the adze along the grain of the wood, but nothing happened.

"Straighten your elbows, and put your weight into the movement," the shipbuilder said.

Nephi gritted his teeth and pressed with all his strength. Next thing he knew, he lost his balance and fell onto the ground.

The man laughed and was joined by the others in the building who had stopped to watch the strangers.

Nephi rose sheepishly and brushed off his clothing.

"You are young, but strong. You'll soon learn the art," the man said generously.

Smiling at the audience, Nephi waved good-bye. Sam followed him out of the building, chuckling. "Don't worry. You'll not have to build a ship anytime soon."

A loud scraping sound caught the brothers' attention. They approached a tent where workers were stripping the bark off trees. The men pounded their chisels with wooden hammers, filleting the skin from the smooth trunks.

When a few of the men noticed the watching strangers, Nephi and Sam moved out of the tent. They continued walking through the town and came upon a group of men huddled around a heating pot. A young boy was shucking a coconut husk and throwing the fibers into the water.

"What are you making?" Sam asked.

The young boy looked at the visitors shyly. "We make thread to stitch the ships together."

Nephi crouched next to the boy. Although he had never seen a ship, he knew that the Arabs sewed the planks together. The brothers watched the men remove the softened fibers and spin them into coarse thread.

Sam nudged Nephi. "It's midday."

Nephi glanced at the sky and nodded. "We'd better return."

When the brothers returned to camp, Nephi noticed that their two donkeys were missing. Lehi had purchased another camel.

Following an afternoon respite, Lehi woke the family, and they pressed on past Eloth. Traveling along the eastern coastline of the Red Sea, they headed south into the Arabian wilderness.

* * *

On the third day, the family reached the Wadi Tayyab al-Ism. They traveled through the upper valley, finally reaching the deep canyon where a stream of water bubbled from the ground, creating an oasis. A black tent was set up underneath a group of palms. Lehi held up his hand for the others to stop and wait. He approached the tent and was greeted by a wizened man. After a stilted interchange, Lehi purchased one of the Bedouin's sheep.

Lehi returned to his waiting family, the sheep in tow. "No tribes control this pass," he said to Sariah. "We can continue."

Passing through a narrow gorge framed by steep cliffs, they traveled several miles into the canyon. At the base, Lehi stopped in a valley bordered by the Red Sea and surrounded by towering granite walls. He stood for several minutes and scanned the deep valley, then drove his staff into the golden earth.

Nephi turned and gazed at the long canyon they had just passed through. Walls of granite rose two thousand feet from the floor. The valley into which his father had led them enjoyed a cool breeze, with the canyon walls shading the vale from the fierce heat. Before them was a beautiful beach cove surrounded by palm trees.

Elisheba and Dinah ran to the stream and began to splash in it. Dinah leaned into the current and drank a mouthful. "The water is sweet," she said, laughing.

Nephi smiled and walked into the stream. The cool water refreshed his tired feet. The camels, now free from their heavy packs, grazed freely on the scraggly grass.

Sam and Nephi helped their mother sort the provisions. Lehi had insisted that Sariah have her own tent for her comfort. Sariah thanked them, then said, "It is beautiful here."

"How long will we stay?" Sam asked.

Sariah answered, "Father wants the family tent erected, so at least several days."

"Sam and I will set it up," Nephi said. "You should prepare the unleavened bread. It looks like Father is planning to sacrifice a sheep."

In the distance, Lehi stacked rocks into a crude altar.

Nephi motioned for Sam to join him, and they constructed the two-section tent. The front entrance led to the men's section. There was a second section for their two sisters. Just as they started to erect the tent, Laman walked over.

"Enjoying the women's work?" he asked.

Sam heaved a sigh. "Mother can't do all of this by herself."

"And whose fault is that?"

"What do you mean?" Nephi asked, feeling the back of his neck prickle.

"I don't understand why we have to camp in the wilderness. We should move near a city so Father can continue to work."

"I think Father's safety is more important," Nephi said.

"Of course." Laman smirked. "But what happens when the food runs out? Look at this place. There's nothing here."

Nephi opened his mouth to respond, but a bleating sheep interrupted him.

Lehi was leading the animal to the finished altar. The family followed and assembled around the edifice. When everyone was present, they bowed their heads, and the prophet began to pray. "O Lord, we thank Thee for our safe passage into the wilderness. We are indebted to Thee. Accept this peace offering, and bless us in this new land. Amen."

He held the animal's head firmly and quickly slit its throat. He sprinkled the blood around the altar, saying, "We are in Thy service, O Lord."

When he finished, he turned to his eldest son and pointed at the river. "The name of this river shall be called Laman."

Laman lowered his eyes.

Lehi's voice rose into a chant, "O that thou mightest be like unto this river, continually running into the fountain of all righteousness!"

Clenching his teeth, Laman kept his eyes on the ground until his father finished speaking.

"Lemuel," Lehi said sharply. Lemuel snapped his head up. "I shall name this valley after you," he said. "The Valley of Lemuel."

Nodding mutely, Lemuel cast a furtive glance in Laman's direction.

"O that thou mightest be like unto this valley, firm and steadfast and immovable in keeping the commandments of the Lord," Lehi chanted.

Lemuel's face darkened. He slowly raised his head and met Laman's eyes.

Repeating the words of the *sajc* again, Lehi's voice rose in pitch. When he finished the poetry, he grabbed his staff. "We'll meet for council in the tent while your mother prepares our covenant meal."

Lehi led the way to the tent and held the flap for each of his sons to pass into the cool darkness. He lit the fire just inside the entrance, and the men sat cross-legged on the rugs in a circle. Taking a deep breath, Lehi composed his thoughts. Laman and Lemuel sat next to each other, their expressions a mixture of dread and contempt. Nephi and Sam sat close to Lehi. Their father rarely called councils unless something important had happened.

Lehi began in a low voice. "I have heard your murmurings," he said, looking directly at his two oldest sons. "You are stubborn in the ways of the Lord. Do you not know that God himself commanded us to flee the land of our inheritance?"

His face working in fury, Laman stood. "We could have protected you, Father. You had wealth, power, and influence to use against them."

Lemuel rose next to his brother and spread his arms. "Look around us, Father. There is nothing here. What happens when the food runs out? We will perish in this wilderness of yours—"

Nephi couldn't keep silent any longer and stood to face his brothers. "The Lord guided us here. We arrived without harm. Surely you see His hand in that?"

Laman shook his head furiously and glared at Nephi. "How can you believe the Lord wants us to live in this wasteland? Jerusalem is the land of our inheritance that we will pass on to our own sons. Father has imagined foolish things and supposed that our family has to flee in order to be protected. If God were real, He would defend us in our own land and not lead us away to die."

"When Jerusalem is destroyed, you will see the wisdom of Father's words," Nephi said.

"Our great city of Jerusalem will never fall," Lemuel scoffed. "Foolish old men who call themselves prophets could never know such a thing. And you, little brother, would support

Babylonia along with Father. That is the real reason for the threats on his life. He is a traitor to King Zedekiah!"

Lehi rose to his feet, his eyes burning. He raised both his arms toward the tent ceiling. "Silence!" he commanded, anger rising in his chest. "My own sons would call me a traitor to my people? My own sons would conspire against me and follow Zedekiah and his Egyptian pharaoh into moral ruin? You are no better than the men who tried to kill me. You are equal to the men who cast the prophet Jeremiah into prison. What is the depth of your treachery?"

His questions were met with shocked silence.

Eyes smoldering, Lehi continued, "You are afraid to speak now when just a moment ago you accused me of treason? Do you think this is only about who supports Egypt or Babylonia? Jerusalem will be destroyed because of its moral wickedness alone. God will oversee that destruction and will use any means to accomplish it. I am not afraid to say what I know, what I feel, and who I am." Lehi thrust his fist onto his chest. He moved in front of Laman and Lemuel, inches away from their faces. "You will not mock me, and you will not mock God," he said in a harsh whisper.

They began to shake from the power of their father's words.

Lehi grabbed each of their shoulders, his heart holding a mixture of anger and sorrow. "You will not betray me or your mother. God gave us everything we have, and we will not question Him when He takes it away. You will stay with the family and share the work. God will protect us, and we will serve Him." He let his hands drop in exhaustion.

Laman and Lemuel were speechless.

Lehi was spent. There was nothing more he could do to convince his sons of the importance of God's commandments. "Now, my sons, we will eat the sacrifice and dedicate ourselves to God." He bowed his head and stepped outside the tent.

* * *

It was nearly midnight. Sariah sat up, clutching her stomach. "Oh no," she moaned and hurried out of the tent. When she could no longer control herself, she fell to her knees and vomited. Instantly she felt better. A hand touched her shoulder, and she turned to see Lehi.

"What's wrong?" he asked gently.

Sariah rose to her feet. She smoothed her hair with trembling hands. "It is as I have feared."

Worry deepened in Lehi's face. "What do you mean?"

"I am with child."

Lehi stared at his wife. "How long have you known?"

"I suspected before we departed Jerusalem, but I didn't dare believe it," Sariah said, her chin quivering. "I didn't want to cause any concern."

Lehi drew her into his arms. "Oh, Sariah. You should have told me. There's nothing for you to fear. The Lord has blessed us six times, and if it is His will that you should bear this child in the wilderness, then so be it."

Sariah nodded and wiped her eyes with the back of her hand.

"You shouldn't have carried this burden alone. You've been working too hard and must let the others help you more," Lehi said. He stroked Sariah's hair and kissed her forehead.

"I'm afraid of giving birth in the wilderness with no women to help me," Sariah said quietly. "And in my fortieth year, I am no longer as strong as I used to be."

His jaw set firm, Lehi said, "The Lord will strengthen you, and I will take the midwife's place and help deliver the child."

Sariah sighed and leaned against her husband's chest, burrowing her face into his warm beard. Squeezing her eyes shut, she offered a silent prayer, pleading for strength.

* * *

Lehi remained awake long after Sariah had fallen asleep. His mind went over the possibilities one more time. Sariah's previous births had not been life threatening, but she'd also been well attended to with the comforts of home. Bedouin women gave birth in the desert all the time, but he suspected traditions were followed and cautions were taken even in primitive surroundings. It might be wise to return to Eloth for her confinement period.

Another concern arose—Sariah's age.

As he drifted to sleep at last, Lehi's last thought was that perhaps Laman and Lemuel would be motivated to cooperate more, knowing their mother's delicate condition.

CHAPTER 7

Remember them which have the rule over you,
who have spoken unto you the word of God.
(HEBREWS 13:7)

The following morning, Sariah woke early. The embers from the fire pit still glowed just inside her entryway, warming the cool air. The nausea from the night before had dissipated. She smiled. Perhaps the Lord was already answering her prayers. She hung the cooking pots on the center pole of her tent and picked up the rug she had slept on, carrying it outside.

Several paces away, Nephi crouched before the breakfast fire. He warmed his hands against the early flames. The others were still sleeping, bellies full from the feasting the night before. He turned when he heard his mother exit her tent and shake her sleeping mat. Her bracelets jangled faintly in the quiet morning. He watched as she busied herself outside the tent.

When Sariah saw him, Nephi motioned for her to join him. She walked over quietly and squatted next to him, warming her own hands. She gazed into the flames, lost in thought.

Nephi watched quiet thoughts play upon his mother's face, which was open and still youthful—only faint lines marked her forehead. Her hair was lustrous with intermingling hues of black, and her wide eyes with heavy lashes could smile in an instant, though sorrow often lay beneath her expression. But it was her hands that betrayed her age. Dark spots speckled her skin. The knuckles were large and the connecting bones prominent. Her bronzed skin was a backdrop for the sun-bleached hairs, the veins creating a roadmap of service intersected with love.

Nephi knew his oldest brothers caused his mother great pain. She was a woman who trusted in the Lord and believed in her husband. She had nurtured her older sons and loved them as only a devoted mother could. But they had grown ill-tempered and discontent. Nephi hoped that after last night's council, their hearts would change.

He thought about his father and the absolute faith he had in God. When Lehi had commanded Laman and Lemuel to stay loyal to the family and to God, Nephi knew he had to find out for himself what his father knew. Nephi glanced over at his mother, who was quietly humming.

"I'll be back soon, Mother," he said.

Sariah barely acknowledged him, a far-off look in her eyes.

Nephi stood and stretched his cramped legs. He pulled his coat tightly about him and walked toward the canyon mouth. He knew he was not a prophetic man like his father, but he hoped he would find some answers. Stopping at a crevice in the granite wall, he stepped out of sight. Groupings of grass protruded from the angled rock. He pulled at the jagged green shafts and twisted them in his fingers, pondering what he might say.

In the silence of the morning, Nephi knelt on the hard desert floor. He bowed his head and closed his eyes tightly, as if to make his prayer more sincere. "O Lord," he said, gripping his hands together, "I know my father is a righteous man. I know that Thou hast spoken to him, guided him, and protected him. Above all else, I am grateful for the safety Thou hast given our family." His voice cracked. "But, I want to know for *myself,* Lord. I want to feel what my father feels and to *know* without a doubt."

Nephi felt his eyes burn and his heart ache. His palms grew moist from pressing them together. "Please let me know if we were led by Thee into this wilderness." Nephi paused, the tears flowing freely now. "I never thought it would be so difficult, and the contention with my brothers is almost unbearable. I don't know if I can endure much longer. If it is Thy will, please give me a sure knowledge that we are here by Thy hand."

Shoulders sagging, Nephi's voice fell into labored breathing. Something pushed down on his shoulders, causing his knees to dig into the rocky earth. Nephi gasped at the pressure, then suddenly it was gone, and he felt as if he were floating above the ground.

Warmth spread through his body, and his legs and arms grew numb. Clear and simple thoughts entered his mind, and he began to understand the teachings of his father. The Lord would be with them as long as they had faith. A sudden burst of joy spread through him, and he felt as though his spirit were being lifted up. He knew all of the words his father spoke were true. He knew that Jerusalem would be destroyed and that they had been led into the wilderness to escape their own destruction.

When Nephi opened his eyes, it was as if he'd just awakened from a delicious rest. His mind was clear, his senses keen, and his body energized. "Thank you, Lord," he said, looking up to the sky. "I now know what I must do."

He hurried back to camp, his heart racing. He crept into the men's tent and roused Sam.

"Come with me," he whispered.

Sam rose, sleepiness in his eyes, but he followed Nephi outside. Nephi led the way back to the mouth of the canyon and drew Sam beside him.

"I prayed and the Holy Spirit visited me!" he said breathlessly.

Sam stared at him.

Nephi clasped both of Sam's hands into his own. "Right here," he said, pointing to the ground. "The Spirit testified to me. It's true—all of it. Jerusalem will be destroyed and we have been led by God into this wilderness." Nephi's eyes shone with tears, and he began to laugh. "Isn't it incredible?"

Tears formed in Sam's eyes, and his heart started to pound. "You have been given a wonderful gift, Nephi. And through you, I know too. I hoped our family was meant for greater things than an unruly Jerusalem," he said, placing a hand over his racing heart.

Nephi embraced Sam. "I must tell the others," he said. Before Sam could speak another word, Nephi started running back to the tents.

Laman and Lemuel had just roused from their slumber when Nephi burst through the tent flap.

"I've been visited by the Holy Spirit," he said.

Laman sat up, rubbing his eyes. "Where am I? In the temple?"

With a groan, Lemuel asked, "Isn't it too early for religion?"

Nephi knelt beside their mats, ignoring their comments. "I prayed this morning to understand our journey, and now I know that Father was commanded to leave Jerusalem. We are supposed to stay in the wilderness."

"It appears we have another visionary man in the family." Smiling, Laman winked at Lemuel.

Lemuel slapped his leg and hooted out loud. "And where does the Lord want us to go today, *prophet?*"

Undaunted, Nephi continued. "You heard what Father asked us to do last night. I just wanted to find out for myself."

They looked at each other with amused expressions. "Yes," Laman said. "We heard what *Father* said. But that doesn't mean we have to listen to *you*." He flicked Nephi's shoulder.

"The Holy Spirit is telling me it's time to eat," said Lemuel, rising. Both brothers burst out laughing.

Nephi backed out of the tent, his face ashen. After last night, he thought his brothers would be more receptive. He walked past the breakfast fire, past Sariah's questioning gaze, past Sam's knowing frown, and into the silent canyon.

He found the crevice once again and knelt, leaning against the cold stone. "O Lord," he cried, "please soften my brothers' hearts. They know not Whom they mock—"

Blessed art thou, Nephi, because of thy faith, for thou has sought me diligently, with lowliness of heart.

Nephi's eyes flew open. He looked behind him, then toward the heavens. No one was there. But he had heard the deep voice as if someone had whispered it in his ear.

The voice came again. *And inasmuch as ye shall keep my commandments, ye shall prosper and shall be led to a land of promise, yea, even a land which I have prepared for you, yea, a land which is choice above all other lands.*

Nephi sank to the ground, the voice still whispering to him. *And inasmuch as thy brethren shall rebel against thee, they shall be cut off from the presence of the Lord.* Nephi's eyes began to burn. *And inasmuch as thou shalt keep my commandments, thou shalt be made a ruler and a teacher over thy brethren.*

Tears coursed down his cheeks. He felt overwhelmed—
he was to become the leader over his brothers.

*For behold, in that day that they shall rebel against me, I
will curse them even with a sore curse, and they shall have no
power over thy posterity except they shall rebel against me also.
And if it so be that they rebel against me, they shall be a scourge
unto thy posterity, to stir them up in the ways of remembrance.*

When the voice was silent, Nephi slowly opened his eyes.
His breathing was shallow. Had he had a vision? No, he
thought. He hadn't seen anything. But his ears had heard the
voice of the Lord. Just like his father, the Lord had blessed
him. Nephi bit his trembling lip and wrapped his arms
around his torso. Rocking back and forth, he thought of the
promises—the responsibilities—given him.

He had to write it down, all of it. Staggering to his feet,
he walked in the direction of camp in a trance, not paying
attention to the jeering looks from his brothers who were
tending to the camels.

As Nephi reached his father's tent, Sam grabbed his arm.
"Are you all right?" Nephi moved past him and pushed his
way inside the shelter. He went directly to the parchment
box. Sam followed him and quietly watched. In the dim
light, Nephi wrote the words which the Lord had spoken to
him just moments before.

When he was finished, he stored the parchment at the
bottom of a basket to show his father later. A movement
from the corner of the tent startled him. It was Lehi.

"I didn't realize you were in here, Father," Nephi said.

"I didn't want to disturb your writing," Lehi said. "Bring
it here."

Nephi removed the parchment and gave it to his father.
Lehi motioned for Sam to join them, and he read the words
slowly. When he finished, he looked up at Nephi, tears in his

eyes. "The Lord has spoken to you." He stared at him in wonder. "It is as it should be. The Lord has chosen you to rule over your brothers, and you will become a great leader," he said, rising to embrace him.

Sam stood before Nephi, head bowed. "You will always have my loyalty." The brothers embraced.

"Can you find Mother for me?" Nephi asked Sam.

"Yes."

After Sam had left the tent, Lehi gazed at his youngest son. "Nephi," he said, "I have dreamed a dream."

✶ ✶ ✶

Isaabel trailed her stick in the murky water. Algae had multiplied in the deserted fountain, creating a thin, green covering. Sheltered from the busy market by the grove of trees surrounding the fountain, Isaabel's thoughts turned to worry. It had been over two weeks since Lehi's family had left Jerusalem. Since then, another prophet had been killed, and the great prophet Jeremiah remained in prison.

She sighed. Her sisters would be looking for her, but she wasn't ready to join their chattering group. Rumors had been circulating that Sabtah, son of Levi, was going to make an offer for her oldest sister, Rebeka. She smiled at the thought. Her sister was twenty-three, long past the proper marrying age, but the match would be a good one since Sabtah's first wife died in childbirth and he needed a mother for the three remaining children.

Rebeka would make a good mother, Isaabel thought. *She is certainly demanding enough. Then only three more sisters before . . .* Isaabel jumped at the sound of breaking branches behind her. Someone was approaching the fountain. She ducked behind the nearby bushes and waited for them to pass.

Two men came into view, one stout and one tall and thin. The stout man looked around furtively, and the tall one carried a goatskin vessel.

"Did you bring the map, Gomer?" the tall man asked.

The man named Gomer ignored the question. "Where's the money?"

The tall man held up the goatskin and shook it. "In here."

"How will it happen?"

The other man scanned their surroundings, then said, "First, I will contact the others and choose a night. You'll meet us at Lehi's door and let us in. After we have uncovered all of the treasure, we'll rough you up, and you'll start yelling after we leave. By the time you tell your story, we'll be south of Jerusalem. Let things settle for a week or so, then meet us in Hebron. Just ask for the Cush brothers."

Isaabel suppressed a gasp.

Gomer hesitated. "How can I ensure your word is good?"

The tall man removed a knife from his belt and cut his finger. He grabbed Gomer's hand and sliced his finger. Then he pressed his own bleeding finger against Gomer's. "We are covenant brothers now. No one can break our bond." The man replaced his knife. "Are you sure that Lehi and his family aren't returning anytime soon?"

"You have my word, *Brother*," Gomer promised. "When will the robbery take place?"

"My brother returns from Jericho in two weeks. When he has gone over the plan, we'll set the time. Now let's see Laman's map."

Gomer handed over a rolled parchment.

Isaabel shifted her position slightly to get a better view.

The tall man unrolled the map halfway and scanned the document. Then he clapped Gomer on the shoulder. "You're a good man. Wait a few minutes after I leave before you make your exit."

Isaabel waited behind the bushes until Gomer left. She had overheard many disturbing things lately. Since Lehi's family's departure, she had been listening carefully to what those around her were saying. Her brothers often spoke of the political strife in Jerusalem. Most of the elders favored Egypt. Lehi and other prophets like Jeremiah supported an alliance with Babylonia. The sarim had accused Jeremiah of speaking treason, and Lehi openly supported him.

When Gomer's footsteps were no longer audible, she breathed freely. She had to find a way to stop them, she realized. She rushed back to her sisters in the market square.

"What took you so long?" Tamar asked.

Isaabel avoided her gaze. "I took a wrong turn."

The girls finished making their purchases and walked home. Isaabel stayed in the workroom weaving long past supper. She hoped that she would be able to speak with her father alone. Finally, when her mother retired for the night, Isaabel crept into the dining room and found her father wrapped in a heavy rug, reading a scroll by the firelight.

Ishmael looked up to see his youngest daughter in the doorway. "Ah, I didn't know anyone was still awake."

She sat next to him on the floor rug and looked at his flushed face. "Are you ill, Father?"

He suppressed a cough and shrugged. "It will pass."

"I need to tell you something important," Isaabel said.

A look of concern crossed his face. "By all means."

"I overheard two men by the old fountain planning a robbery," she said quietly.

Ishmael reached for her hand. "You weren't hurt, were you?"

"No, they didn't know I was there."

He frowned. "What were you doing spying on them?"

"I didn't mean to. I heard someone coming and hid behind the bushes. Two men appeared, and one gave the other a map."

"A map of what?" Ishmael asked.

"Lehi's estate," Isaabel replied, her voice uneven. "They are staging a robbery of his valuables."

He stroked his beard. "Hmm. Are you sure it is the same Lehi we know?"

"They also mentioned Laman's name," she said.

Ishmael patted his daughter's shoulder. He began coughing, shallow at first, then deeper.

Isaabel knelt by her father's side, took his hand, and waited for his cough to dissipate. "You don't look so good."

Her father brushed off the comment. "You did the right thing by telling me. We certainly don't want Lehi's property robbed. Did they say when the family might be returning?"

"Neither of them said anything."

A knock sounded at the door, making both of them jump.

Ishmael placed his hand on his daughter's arm. "Stay here." He shed the covering about his shoulders and left to answer the door.

"Who is it?" Isaabel heard him ask.

"I have a message for Ishmael," came a deep voice.

Ishmael cracked the door open and took the rolled parchment extended to him. "Thank you," he said, and shut the door.

He walked to the table and sat down. He shook his head when he saw the scarlet insignia sealing the document. Breaking the wax, he unrolled the paper and read the message.

"Curses," he muttered.

"What's wrong, Father?" Isaabel asked.

Ishmael looked at her in surprise, as if he'd forgotten her

presence. "Uh . . . it's just a letter from someone I don't particularly like." He placed the letter in his sash. "You should be sleeping. Good night."

Isaabel kissed her father on his too-warm cheek and left the room. Before exiting, she heard her father mutter, "Laban, I will not join your marzeah."

* * *

The following day, Isaabel woke with the late morning sun on her face. She sat up and realized that her sisters had already begun their chores. She was surprised they hadn't awakened her.

Climbing out of bed, she looked at her sleepy face in the polished metal. Black eyes stared back at her. She pinched her cheeks and watched the color spread. Then she quickly brushed her wavy hair and pinned it into a knot. The prattle from her sisters floated through the bedroom window.

"Maybe he will visit today," Anah said.

"It is bad luck to speak of it," Rebeka replied sharply.

Isaabel sighed. Her oldest sister was always afraid of bad luck.

She went into the hallway, passing her parents' room. She paused when she heard her mother's sobbing voice. "Rebeka will not become that cruel man's wife!"

Isaabel froze in her steps. Her father said, "Sabtah has not even come to our house yet."

"You must put a stop to this before he does, or we'll all be disgraced. If the rumors are true about him, he'll beat our daughter until she miscarries too."

Covering her mouth, Isaabel crept into the dining room. A jug of water and some flat bread still remained on the table. She bit into the bread hungrily, her heart thudding. She thought about her mother calling Sabtah a cruel man.

Even though she knew her parents must be anxious to marry off their oldest daughter, they would not stoop so low. Voices came into the hallway.

Ishmael said, "We don't know if the rumors are true. Sabtah may be the only one willing to take such a meager dowry."

Her parents entered the dining room. Isaabel felt her face flame when they saw her sitting at the table.

Her mother wiped her eyes quickly. "Why are you not outside with your sisters?" she demanded.

Isaabel opened her mouth to explain, but Ishmael cut her off. "She was awake into the night, talking to me."

Bashemath glared at Isaabel. "What about?"

Isaabel swallowed and looked at her hands.

"She overheard some men plotting to rob Lehi's property."

"So?" Bashemath asked with a shrug. "I'm sure Lehi took all his valuables with him." She looked directly at Isaabel. "How did you happen to overhear those men?"

Ishmael held up his hand. "Isaabel is not at fault, Bashemath. Lehi is my cousin, and I need to find a way to prevent this robbery."

Folding her arms, Bashemath pursed her lips. She could not disagree with protecting one's own family.

CHAPTER 8

Ye shall diligently keep the commandments of the Lord your God,
and his testimonies, and his statutes,
which he hath commanded thee.

(DEUTERONOMY 6:17)

Nephi sat across from his father. The fire's dying embers cast shadows around the tent. Lehi spoke quietly. "My kinsman Laban has the record of the Jews and our genealogy engraven on plates of brass."

Nephi knew genealogy records were kept in the elders' homes. Laban must be one of the elders.

Lehi continued, his heart aching because of the words he must say, "The Lord commanded that you and your brothers should go to the house of Laban and seek the records to bring them into the wilderness."

Nephi stared at his father. The Lord wanted them to return to Jerusalem? A slow burning began to grow in his chest. As incredible as the request seemed, he knew the Lord was guiding his father.

"I have told your brothers, and they murmured, saying it is too difficult. But *I* have not required it of them—it is a commandment of the Lord." His eyes implored Nephi's, as if begging him to accept the Lord's request.

Nephi gripped his father's outstretched arms and nodded.

Warmth spread through Lehi's bosom as he realized Nephi understood. "Go with my blessing, my son, and you'll be favored of the Lord because you have not murmured," Lehi said.

Leaning forward, Nephi embraced his father. "Thank you. I will go and do the things which the Lord has commanded. I know He will prepare the way for us to accomplish His will."

"We would accompany you, but your mother is with child," Lehi said, his eyes growing moist. "May God be with you, son."

Nephi stepped out of the tent and looked around the camp. His three brothers were still eating breakfast, and Laman and Lemuel were laughing. Sam saw Nephi emerge and stood to meet him. But the questions in Sam's eyes would remain unanswered for the present. Nephi ate his share of the meal quickly and left to gather the camels.

Laman and Lemuel sauntered up to Nephi. "What are you doing?" Laman asked.

Tossing the rope halter on the camel, he turned. "Preparing for our journey back to Jerusalem," he said.

"You're coming too?" Lemuel asked.

Nephi tightened the rope around the camel's neck. "Father wants all of the brothers to go."

"Lemuel and I can make the journey on our own," Laman said, his face discoloring.

"Perhaps he thinks you'll need help obtaining the brass plates from Laban." Nephi pulled the protesting camel forward with the rope and started walking to the tents.

Laman clenched his fists together, and Lemuel grabbed his elbow. "Let's speak with Father."

The brothers pushed their way into their father's tent, leaving Nephi behind.

Sam rushed to Nephi when Laman and Lemuel disappeared into the tent. "What's happening?"

Nephi told Sam about the assignment. Sam shook his head. "I believe the Lord is guiding us too, but do you think we should leave the women behind? Father will be the only one here to protect them."

Nephi lowered his voice. "Mother is with child, so it would not be good for her to make such a quick journey. He will stay behind to take care of her."

Sam frowned. "Will Mother be all right giving birth in the wilderness?"

"The Lord will keep her in mind and provide a way. Besides, I think we are the ones who will be in danger," Nephi said.

"What do you mean?" Sam asked.

"The elders of Jerusalem don't exactly favor Father. If Laban is anything like those who oppose Jeremiah, we'll have trouble," Nephi said.

Laman and Lemuel stumbled out of the tent before them. "We leave tonight," Laman said, his face twisting in anger.

At sunset, the four brothers stood before their camels. Sariah embraced each of her sons, trying to hold back tears. But as they mounted their camels, her resolve broke. Nephi held his mother's hand, trying to reassure her. "We'll return soon."

Sariah nodded and wiped her eyes, releasing Nephi's hand. Nephi turned his camel and followed the others. His heart was heavy with anticipation. It would take almost a month to make the round-trip journey, and he worried about his parents' well-being.

From a distance, Lehi watched his sons' departure. He'd already bid them farewell, but the moment of leaving was bittersweet. Never had his sons made such a journey without him. Silently he prayed for their safety, not only against outside danger, but against their own dispositions.

Laman and Lemuel took the lead into the canyon along the River Laman. Nephi and Sam discussed the instructions Nephi had received from the Lord.

"What will our brothers do when they learn you are to be their future leader?" Sam asked.

Nephi gripped his reins. "Hopefully they'll choose to follow the Lord. We are nothing without God, so we must follow the commandments given us."

Sam watched as his younger brother pulled ahead of him. He had seen him grow from a boy to a man in just a few weeks. The Nephi returning to Jerusalem was not the same youth who had left it.

* * *

Ten days later, the four brothers reached the outskirts of Jerusalem. The cooler months had enveloped the land, and the hills were losing their green luster. But the early morning sunlight had turned the ivory buildings to amber. With a lump in his throat, Nephi realized that he had missed the rolling hills of his home.

Traveling had been easier without the rest of the family, but the meals were not the same without the women. The fruits and vegetables purchased in Eloth were long gone, and no one had the patience to make bread. Laman and Lemuel had ignored Sam and Nephi most of the time.

They decided to camp on a slow-rising hill a short distance from the city walls. They found a relatively clear area behind a grove of olive trees. It was far enough away from the city so as not to draw too much notice.

Nephi threw his mat onto the ground, and Sam helped him erect the small tent which they shared. Laman and Lemuel were already resting in the shade of theirs. The rising sun would soon spread its merciless heat on the tired travelers. Nephi climbed into the tent and lay down on his bedroll. *This time tomorrow,* he thought, *we will be leaving Jerusalem.*

Sam sighed next to him. "Do you think Laban will just hand over the records?"

Nephi opened his eyes. "I don't know. It depends on the type of man he is and whether or not he is sympathetic to Father."

With a grunt, Sam rolled over onto his side. Minutes later, Nephi heard his soft snoring. Nephi closed his eyes, thinking about the last time he'd seen his home. It seemed so long ago now. Then he remembered a face he hadn't allowed himself to think about in over a month. The face of a young woman he thought he'd never see again.

* * *

"They're up," Sam whispered.

Nephi woke with a start. "Who?"

"Laman and Lemuel. They're outside."

He drew open the tent flap and saw them squatting on the ground, drawing pictures in the sand.

"Oh, look who's awake," Laman said with a grin.

Nephi stumbled out of the shelter and approached them.

Laman handed Nephi a pebble. "Let's cast lots."

The four brothers placed their pebbles into a clay vessel. Laman shook the jar and poured the stones onto the ground. Laman's landed the farthest from the group. His face went bright red. "So be it. It's fitting for the eldest to represent the family anyway. When the sun sets, I'll begin the journey."

At sundown, Laman climbed upon his camel, his brow set firm. He threw a halfhearted look at the others. "I'll be back soon," he said.

Lemuel smacked the camel's rump and stood watching until Laman disappeared from view. Nephi went into his tent and offered a prayer in behalf of his brother.

* * *

Several hours later, Lemuel spotted a camel approaching their makeshift camp. "It's Laman. He's back," he said.

The camel halted, and when it dropped to its knees, Laman climbed off. His face was a mask of stone.

"Did you get them?" Nephi asked.

Laman looked hard at Nephi. "I went to Laban's house. His servant showed me into his chambers. There he sat—in his fine clothes and jewelry. A feast was set out before him of the most delectable foods imaginable. Sliced lamb, breasts of chicken, sweet cakes, red wine . . ." Laman brought his focus back to his brothers. "He listened to my plea, and suddenly," Laman paused, "Laban flew into a rage and called me a robber, then screamed for his servants to seize me so that he could slay me—" He gripped the knife under his belt.

The three brothers stared at him in disbelief.

"I fled his house and the city. I'm sure his men are still hunting for me," he said, his voice sounding panicked.

Nephi moaned. "Laban must be against Father," he said.

Sam spread his hands in helplessness. "Now what do we do?"

"I'm leaving. There's an order for my head, and I'm not waiting around here for it to be served," Laman said.

Lemuel looked around. "Laman's right. We can't stay. It's too late to negotiate with the tyrant."

Nephi raised his hand. "Wait. We can't leave now—not after coming all this way. The Lord commanded us to recover the records. Maybe we can make a trade with Laban."

"What do you mean?" Lemuel asked, confusion creasing his forehead.

"Let's gather the gold and silver that Father left behind. Laban will give us the plates when he sees what we have to offer," Nephi said.

"Laban will try to kill us the moment he recognizes Laman," Lemuel protested.

"Not with our father's riches, he won't," Nephi said. "I don't think he'll mind trading some old plates for our property."

Laman nodded. "Perhaps you're right."

"We have to try," Nephi said in earnest.

"We'll leave tomorrow night then, under the cover of darkness," Laman said, sighing.

* * *

The following evening, the brothers loaded their provisions onto the camels in the gathering dusk. They traveled with heavy hearts until they reached their father's estate.

When the house finally came into view, Lemuel noticed several lanterns lighting the courtyard. "Gomer must be there," he whispered to Laman.

Nephi climbed off his camel. "Why are there lights?"

Lemuel cleared his throat. "A friend is watching over the place for us."

"What do you mean?" Nephi glanced from Lemuel to Laman.

Suddenly a man appeared in the courtyard. "Who goes there?" he called out.

Laman stepped forward into the light. "It's Laman and Lemuel."

Gomer embraced the brothers and then stood back. "Who are the others?"

"Our younger brothers."

"So you've returned already?" Gomer looked back and forth between the men nervously.

"I trust everything is in order?" Lemuel asked.

Gomer nodded, glancing furtively at the ground.

The grunt of an animal made them all turn. Three camels entered the courtyard. Gomer stepped forward, fear in his eyes. "Identify yourselves."

The old man in front climbed off his camel. "I am Ishmael, cousin to Lehi."

Gomer shrank back, but Lehi's sons embraced the man. "What are you doing here?" Nephi asked.

Ishmael stared at the brothers. "I thought you had left Jerusalem."

"We've returned on a mission for our father," Laman said.

Ishmael smiled and looked about the group. "You are in luck then. I have a story to tell you."

"We're in need of a good story," Laman said with a grin. "Come into the house, and we'll find something to drink."

Ishmael motioned for the other two men who were with him to follow. "You remember my sons, Raamah and Heth?"

Laman and Lemuel greeted them and led the way into the house. The men entered the front room and gathered around the hearth. "Is there anything to drink, Gomer?" Laman asked.

Gomer's face went pale, but he nodded and left the room.

"Ah, so he is Gomer," Ishmael said, stroking his beard.

"He has been protecting our property in our absence," Lemuel said.

In a low voice, Ishmael said, "He can't be trusted."

Laman eyes narrowed. "Why not?"

Ishmael leaned into the circle of men and whispered, "He is staging a robbery of your father's property."

Lemuel shot to his feet. "Impossible. Gomer and I are as close as brothers—"

"Wait." Ishmael interrupted. "There is more."

Lemuel folded his arms, and the others held their breath.

"His friends are coming here tonight. They have a map of where your father's valuables are buried," Ishmael said, his voice rising. "Gomer was to pretend to be assaulted and later meet them in Jericho to share in the fortune."

Murmuring rose among the group. Ishmael continued, "I brought my sons with me tonight to turn out Gomer and lie in wait for the others."

Raamah and Heth grinned and opened their coats, revealing long knives.

"Let's ask Gomer if this is true," Laman said over the murmuring.

Rising, Lemuel stomped into the next room. The men heard him calling for Gomer, but there was no answer. Lemuel appeared at the doorway, his face red. "He has fled! Let's chase after the scoundrel."

Laman jumped to his feet and followed Lemuel outside.

A few minutes later the two brothers returned, panting. "He's gone," Lemuel sputtered.

Ramaah shrugged his shoulders. "So be it. His friends will receive a surprise when they arrive and find us here."

"Not necessarily," Nephi said. "Gomer will warn them. We won't see their faces in Jerusalem again."

All heads nodded.

"Our business is finished here." Ishmael stood. "Let us leave Lehi's sons to theirs."

Nephi and his brothers thanked Ishmael. Sam and Nephi
followed them out to their camels.

"How are your parents?" Ishmael asked Nephi.

"They're well, but anxious for our return," Nephi said.
The two men embraced.

"Can I be of further service?"

"Not unless you are good friends with Laban."

Ishmael's face drained of color. "Unfortunately, I am not
well thought of in his circle." A heavy cough erupted.

Concerned, Nephi asked, "Are you feeling well?"

"It's been a long day, but I'll be fine."

Nephi agreed, then asked, "How did you happen to
discover the robbery plans?"

Ishmael's eyes lit up and some color returned to his face.
"Ah, there's a tale. My youngest daughter overheard the
scheming men. She couldn't bear to see harm done to your
family."

Nephi bowed his head. "We're indebted to her service."

"Indeed. I'm lucky to have such a daughter."

Nephi answered quickly, "Thank you again." Even in the
dark, he found himself trying to suppress his smile as he
watched Ishmael and his sons leave.

When he turned, he saw Laman standing in the courtyard watching him. "So little Isaabel saved our inheritance,
eh?" Laman asked.

The last thing Nephi needed was for Laman to know
that the thought of Ishmael's youngest daughter made his
blood race. He lifted a shoulder nonchalantly.

Laman grunted. "Let's start digging."

CHAPTER 9

Take heed unto yourselves,
lest ye forget the covenant of the Lord your God.
(DEUTERONOMY 4:23)

"Cover your trails," Laman instructed.

The brothers had spent over an hour digging the metal boxes out of the ground.

"Will the camels be able to hold all of this?" Sam asked.

Lemuel grimaced. "They'll have to. We'll need to conceal it, though."

Laman and Lemuel heaved the final box from the earth and carried it to the courtyard. Sam and Nephi worked quickly to fill the hole, then hurried back to the camels.

While Laman and Lemuel lifted the heavy chests onto the protesting camels, Sam lashed the treasure to the saddles. Nephi brought out the best rugs from their house and arranged them on top of the precious goods.

They climbed onto the laden camels. Nephi patted his animal and said, "It's just for a little while. Then you'll only have to carry the tents."

When they reached the city, Laman led them through the winding streets of Jerusalem. Dark had long fallen, and only an occasional torch lit the way.

Laman paused when they reached the outer courtyard to Laban's two-tiered home.

Lemuel nudged him. "Offer the guard a few coins."

The guard eagerly accepted the money and commanded them to tie the camels to the gate. When the brothers refused to leave their camels, they were led to a private courtyard.

"Is this where you were before?" Sam asked in a whisper.

Laman nodded his head, his face pallid.

They waited for several moments before a servant appeared. The servant looked around nervously and asked, "What do you want?"

Lemuel stepped forward and cleared his throat. "We've brought gifts for your master."

The servant's expression relaxed. "Camels?"

"No," Lemuel said. "The gifts are what the camels are carrying."

Nephi untied a metal box and opened the lid. The servant's eyes widened when he saw the gold coins spill out. "I'll report to my master," he said.

Moments later, a large man appeared with several servants in tow. He wore a bronze breastplate emblazoned with Zedekiah's crest. The jewels on his turban twinkled in the light of the torch he held.

"Who are you?"

Lemuel stooped into a bow. "We have brought gifts from our father, Lehi, of the tribe of Manasseh."

Laban stood before the men and crossed his massive arms over his chest. "And what does your father want from me?"

"In return for our precious cargo," Lemuel said, spreading his arms wide, "we would like the genealogical record of our ancestors that you keep."

Laban squinted in the darkness, trying to identify their faces. "I thought I took care of this already."

Nephi and Sam pulled the rugs from the camels. The servants surrounding Laban gasped.

"Well, look at what we have here," Laban said, a broad grin stretching his face. "All of this is your father's?"

Lemuel spoke with authority. "Yes, sir."

Walking between the camels, Laban fingered the fine pottery, vases, and metal artwork. "What's in these chests?"

Nephi and Sam unloaded the metal chests and opened the lids, revealing silver mixed with gold coins. Laban squatted and ran his fingers through the coins in a trunk. He plucked a single gold coin out and held it up to the light. Then he bit down on the metal. Dropping the coin back into the chest, he looked at Lemuel.

"Unload everything. While my servants make a tally, I will consider your offer and return with an answer."

Laban turned and left the courtyard, flanked by his groveling servants. Two remained behind and silently counted the goods as the brothers unloaded them.

After the servants finished, they left the brothers alone.

"Something's not right," Sam warned.

"Shhh," Nephi said, "they may be listening."

The brothers stood together and waited in silence. Laman whispered, "I don't think he's going to let us live."

Lemuel wiped the sweat beading on his brow.

After motioning for his brothers to remain still, Nephi crept to the opening of the courtyard and peered around the sculpted foliage. He watched as armed men noiselessly gathered in the next courtyard. Laban stood in their midst, smiling and counting their heads. When the number reached a dozen, he nodded. Nephi backed away, his heart beating rapidly. He rushed to his brothers.

"He's assembling his guards," he said.

Laman withdrew his knife and gripped the shaft. Lemuel and Sam unsheathed their weapons. Nephi hesitated, then whispered, "Let's make our escape." He climbed onto his camel, followed by his brothers. He whipped the camel's rump. It jolted forward, and Nephi maneuvered it through the scattered palms in the broad courtyard, then bolted toward the gate. His brothers tagged close behind. Shouts arose behind them, but Nephi pressed on until they reached the gate.

Nephi ordered his camel to a stop and the others followed. "We'll rush the gate and the guard won't be able to stop us."

The brothers whisked the camels into a frenzy until their knobby knees obeyed. On stampeding camels, their turbans flying, they stormed through the gate. The guard leaped out of the way and was left to choke on billowing dust.

Nephi and his brothers rode hard through the dark streets of Jerusalem. Once they reached the outside walls, Nephi slowed and turned to see if they were still being pursued. A dozen men on camels soon came into view.

"They're not giving up!" Laman shouted.

"Hut! Hut! Hut!" Nephi cried, urging his camel on.

They left the main road and headed across the hills in the moonlight until they realized they were no longer in danger of being overtaken.

"Let's stop here," Nephi said, panting. He climbed off his heaving camel and scouted the nearby caves. Sam alighted and followed Nephi.

Sam stopped in front of a cave. "This one is large enough for all of us and the animals. It will be a good lookout."

Nephi eased himself to the ground.

Laman and Lemuel watched the landscape for a while, then joined their younger brothers in the cave. Laman stood over their reclined figures and prodded Nephi with his staff. "This is all your fault. Now we have no inheritance," he said through clenched teeth.

Nephi and Sam rose to their feet. "We couldn't know that Laban was an outright thief," Nephi said.

Laman sneered, his eyes narrow slits. "After what he did to me?"

"The Lord has commanded us to—"

"To die?" Lemuel cut Nephi off, then shouted, "What purpose would that serve?"

"You are worse than those who plotted our father's death, worse than a visionary man leading his entire family to perish in the wilderness. You are nothing!" Laman struck Nephi with his stick.

Sam tried to block the blow, but he was hit from behind by Lemuel.

Another blow from Laman, and Nephi was knocked to the ground. He shielded his head with one hand while he scratched the ground for a rock or anything else he could use to defend himself.

Several feet away, Sam cried out in pain. "Stop . . ."

With each strike, Laman and Lemuel became more ferocious. Nephi's head was spinning, his body numb from the blows. He clawed at the ground and tried to rise to his knees, but the strikes kept coming.

"Why do ye smite your younger brother with a rod?" came a deep, solemn voice.

Nephi's ears were ringing. He realized that his brothers had stopped beating him.

The voice came again, strong and firm. "Know ye not that the Lord hath chosen him to be a ruler over you, and this because of your iniquities?"

Nephi saw that the ground was bathed in a glowing light. He half-turned and raised himself to his elbows. A man with golden hair and long, white robes stood in front of Laman. Nephi lifted his bloody hand to shield his eyes from the brightness. Then Nephi noticed that the man wasn't standing on the ground at all. He was floating just above it. Heat seared into Nephi's heart as he realized the being wasn't a man—he was an angel.

The messenger continued, "Behold, ye shall go up to Jerusalem again, and the Lord will deliver Laban into your hands."

Laman sank to the ground next to Nephi, his face contorted in shock. Lemuel hit the earth with a thud. Nephi stared at his fallen brothers, then looked to the angel. But the heavenly being was gone.

A few feet away, Sam scrambled to his feet, gaping at the now vacant spot where the angel had appeared.

Nephi sat up, his thumping heart seeming to echo in the electric silence.

Lemuel rubbed his eyes. "I don't believe it . . ." he said in a hushed whisper.

The sound of cracking wood startled Nephi. Laman staggered to his feet, moaning in anguish. "What have I done? I have sinned against my own brothers." He grasped Nephi's shoulder with a heavy hand. "Are you all right?"

Nephi placed his hand over Laman's. "We have all been chastened for not obtaining the records." Laman pulled Nephi to his feet, and they embraced.

"Forgive me," Laman said.

"The angel told us to return to Jerusalem," Sam interrupted.

Laman nodded gravely and went to help Lemuel stand.

A look of fear crossed Lemuel's face. "How can we return to Jerusalem? Doesn't the angel know that we were nearly killed?" he asked.

Laman stiffened, his eyes growing wild. "Lemuel's right. It would be a death sentence if we returned. Unless you think the angel is going to follow us and fight off Laban's men."

"Maybe we won't have to fight them," Sam suggested, his mind coming into focus. "We've received a direct commandment from the Lord. There must be a way."

But Laman was not deterred. He looked around at his brothers in earnest. "Did you see how mighty Laban was? He could fight fifty men by himself."

Nephi couldn't remain silent any longer. He spoke, his voice full of authority. "An angel of the Lord just commanded us to return. Do you think we won't be protected? We must keep the Lord's commandments. He is mightier than Laban and his fifty. He is mightier than even Laban's tens of thousands."

Moving to Nephi's side, Sam said, "He's right. We should not fear a weak man such as Laban when we have the Lord with us."

Nephi's gaze bore into his brothers. "Let us be strong like Moses, who divided the Red Sea. Did he not lead the children of Israel out of the land of Egypt with Pharaoh's army in pursuit?"

Laman kicked at the ground, sending a spray of fine sand about their feet.

"You know this is true," Nephi continued, pointing to the place where the angel had appeared. "An *angel of God* just visited us. How can you even think of leaving without the plates? God will destroy Laban as the Egyptians were destroyed."

"If you want to get yourself slain, Nephi, then it's your choice," Lemuel said. "But we aren't carrying your dead body back to Father."

Laman grunted in agreement, all repentance gone from his countenance. "We'll leave you to rot in the streets of Jerusalem."

* * *

The daylight hours passed slowly as they waited for dark to settle over the land. Nephi and Sam nursed their wounds while remaining in the cave. During the heat of midday, Nephi fell into a restless slumber. He found himself half-praying and half-sleeping. *Protect us from harm and death,* he pleaded throughout his dreams.

When Nephi awoke, his robe beneath him was soaked in perspiration. He had the distinct impression that he was to make the journey alone. Sam was leaning against the wall of the cave, his eyes closed.

"Sam," he whispered, so as not to draw attention from Laman and Lemuel, who were asleep a little farther back in the cave.

Sam opened his eyes and focused on Nephi.

"Returning to Jerusalem is something I must to do by myself."

Shaking his head, Sam mouthed the words, "No. I'm coming too."

Nephi joined him against the wall. "You must trust me. The Spirit has made it known to me."

Sam let out a long breath. "I do trust you, but I fear for your safety."

"The Lord has protected us this far. He won't let us down now."

Sam stared at the ground for several moments, mulling over Nephi's words. He knew what his brother said must be. "You'll be in my prayers, little brother. May God be with you."

The brothers sat together in silence, each thinking about the task that lay ahead.

CHAPTER 10

It is better that one man should perish
than that a nation should dwindle and perish in unbelief.
(1 NEPHI 4:13)

"Hide in the grove, and wait for me there," Nephi said. In the gathering gloom, he watched as his brothers entered the cluster of trees with the camels and disappeared from view.

Nephi straightened his mantle and gripped his knife with his sore hand. He swallowed nervously and started walking toward the city gate. "The Lord has prepared a way," he whispered to himself.

Soldiers guarded the gates of Jerusalem at night, and it was difficult to obtain entry without suspicion. If Nephi were younger, the guards might assume he was just a youth who'd stayed playing in the fields too late. But he was the size of a grown man and couldn't possibly enter without questioning.

As he drew closer to the gates, he veered off to one side before he could be spotted in the darkness. The terrain was rocky so he proceeded carefully, as it was easy to stumble even in the moonlight. Several dozen paces from the main entrance was a place where he and his friends had scaled the wall many times.

When Nephi reached the outer wall, he crouched at its base, catching his breath. Then he felt along the rising rocks for the first protrusion. It was still there. Relieved, Nephi grasped at the projecting rock and slowly began to climb. As he neared the top, he hesitated, looking in the direction of the guards. There was still no unusual movement from them. Nephi hoisted himself to the top of the wall and looked down the other side. The street below was dark and silent as he had hoped. Carefully, he clambered over the top and down the other side, landing with a quiet thud.

The dark streets of Jerusalem were not a friendly place at night. All citizens who wanted to avoid trouble kept to their quarters. Nephi drew up his outer garment to cover his neck and lower half of his face. Now was not the time to be recognized. He took a few tentative steps forward. The sound of a falling rock came from behind him. He turned and peered through the inky darkness, his heart hammering, but he saw nothing. In front of him, the echo of a donkey's hooves grew closer. Nephi felt his way along a nearby wall and found an alcove to step into. The unseen donkey and rider passed by without incident.

When he reached the deserted marketplace, a beggar woke at Nephi's footsteps. The one-legged man held out his crippled hand for alms. Nephi stretched open both his hands, demonstrating his absence of money. The beggar continued to call pitifully after him until Nephi rounded a corner.

Nearing Laban's house, Nephi came across a man lying in the street. He crept past the crumpled figure, not knowing whether he was dead or alive. Then he felt compelled to stop and turn around. Something caught his eye. In the moonlight, jewels glittered on the man's hands. Nephi retraced his steps and bent over the still body. The man was alive.

It was Laban.

The stench of sour wine rose into Nephi's nostrils. He straightened, not wanting to wake the sleeping giant. Laban's open coat revealed a long, curved sword with a hilt of gold. Nephi drew his breath in sharply. The intricate workmanship of the sheath and hilt fascinated him. Only aristocrats carried such ceremonial weapons.

Nephi stooped and fingered the golden hilt, then withdrew the sword from its sheath. In an instant he knew the blade to be Damascus steel, the finest in the world. Laban was wearing his full armor. Nephi wondered what sort of place Laban had been returning from that would require such dress.

Slay him.

Nephi spun around, his heart pounding. But only emptiness greeted him. He turned back toward Laban.

The Lord hath delivered him into thy hands.

He closed his eyes. Was this what the angel meant when he said that Laban would be delivered into their hands? His stomach began to churn, and he fought the rising bile in his throat. He knew Laban was cruel and greedy and had sought to kill him and his brothers. Laban had also stolen his father's property, but Nephi couldn't take his life.

No, he decided. With Laban passed out, he would be able to find a way to procure the brass plates from someone in Laban's household. He slid the sword back into its sheath.

Slay him, for the Lord hath delivered him into thy hands. Behold, the Lord slayeth the wicked to bring forth his righteous purposes. It is better that one man should perish than that a nation should dwindle and perish in unbelief.

Nephi sank to the ground and buried his face in his hands. In the wilderness, the Lord had promised him that, if he would keep the commandments, his family would prosper in the promised land. Nephi moaned. The Lord's commandments were written on the plates of brass. And it was up to him to obtain those plates. Without them, he knew, his posterity would not learn the laws of Moses.

Nephi sighed with heavy dread. Wearily, he stood up.

He grabbed Laban's ankles and dragged him into an alley. Closing his eyes for a moment, he listened to his pulse racing through his body. "Do it now," he told himself. Gritting his teeth, he withdrew the gleaming sword from Laban's sheath and clasped it tightly, raising it over his head. With all his strength, Nephi brought the blade down swiftly onto Laban's neck. He released the hilt and let the blade rest where it separated Laban's head from his body.

It was done.

Fighting his turning stomach, Nephi carefully removed the dead man's breastplate and outer garment, covering his own body with them. Without looking at the spreading blood, he unfastened the leather sandals with trembling hands and put them on. He removed the precious rings from Laban's lifeless, but still warm, fingers. Nephi unwound Laban's turban and wrapped it around his own head, complete with the band of gleaming jewels. Then he wiped the blood off the sword with Laban's inner tunic. Finally, Nephi placed the sword in its sheath and hung it from his own waist.

Nephi rose, now transformed into the man he had just slain. He knew what he had to do. He strode to Laban's house and stopped in front of the formidable gate. A sleepy guard stood at attention and waved him through. Nephi released an inaudible sigh, and passed through the gates. The silence only made his heart pound faster. He walked to the center courtyard, painfully aware of Laban's too-narrow sandals cutting unfamiliar grooves against his feet.

Stopping in the courtyard, Nephi hesitated. He assumed the treasury was behind the main buildings and courtyards. The sound of rushing footsteps to his left startled him. From the darkness, a tall, thin man rushed forward.

"Sir, you've returned early," the man said, bowing.

Nephi was grateful for the inadequate light. "Come with me to the treasury," he said in a rough voice, mimicking Laban's. He motioned for the servant to lead the way.

The servant turned toward the direction he'd come from and moved quickly to the side of the main house. The shadows deepened, and he raised his dim lantern before him. "How was the meeting with the elders?" he asked.

Trying to avoid speaking, Nephi grunted as they passed through a narrow alley, which then opened into another, smaller courtyard.

"Do they want more money?" the servant asked.

Nephi was surprised at the bold question. "I need to find the plates that contain the record of the Jews," he answered, hoping that would silence the curious man.

The servant stopped in front of a stone building with a plain door. A scuffing sound came from beneath the tree next to the entrance. A guard rose to meet them, bringing a hand to his sword hilt.

When he recognized the visitors, he bowed. Nephi avoided eye contact with the guard, keeping his gaze forward. The guard quickly unlocked the door and stood back so they could enter.

As the door swung wide, the light of the lantern revealed stacks of trinkets and metal boxes, undoubtedly filled with gold and silver. Nephi recognized his father's property stacked haphazardly in a corner.

"I think I know where those plates are," the servant said. He left Nephi in the doorway and nimbly moved to a stone shelf. Moments later, he turned, staggering underneath the weight of a metal chest.

Nephi lifted the lid and scanned the top plate. It was a genealogical record of the Jews. "These are the ones," he said. "Bring them."

The servant shouldered the chest and followed Nephi. "Where did the meeting take place tonight?" he asked.

Nephi realized that this servant must be a close confidant of Laban's. "Outside the gates."

"You're becoming more cautious then," he said.

Nodding, Nephi ducked into an alleyway. "In here," he whispered. They waited for a group of men to pass.

"The people in the marketplace started a riot today. Did the elders discuss the arrests?" the servant asked.

Nephi peered about the empty streets. "Quiet. We must hurry."

The servant fell silent until they reached the outer walls. The guards recognized Nephi as Laban and let them pass through a small door in the gate without questioning.

Once they were outside the walls, Nephi felt a burden lift. Next to him, the servant hesitated, staring into the blackness. "It's too dark to see anything out here," he said.

Nephi hid a smile. This man was not an experienced desert dweller.

"The elders are over there," Nephi said, motioning with his head.

As they neared the grove, Laman stepped out from behind a tree. He froze at the sight of the man in Laban's clothes and the servant next to him. He yelled, "Run!"

Nephi watched his brothers tear out of the trees on their camels, urging them to gallop. "Wait," he called, charging after them. "It's me, Nephi!"

The brothers slowed the camels and stopped. "Look," he said, pulling off his turban. "I'm not Laban."

Laman jerked his camel around to face Nephi, staring, then laughing weakly. "I could have sworn you were Laban."

Sam and Lemuel joined Laman and grinned with relief.

"Did you bring company?" Lemuel asked, looking behind Nephi.

Nephi turned and saw Laban's servant backing away from the group. Realizing that he had been tricked, the man dropped the brass plates and turned to flee. Nephi sprinted the short distance and leaped onto him.

The servant hit the ground hard, pinned by Nephi's weight. "Have mercy," he cried.

Nephi straddled his writhing body and covered his protesting mouth. "If you want your life spared, keep quiet."

The man stopped struggling and fell silent. Laman, Lemuel, and Sam joined Nephi. "I'm going to turn him over. Help me hold him down," Nephi instructed his brothers.

With Laban's servant lying face up, Nephi continued to hold his hand over the man's mouth. "If you'll listen to my words, as the Lord lives, and as I live, we'll spare your life. Do you understand?"

The servant barely nodded. Nephi slowly released his hold and the servant sat up. Nephi gripped his shoulders and stared into the man's eyes. "Don't be afraid. You'll be a free man if you come into the wilderness with us. The Lord commanded us to retrieve the brass plates from Laban, and we've been faithful in keeping that commandment. If you'll join our father in the wilderness, you may live in peace with us."

His mouth formed silent words, his breathing labored.

"What's your name?" Sam asked.

"Zoram," he said with great effort. When his breathing steadied, he looked at each brother with liquid eyes. "By my life, I will go into the wilderness with you to your father. And as the Lord lives, I will not try to flee again."

Nephi grabbed Zoram's hand and hoisted him to his feet. He knew that Zoram couldn't return to Jerusalem. Once the brass plates were discovered missing and Laban was found dead, Zoram would be accused and executed. "You'll ride with me," Nephi said.

* * *

"Let's stay in Eloth a little longer," Lemuel said.

Nephi glanced at the sun in the sky, noting the lateness of the afternoon. "Father and Mother will be worried. We've already been gone longer than planned."

Laman spat on the ground. "One more day won't make a difference." He threw his arm around Lemuel's shoulders, and they walked toward town.

Watching the departing brothers, Zoram sighed and picked up a ripened date, polishing it against his sleeve. "Your brothers have no respect," he said. "Now what will we do?"

"They won't return until morning," Nephi said, clenching his jaw. He sat in the shade beneath a palm, next to Zoram and Sam.

Zoram chewed on the date. "Tell me more about your father and his dreams."

Nephi leaned against the tree and stretched his legs. "My father has always been a man of God. As a wine and oil merchant, he traveled many weeks at a time. I suppose all that time in the desert brought him closer to the Lord. Each time he had a vision, he would record it on parchment. He shared the messages with our family, but Laman and Lemuel hardly listened."

Zoram spit out a seed. "What made him decide to leave Jerusalem?"

Reaching over, Nephi grabbed a date from Zoram's collection. He rubbed it slowly against his robe. "When the prophet Jonas was killed, my mother became fearful. My father had already experienced public confrontations, and I felt nervous myself. But he wouldn't deviate from his mission. It took a vision from God to make him leave."

"You mean God actually told him to leave?" Zoram asked.

"The Lord made it clear that if he didn't flee into the wilderness, his life would be taken," Nephi said.

"Your father was lucky," Zoram said, chewing thoughtfully. "I remember when Jonas was killed. Laban had a meeting that night and came home drunk, as usual. He carried stolen valuables from Jonas's home. The elders had looted his property and divided the goods among themselves."

Sam stared at Zoram. "What happened to his wife and children?"

"They had already fled, probably to a relative's home."

Nephi let the date fall into his lap, no longer interested in the fruit. An eager fly landed on top of the date. "What gives the elders the right—"

"You forget, Nephi. Your father was once esteemed among them," Zoram interrupted.

Nephi shooed the fly away and nodded gravely. "Yes, before he discovered that the people were breaking the Sabbath and marrying women from other ethnic and tribal groups."

Zoram laughed bitterly. "Oh, it's far beyond that."

"What do you mean?" Sam asked.

"Some of the elders have designated sacred trees as alternate worship sites," he said. "They are burning incense and worshipping foreign deities."

Nephi grimaced, and Sam shook his head.

"It gets worse," Zoram said.

They stared at him.

"There's rumor of 'sacred prostitution' occurring in underground chambers beneath the holy walls."

"The temple has been desecrated then." Nephi stood. "I've heard enough." He walked away, his eyes stinging and his stomach weak.

A breeze picked up, shifting Nephi's robes. He gazed at the clear sky. No clouds were in sight, but that didn't mean a windstorm wasn't on its way. The palm trees began to sway above him. The late afternoon sun glowed pink—an unmistakable sign of trouble.

Nephi hurried to Zoram and Sam. "Let's set up a tent and secure the camels. It looks like we're in for some foul weather."

By the time the tent stood, the wind was violently lashing through the camp. Though it was daytime, the sky was dark from the swirling sand.

"What about your brothers?" Zoram yelled through the driving wind.

Nephi spread his arms helplessly. "They'll find shelter somewhere," he called over the rising pitch. He knotted his turban securely about his head, then ran to the camels. Sam had already tied two of them together. Nephi tied the remaining camels and secured them to a swaying palm tree.

The sand whipped around the camp, and Nephi covered his mouth to keep from ingesting the bits of dirt.

Zoram's thin figure struggled against the billowing tent, trying to keep it in place. Nephi used his weight to hold one side down while Sam hammered in additional spikes. By the time the tent was secured, the three men were exhausted and covered in dust. They staggered into the tent and removed their sand-encrusted turbans.

Coughing, Zoram reached for the water gasket. "Can it get any worse?"

Nephi blinked sand from his eyes. "Let's pray our tent holds."

The storm surged through Eloth, scattering flocks and razing entire campsites. Everything shut down in the busy town, and people huddled in their shelters and homes.

Hours later, the wind abated, but the sky remained dark with the fallen night. "Let's check the camels," Sam said.

The three men stepped from their tent. The night was calm, belying the ferocious storm that just passed. Sand hills appeared where there had been flat ground just hours before. Nephi stroked a complaining camel. "We'll load, then search for Laman and Lemuel."

As Sam hoisted the last bundle onto the camels, two men came into view.

"Where have you been?" drawled one.

Nephi recognized the slurred voice. "Waiting for you."

"We were waiting for *you*." Lemuel's unmistakable laugh echoed through the night.

Climbing on his camel, Nephi urged it forward. Sam and Zoram followed. After a few paces, they paused and watched Laman and Lemuel making a spectacle as they climbed onto their animals. First Laman missed the saddle and fell off the other side. Then Lemuel jerked the reins too tightly, and the camel tried to bite him.

Laman started singing loudly as his camel loped forward. "O, that thou mightest be like unto this river . . . O this river . . . run into the fountain of righteousness . . . I am the river . . ."

Nephi cringed at Laman's words. He increased his camel's pace, hoping the night air would sober his brothers. He was relieved when the sloppy interpretation ended with the sound of vomiting.

"They get better when there's no wine around," Sam whispered to Zoram.

Zoram shook his head as they increased their distance from the intoxicated men.

CHAPTER 11

So all Israel were reckoned by genealogies; and, behold,
they were written in the book of the kings of Israel and Judah.
(1 CHRONICLES 9:1)

Two days later, they reached the Wadi Tayyab al-Ism. "We're almost to the camp," Nephi said, turning to the exhausted Zoram.

Zoram could only nod, his strength depleted.

Nephi smiled in understanding. Eventually Zoram would adjust to desert life like the rest of them. Nephi pulled his turban over his ears. The sun would soon rise, but the morning air was chilly. In the early light, he gazed at Zoram's profile. He judged him to be at least thirty years old. Nephi wondered why he'd never married. Surely with Zoram's position in the house of Laban, he would have his pick from the servant women.

Zoram's face and protruding chin were pocked with indented scars, hinting at a childhood disease. His honest eyes were framed by heavy brows, and he had the habit of curling his lip when he spoke of something unpleasant. Nephi sighed to himself when he thought about the persistent questions Zoram asked. He hoped Zoram's talkative nature wouldn't be a nuisance to his father.

In the cool canyon, Nephi felt his heart pound. He anticipated when they would present the plates of brass to his
father. Joy spread through him, coupled with concern for his
family. Had they fared well?

The first thing Nephi spotted as they came upon Lehi's
camp was a stream of smoke billowing from the morning
fire. His mother's form sat hunched over a cooking pot. He
couldn't wait to see the surprise on her face.

Dinah saw them first. "They're here!" she screamed for
all the desert creatures to hear.

A flurry of legs and arms ran to meet them. Nephi
laughed and climbed off his camel to greet the reception of
embraces.

Zoram was introduced to the others as a former servant
of Laban and received a warm welcome. Lehi raised his
eyebrows, but his questions remained silent.

Nephi embraced his father. "We've brought the plates."

Lehi's eyes glistened as he kissed each of his sons.

Sariah made her way to each one. By the time she
reached Nephi, she was trembling with emotion. She threw
her arms about his neck and wept. Her voice was lost and
she could only emit weak cries.

Several minutes passed before Sariah could compose
herself. "I-I thought you had perished in the w-wilderness,"
she stammered.

Nephi and his brothers smiled. "We're safe, Mother,"
Sam said.

Sariah swallowed deeply. "I disrespectfully called your
father a visionary man."

Nephi was startled. He had not expected his mother to
doubt her husband's authority.

Lehi put an arm around Sariah. "And I agreed. I am a
visionary man." He looked at her tenderly. "Had I not seen

the things of God in a vision, I wouldn't have known the goodness of God, and we would have stayed and died in Jerusalem."

Sariah wiped her eyes.

Lehi continued, "We have traveled this far safely. I knew the Lord would deliver my sons out of the hands of Laban and bring them back to us."

Stepping forward, Sam held out the metal box. Lehi looked at the container with curiosity. "Are those the plates?"

The brothers all nodded.

Lehi moved closer and peered into the box. A hush fell over the group as they watched him touch the engraved words. With tears pricking his eyes, Lehi looked at his sons. The Lord had truly guided and protected them. "Thank you. We have been blessed through your sacrifice."

The family walked to the camp together. Following the morning meal, they remained sitting around the fire.

After several moments of silence, Sariah cleared her throat and looked at her sons. "My sons," she began, "I know the Lord commanded us to flee into the wilderness. The Lord protected you and delivered you out of the hands of Laban." She looked at the ground, then raised her head, her eyes bright. "Please forgive me. I was wrong not to trust in the Lord." She stood and walked around the circle, kissing each son.

Nephi gazed at his mother, understanding how difficult it must have been for her when they hadn't returned when expected. He embraced her tenderly, then sat down when Lehi rose.

Standing before the family, Lehi said, "Tell us about your journey and how Zoram came to travel with you."

Laman looked at the other brothers. "Nephi insisted Zoram travel with us and told him he would be under our care."

"We couldn't afford to have a servant of Laban reporting what had happened. Zoram has promised to follow the Lord's commandments," Nephi said.

"What did happen?" Lehi asked.

Zoram and the brothers looked at Nephi. He flushed and bowed his head. After a few moments, he looked at his father. "Laman went into Laban's house and was threatened with his life."

Sariah gasped and looked at Laman.

Nephi continued, "He wanted to return to the wilderness, but we decided to follow the Lord's commandments and—"

"Nephi thought we should offer the gold and silver from our estate in exchange for the brass plates," Sam cut in.

Nephi spoke in a grave voice, "We traveled to our home and found a man living in our house."

Lemuel shot to his feet. "It was Gomer, a friend I asked to protect our property."

"Gomer was a thief." Laman laughed. "We learned from Ishmael that a robbery had been planned for that very night."

Lehi looked from Laman to Lemuel. "Ishmael my cousin?"

"Yes, apparently one of his daughters overheard Gomer planning the robbery," said Sam. "We arrived just in time. Gomer disappeared, and we unearthed the caskets of gold and silver. We took the valuables to Laban's house and presented our offer."

Lemuel spat on the ground and glared at Nephi. "Laban sent his men to kill us, and the property was stolen—"

Lehi interrupted. "I'm not concerned with the property. Tell me what happened next."

"We were pursued by Laban's men and fled into the wilderness," Sam continued. "Laman and Lemuel took it upon themselves to beat us with their sticks."

Sariah covered her mouth, tears forming in her eyes.

Laman's face turned red. "They deserved the beating."

Lehi's eyes filled with pain.

"But an angel stopped us," Laman said. Everyone stared at him.

Nephi spoke quietly, "The angel commanded us to return to Jerusalem. He promised that Laban would be delivered into our hands."

He closed his eyes for a moment. "I went alone to Laban's house. I didn't know what I would do, so I relied on the Spirit to guide me. Outside his estate I came across a drunken man passed out in the street. It was Laban. As I examined his fine sword, I heard the Spirit speak to me."

As Nephi spoke, no one moved or made a sound.

"The Spirit told me to slay Laban. I shook off the horrible thought, but it returned a second time. The Spirit reminded me that the Lord had delivered him into my hands. I still could not obey. Then a third time, the voice came to me and said, 'Behold, the Lord slayeth the wicked to bring forth his righteous purposes. It is better that one man should perish than that a nation should dwindle and perish in unbelief,'" Nephi said.

Sariah choked back a sob, and Lehi put his arm around her.

Nephi reached into his robe and withdrew Laban's sword from his girdle. He placed the gleaming weapon on the ground before him. "I obeyed the voice of the Spirit. I took Laban's own sword and cut off his head."

A cry erupted from Sariah. When she regained her composure, Sam said, "Nephi put on Laban's clothes and went into the house. He met Laban's servant Zoram, and they brought the plates out of the city."

With tears streaming down his cheeks, Lehi rose and spread his arms, commanding everyone's attention. "We shall prepare the sacrifice and thank our Lord for your safe deliverance. Then we shall offer burnt offerings to rid our family of the sins that have been committed." Lehi looked at each face. "We know our sins and will be cleansed of them on this day."

The family proceeded to the rudely constructed altar. Lehi brought forth a sheep, purchased from the Bedouin who lived in the upper valley, and a bird for the burnt offering.

Laman, Lemuel, and Sariah each placed their hands upon the head of the burnt offering, transferring their sins to the fowl.

Lehi slew the sheep upon the altar and sprinkled its blood on the rocks. After his prayer, he built a fire and burned the bird.

* * *

Lehi spent the next several days poring over the records contained on the brass plates. Because of the difficulty of obtaining the plates, their importance was compounded. Even Laman and Lemuel seemed to sense their value. Each evening Lehi shared what he had learned with his family. Nephi was astounded at the amount of information the plates contained.

"Nephi," Lehi said one evening.

"Yes, Father?"

"Come into the tent with me, and see what I've been reading."

He followed his father into the dim interior. Nephi placed wood on the fire and watched the blaze leap into the air. Settling across from his father, he waited for him to begin.

"First, tell me how Ishmael came to learn of the robbery planned for our estate," he said.

"As you know," Nephi said, "his youngest daughter overheard the men plotting."

Lehi stroked his beard. "Are any of Ishmael's daughters married?" he asked.

"I don't think so."

Lehi remained silent for a moment, then touched the brass plates before him. "I want you to treasure these records and always protect them."

"I will," Nephi said.

"The five books of Moses are recorded on them, giving us an account of the creation of the world and of our first parents, Adam and Eve."

Nephi watched his father's eyes grow damp.

"The record of the Jews from the beginning down to the commencement of the reign of Zedekiah lies within these plates. The prophecies of the holy prophets from the beginning—even Jeremiah—are also in them."

He moved closer and peered over his father's shoulder.

Lehi turned several plates and pointed to an inscription. "The genealogy of my fathers is written here. I am a descendant of Joseph who was sold into Egypt and preserved by the hand of the Lord. Joseph kept his father, Jacob, and his household from perishing with famine. Through the Lord, he led his people out of captivity and out of the land of Egypt."

Nephi stared at the engraved writing. "Why was it in Laban's house?"

"Laban was also a descendant of Joseph." Lehi rocked back on his heels and stood. "Gather the others. I have something to say."

Nephi left the tent and called the family together. Sam heard the call and ran to inform Laman and Lemuel, who were fishing down at the beach. When the family had gathered, Lehi stood before them and raised his staff.

"I have read the plates of brass and wish to speak concerning them." He gazed at each family member. "These plates shall go forth unto all nations, kindreds, tongues, and all our posterity. They will never dim or perish. We will carry them as we journey to the land of promise. Each of us will protect them with our lives."

Laman hunkered down beneath his mantle, and Lemuel stifled a yawn. Nephi looked at his older brothers and felt the hair on his neck rise. His father had mentioned the promised land. Nephi smiled at the thought. He hoped they would reach their destination soon. Then a shadow crossed his face. Lehi had also mentioned their posterity.

CHAPTER 12

*For the Lord shall comfort Zion: he will comfort all her
waste places; and he will make her wilderness like Eden,
and her desert like the garden of the Lord.*

(ISAIAH 51:3)

Isaabel lay on her bed, propped up on her elbows. She
stared out her small window at the clouds racing across the
sky. It had been two weeks since her father had traveled to
Lehi's house and intercepted the robbery. She rolled over
onto her back and placed her hands across her abdomen.
Closing her eyes, she thought about what her father had said
upon returning.

She had been waiting anxiously in the courtyard and was
the first to hear the arriving camels. After her brothers,
Raamah and Heth, climbed off their camels, they led the
beasts behind the house. When they were out of sight,
Isaabel rushed to her father.

"What happened?" she whispered.

Ishmael chuckled and kissed his daughter's forehead.
"You were wise to discover the plot, Isa." Isaabel stared at
him with wide eyes. "Did the robbers come?" she asked.

Her father grinned. "Ah, right to the point as usual."

"Father," Isaabel protested, tugging his sleeve.

"Let's go inside, and I will tell you what happened."

As soon as Ishmael made his way to the table and settled against some pillows, he said, "Please bring me a drink."

"As you wish," Isaabel said and rushed out of the room.

Raamah and Heth entered. "Good night, Father," Raamah said.

"Thank you for your help. We accomplished a great service tonight."

The brothers bowed out of the room just as Isaabel reentered. She carried the cup of tea to her father and sat next to him on the edge of a cushion, her hands clenched together.

Ishmael took a sip and sighed. He closed his eyes for a moment. Then he leaned his back against the wall and looked above his daughter's head, as if he were watching the event again. At last he began. "We arrived just after dark to find Lehi's home brightly lit. Even the courtyard was lined with torch lights. We came upon five men—"

"You had to fight five of them?"

Ishmael chuckled. "We didn't have to fight. Four of the men were Lehi's sons," he said. "The other was Gomer, the man you heard plotting."

"Lehi's family has returned, then?" she asked, clutching her bodice.

"No, only his sons came to complete business for their father. They are probably on their way back into the wilderness now."

"They are already gone?" Isaabel asked quietly, disappointment crossing her brow. "What happened with the robbers?"

"We foiled the plans. Once Gomer discovered that I knew his plot, he disappeared and no doubt informed the others."

With a sigh of relief, Isaabel asked, "When is Nephi, I mean Lehi's family, returning?"

"Patience, my daughter. They mentioned that they had been traveling for almost two weeks, but I did not inquire of their plans. I assume they'll stay in the wilderness for a while longer," Ishmael said. "But I am tired now and must rest. These bones of mine aren't getting any younger."

Isaabel fought the rising questions. She wondered how far into the wilderness they were going. But her father must not see too much interest. She rose and kissed him on the cheek and bid him goodnight.

"I am happy everything turned out so well and you are safe," Isaabel said.

Since that fateful night, Isaabel couldn't help but wonder what had happened to Lehi's sons. What had they come back for and how long would they stay in the wilderness? Voices from outside interrupted her thoughts.

Her oldest sister, Rebeka, had been extremely short-tempered since she'd been ignored by Sabtah. He never did come to visit the home and ask her parents for her hand in marriage. Even if it were to replace his first wife, such a betrothal would still have been an increase in status. Isaabel had overheard her sister whisper that if Father were more prominent and wealthy, he would have no trouble marrying his five daughters.

Isaabel cringed at the thought of her sister disrespecting her parents. Rebeka owed her life to them, and she had no business slighting them. She strained to hear the words floating into her room. It was Rebeka again.

"I saw Sabtah's sister in the marketplace this morning," she said.

"Did you speak with her?" Anah asked.

Rebeka sighed. "She wouldn't even look at me."

"I don't blame her. She's protecting her brother," Anah said.

"Have you asked Father about Sabtah yet?" It was Tamar.

"I don't want him to know I hoped to make the match. If he wanted me to marry him, then he would have arranged it."

Tamar said, "I'm not so sure."

"What do you mean?" Rebeka asked.

"Isa overheard something Mother said to Father," Tamar said.

Isaabel sat up in the bed. How dare her sister break a confidence! She knew Rebeka would be furious.

Seconds later, she heard her name called through the hallway.

"I'm in the bedroom," Isaabel said, swallowing hard. Her four sisters instantly appeared in the doorway. Tamar's face was drawn.

Isaabel glared at her betraying sister.

Standing before her, Rebeka folded her arms. "I think you know what I've come to ask you."

Isaabel's shoulders slumped. *It might be better that Rebeka knew the truth anyway,* she thought. She raised her eyes and met her sister's. "I overheard Mother and Father arguing. Father was ready to accept Sabtah, but Mother was set against the union."

Rebeka's eyes widened at the news. "I thought Mother wanted me to marry him," she said.

"Mother thought there was truth in the rumors about Sabtah—that he hurt his first wife and caused her to miscarry," Isaabel said quietly.

"Sabtah's wife bore him three healthy children. No sensible man would beat a pregnant wife," Rebeka said.

"I don't know what's true," Isaabel said with a shrug. "Mother just wanted to protect you with the knowledge she had."

Rebeka's eyes narrowed. "Next time, little sister, don't keep secrets from me." She turned and left the room, the others following.

Hot tears burned Isaabel's eyes. She lay on her bed and turned toward the wall. She was trapped within the walls of her family. With four older sisters, she would never marry, she decided. A lump formed in her throat as she realized that, even worse, she would never again see Lehi's youngest son.

A movement in the room startled her. Isaabel turned and saw Tamar hovering in the doorway.

Tamar braved an apology. "I'm sorry, Isa. I shouldn't have told your secret," she said.

Isaabel sat up and wiped her eyes. "I thought I could trust you."

Distress crossed Tamar's face. "You can. I made a mistake, and it won't happen again." She crossed the room and sat next to Isaabel. "Mother should have spoken to Rebeka about this. It's not your fault you overheard."

Isaabel nodded, and Tamar put her arm about her. "I know what will make you happy," Tamar said. "Let's go to the mapmaker's shop and buy a map."

"What for?" Isaabel stared at the ground.

"So we can speculate where Lehi took his family," Tamar said, squeezing Isaabel's shoulder.

Isaabel brought her head up. "Why would we want to do that?"

Tamar's eyes twinkled. "Come on. It will be fun."

* * *

The two sisters stepped into the musty shop. An ancient, wrinkled man sat behind a table, poring over large parchments. Behind him, shelves crammed full of dusty scrolls climbed the walls. He raised his head in surprise and surveyed his visitors with one eye. His other eye seemed to be looking just to the side of them.

"May I help you?" he asked.

Isaabel looked at Tamar, who spoke. "We are looking for a map."

"A map? For your father?"

Isaabel cleared her throat. "Yes."

The man stood and rubbed his brown hands together. "And your father gave you instructions to come here?"

Tamar glanced about the shop. "Are you not a mapmaker?"

"Indeed, I am. But the maps I draw are not of the land of Judah," he said, squinting at the two girls.

"We want a map of Arabia," Isaabel burst out.

The man arched a brow. "Is your father a merchant, then?"

"Yes," Tamar answered.

"Perhaps I know him. What is his name?"

Isaabel couldn't pretend any longer. "Actually the map isn't for our father. It's for us. We have a friend who is traveling in the desert. And—"

"Say no more." The man held his hand up, then shuffled about the shop. "I understand your plight. You're interested in the safety of your friend, but don't want your family to know about it," he said, with a knowing look in his one good eye.

"How did you know?" Tamar asked.

"You are not the first to visit the shop under false pretenses," the shopkeeper said. He tugged a large scroll from a high shelf behind him. The movement caused several others to tumble to the floor, but the man didn't seem to mind. "I think this is what you are looking for." He unrolled the scroll and spread it across the table. Then he placed camel-shaped weights on each curling corner.

Isaabel and Tamar stepped closer and peered at the odd markings.

The man's long finger pointed at a red star. "This is Jerusalem here," he said. The girls nodded. "And here," he said, pointing at a blue marking, "is the Dead Sea. Do you know where your friend is traveling to?"

Isaabel shrugged her shoulders. "No."

"How long have they been gone?"

"They left six weeks ago, but they returned to Jerusalem after being gone for four weeks."

The mapmaker stroked his chin. "Yes, they probably have a camp approximately two weeks' travel from Jerusalem. But the question is which direction did they go?"

Isaabel sighed. She knew it was hopeless.

But the shopkeeper wasn't swayed. "Tell me more about your friend and what his trade is."

She looked about the shop cautiously. Isaabel didn't want to reveal their true identity, especially since Lehi's life was in danger. "The family is in the merchant business."

"Such as?" the mapmaker prompted.

"Wine, oil, figs, honey . . . I think," she said.

The man stretched his thin arm and pointed to a set of black markings on the map. "Here is Jericho. If your friend is a merchant then he would likely stop there." Isaabel and Tamar exchanged glances. "Or perhaps he traveled to Hebron," he said, pointing to another marking. "Nevertheless, your friend would most likely travel in a southern direction." The shopkeeper moved his finger along the Dead Sea. "He could have traveled around either side of the Dead Sea until he reached Eloth."

"How long does it take to reach Eloth?" Tamar asked.

"Depending on the size of the caravan, it would take at least ten days."

Isaabel looked at the place the mapmaker pointed to. "What is the blue part?" she asked.

"The Red Sea. Eloth is a gathering station for many merchants."

Isaabel nodded. *Perhaps Nephi is living in Eloth,* she thought.

The mapmaker looked at the sisters. "After Eloth, it's just desert and arid mountains. Only the staunch Bedouin could survive such conditions."

"What do you mean?" Tamar asked.

"Your friend would have to be a skilled desert traveler in order to survive the weather conditions and rough terrain. Food is scarce, and travel is difficult. And . . ." he paused. "The desert tribes are bloodthirsty people."

Isaabel shuddered. She hoped Lehi's family lived in Eloth. It would account for the time it took for them to travel back to Jerusalem.

The sisters thanked the mapmaker and left the shop without buying the map. Tamar linked her arm through Isaabel's. "See? Didn't that take your mind off your worries?"

Isaabel smiled at her sister. But inside her heart, a new fear started to grow.

CHAPTER 13

Lo, children are an heritage of the Lord:
and the fruit of the womb is his reward.
(PSALM 127:3)

Nephi wiped his brow. The late morning sun's heat indicated that it would be a scorching afternoon. He and Sam had spent the past several mornings fishing in the early light. Later, his sisters cleaned and dried the meat. Laman, Lemuel, and Zoram had gone hunting, hoping to find some wild animals.

His mother seemed content at her work. Nephi often heard her humming to herself. He wondered if she was lonely for her women friends. He glanced in the direction of the tents and saw his father exit and walk toward the water. Lehi stood for some time before the gurgling stream.

Nephi crossed to him. "Is everything all right?"

Lehi met his eyes and answered quietly, "I've had another vision."

"Should we wait for Laman and the others to return to camp?" Nephi asked.

"This can't wait," Lehi said slowly. "Gather the family members who are here."

Moments later the family sat on rugs spread around the fire. Lehi said, "The Lord has spoken to me concerning our posterity."

Nephi stared at his father. He had wondered about that exact thing.

Looking at Sariah, Lehi said, "The Lord doesn't want our family to journey into the wilderness alone. Our sons need wives so they might raise up children unto the Lord in the land of promise."

Sariah nodded, but a look of bewilderment crossed her face.

Taking a deep breath, Lehi came to the point. "The Lord has commanded that our sons should return again to Jerusalem and bring the family of Ishmael into the wilderness."

Sariah clapped her hands over her mouth.

Nephi stood, his heart pounding. The fact that they had just returned from Jerusalem didn't bother him—he would see Isaabel again. He glanced at Sam, who nodded. "We will prepare for the journey, Father."

Lehi breathed a sigh of relief, although he'd expected such a reaction from his younger sons. He embraced Nephi and Sam. Then Nephi took his mother's quivering hands. "We will go and do what the Lord has commanded, Mother. All will be well."

Sariah nodded through her tears and kissed Nephi's cheek. "I know the Lord will protect you," she said.

A shout sounded from the canyon. Laman, Lemuel, and Zoram had returned. Their hunt had been successful, and several wild goats lay across their camels. When they neared the center of the camp, they were greeted with much joy.

"You'll have enough meat for your journey," Sariah exclaimed.

Stiffening, Laman asked, "What do you mean *our* journey? We are all traveling together." He looked from Sariah to Lehi.

Lehi explained his vision and the commandment to bring Ishmael's family into the wilderness a second time.

Laman's mouth dropped open. "We are returning *again?* Don't they have women in the so-called promised land?" he asked. No one answered.

Sorrow pierced through Lehi as he watched his two oldest sons turn away in disgust.

Nephi and Sam unloaded the carcasses. In silence, they began to skin and clean the beasts.

Zoram, Laman, and Lemuel walked to the river to wash themselves. Laman looked at the sky. "Why is this happening to us?" he asked.

Lemuel sneered. "You think the sky has the answer?"

"If the Lord can speak to Father and Nephi, why doesn't He speak to us?"

"You want to be a prophet?" Lemuel chuckled.

Laman shoved him hard. "Of course not. But none of this makes sense. The Lord commanded us to flee for our lives into the wilderness. Then we are to return for the brass plates. Why? Couldn't we have taken them before we left the first time?"

Zoram broke in. "Not if your father's life was in imminent danger."

Throwing a glare in Zoram's direction, Laman said, "Now we have to return to Jerusalem again—to fetch ourselves wives. Jerusalem isn't the only city in the world with eligible women."

"It is if you want to marry an Israelite bride," Zoram said.

Laman spit on the ground, ignoring Zoram's answer. "What I'd like to know is where this land of promise is."

Lemuel laughed. "Perhaps it's our graves."

They had reached the stream, and Zoram knelt beside it. He splashed cool water on his face and neck. "How many daughters does Ishmael have?" he asked.

"Five," Lemuel said.

"How many are married?"

Laman looked puzzled. "I don't think any of them are. His two sons have families, though."

"So the daughters must be young?" asked Zoram.

Lemuel's expression lightened. "No. In fact, the youngest is marriageable age." A slow grin spread across his face. "Remember her, Laman?" he asked, elbowing his brother.

"I do." Laman's eyes brightened. "This might be interesting after all."

Lemuel hooted. "We might even let you have one, Zoram." He shoved Zoram's back, making him stumble into the water. Soon, all three men were splashing each other, laughing.

* * *

In the center of camp, Sariah and her daughters prepared bread dough to be taken on the journey. She watched her sons and Zoram splash in the water. Nostalgia crept through her breast. She remembered Laman and Lemuel in their youth and how well they had played together. It wasn't until a few years ago that they began to doubt their father's faith. She wished they could still be as devoted as Nephi and Sam.

A shadow fell over her. Sariah looked up and saw Nephi standing above.

"How are you, Mother?" he asked.

She rose and squeezed his hand. "I am happy my sons will be marrying soon."

Nephi looked at his mother's trusting face. "I hope Ishmael will be easily persuaded."

Sariah looked closely at Nephi. "Ishmael is a good man. He has limited means and may appreciate the opportunity to have all of his daughters marry." She hesitated, then said, "And I will welcome the company of Bashemath and her daughters. They will be helpful during the upcoming birth." She turned her attention back to the dough.

"Yes. An experienced woman in the camp will be helpful in your time of need." Nephi crouched beside his mother. "Do you think we'll have any say in whom we are betrothed to?"

Sariah glanced sharply at him, wondering why he asked. "I haven't thought about it. I suppose we'll match the oldest with Laman, and so on."

Nephi looked away. "We can't be sure that none of them are betrothed."

"You're right," she said. "You may not be returning with all five daughters."

Nephi's shoulders sagged, knowing he might not have a say in which one he married.

Sariah studied her youngest son. She knew something was bothering him. Then her expression lightened. "Is there a specific daughter who you think would make a fine wife?" she asked. By Nephi's expression, she knew she'd guessed the concern.

His face was warm. "You are perceptive, Mother . . ."

Sariah laid her hand over Nephi's. "When you have returned with Ishmael's daughters, come and tell me if there is one whom you most desire. I'll see what can be arranged."

He kissed his mother gratefully and left to prepare the camels for the journey.

* * *

The singing grew closer. Nephi froze at the words coming from his brother's mouth.

"O Isaabel, thou fairest maid of all . . ." sang Laman.

The men had returned from the river, and instead of glowering, they were actually rejoicing in the upcoming journey.

Lemuel ruffled Nephi's hair. "We'll soon be married."

He glanced away. "We'd better load our provisions."

"Why so serious, little brother?" Lemuel asked.

"We still have to persuade Ishmael to leave his home," Nephi said, eyeing him.

Lemuel slapped him on the back and guffawed. "That shouldn't be hard for a man of God such as you."

Nephi reddened and turned his back. Eventually Lemuel left, whistling merrily, to gather his things.

Feeling a hand on his shoulder, Nephi was relieved to see Sam. "We'll convince Ishmael, I know it," Sam said. "Father has given me instructions of how to contact one of his debtors. We'll be able to procure the mohar."

Nephi faced him. "The bride price? I hadn't considered that. How will we purchase the gifts without Laban's house discovering our presence?"

"We'll put our faith in the Lord," Sam said quietly.

The difference between Sam and his older brothers never ceased to astound Nephi. "You're right. With the mohar in place, all that will be needed is for the Lord to soften Ishmael's heart." Nephi looked past Sam, his jaw tightening.

"Is there something else that's bothering you?" Sam asked.

Nephi hesitated and then asked, "Did you hear what Laman was singing?"

Sam shook his head, surprised at his brother's vehemence.

"He was singing about Isaabel, Ishmael's youngest daughter. It makes me sick to think of him marrying her . . ."

Sam's eyes widened. Now he understood. "Don't worry. Laman will probably marry the oldest daughter."

"But what if the oldest daughter is already betrothed?" Nephi asked.

Sam paused a moment before answering. "Because of our birth order, either you or I will marry Isaabel. If I'm given her, I'll ask Father to reconsider." He placed a hand on Nephi's shoulder. "Isaabel will be your bride."

Nephi stared at him. "But—"

"Don't try to tell me you don't want her. I can see it in your eyes," Sam said. "I won't tell the others."

Nephi was embarrassed he had let his feelings show. "If Laman or Lemuel suspect, they will—"

"Shhh. Zoram's coming." Sam moved away and secured the ropes on the camel. Nephi busied himself checking the provisions.

Zoram approached the brothers. "Do you know Ishmael's family well?"

Realizing Nephi wasn't going to answer, Sam spoke up. "Ishmael is Father's cousin. He has two sons and five daughters."

"Your brothers thought I might be able to marry one of the daughters," Zoram said.

Sam hesitated. "Perhaps they're right. The number will match up perfectly, provided none of them are betrothed to someone else."

Zoram left, whistling as he went.

Turning to Nephi, Sam nudged him. "Did you hear that?"

Nephi raised his head. "If all five daughters are available, it only makes sense that Zoram would marry one too."

"Why do you think he's never married?" Sam asked.

Nephi straightened and looked at Zoram's retreating figure. "Maybe his position in Laban's house didn't allow it. It's apparently not from lack of desire," he said.

Sam smiled. "Things are going to become very interesting."

* * *

Isaabel scowled at Tamar. "Can you hurry? We're late."

"Be patient," Tamar said, grinning. "I want to try one more scarf."

She rolled her eyes. Her sister was obsessed with trying on bridal clothes. If her parents knew their two youngest daughters practiced dressing as brides, they would be furious.

Stepping from behind the curtain, Tamar asked, "How do you like it?" She spun around in the silk tunic intricately embroidered with delicate flowers. The bridal mantle covered her dark hair and cascaded down her back. Silver threads intertwined, creating a leaflike pattern. Most arresting of all was Tamar's golden face beaming at Isaabel.

"It's beautiful," Isaabel said, "but take it off, quick."

Tamar groaned and disappeared behind the curtain. Isaabel glanced furtively in the shop owner's direction. He was busy with a customer arguing over the price of a nose ring.

Last week when the sisters had ventured into a different dress shop, they were pressured to buy something. The shopkeeper was irate when he found out neither of the girls was betrothed. But in this shop, the owner didn't mind them browsing.

Tamar appeared with a grin, and Isaabel grabbed her hand. "Come on. We haven't even bought the meat for Mother yet," she said, tugging her sister along.

The sisters stepped out of the shop into the glaring sun. Isaabel squinted. "Which one should we go to?" she asked. Typically, they bought their meat at Japeth's stall, but he was Sabtah's uncle. Since the disaster with Rebeka and Sabtah, they had changed loyalties.

"Mother went to Havilah's stand yesterday," Tamar said.

Isaabel frowned. "That's by the west gate. By the time we reach home, it'll be too late to start the cooking."

Tamar crossed her arms over her chest. "Then we'll buy from Japeth."

Her shoulders sank. Isaabel knew her mother would ask what had taken them so long. Gripping Tamar's sleeve, she said, "Let's go to Havilah's then, but we must hurry."

Tamar and Isaabel rushed through the narrow alleys of the inner city. Merchants called out to the hastening sisters, promising the best prices for quality goods. Isaabel clutched her basket tightly as they moved through the Phoenician part of the bazaar. Skinned carcasses hung overhead and the smell of hot pastries reached Isaabel's nose. "I wish we could just buy meat here," she whispered.

Tamar shook her head. "You know it's not clean."

She knew. Isaabel brushed past a shopkeeper's outstretched hand. Gold bracelets dangled from his exposed arms. "You're beautiful. I have a present for you," he said, leering.

Isaabel ignored him and pressed on. Another hand reached her. "Gold earrings for the beautiful woman. I will give you a special price," the grinning man said.

Tamar linked her arm through Isaabel's, and they pushed their way through the remainder of the quarter, leaving the smell of roasted sesame behind. "Do we have to return the same way?" Isaabel asked.

"We could walk along the outer wall, but it will take longer."

With a grimace, Isaabel said, "I don't know if I can go back through the bazaar again."

"You have to be stronger, little sister," Tamar said, pulling her closer. "Hang onto me, and don't make eye contact."

After they purchased their meat, the sisters returned through the Phoenician market. Isaabel did just as she was told and clung to her sister. She even closed her eyes a few times when they passed the pushy shop owners. One called after her, "You came back. Come and see the earrings I have for you. They are made of Egyptian glass. Very rare . . ."

Dusk had fallen by the time the sisters reached home. As they stepped through the gate, Isaabel said, "Mother and Father are—" She stopped and stared. Four camels were tethered in the courtyard. She walked slowly around the beasts. Usually the rugs on the camels gave a clue to whom they belonged. They were desert camels she'd never seen before. It was rare for her father to receive guests who traveled by camel.

"Let's go through the back entrance," Tamar suggested.

Isaabel followed numbly. Her heart pounded, and she knew her mother's wrath would be full. A thought jolted through her mind. *What if the travelers were the sons of Lehi?* As soon as she thought it, she was filled with regret. She pinched herself and ordered her foolishness to stop. The sisters entered the cooking room through the rear door where their mother and sisters were feverishly preparing food.

Bashemath stared at Tamar and Isaabel. "What happened? We have visitors tonight, and you had to pick this day to be late." She wiped the sweat from her brow.

Tamar spoke first. "We bought meat from Havilah on the west side."

"Why not buy closer to home?" Her mother frowned. "You know I was expecting you."

Tamar ignored the sharp reprimand. "Who are the guests?" she asked casually.

Isaabel held her breath and waited for the reply.

Bashemath turned to stir the cooking pot and said over her shoulder, "The sons of Lehi have returned to meet with your father."

Isaabel choked back a cry. She looked at Tamar who merely grinned. Isaabel lowered her hand and crossed to the other side of the table. She gripped the corner to steady her legs. Swallowing deeply, Isaabel sat down at the table and began to husk the coconuts in front of her.

CHAPTER 14

The Lord . . . heareth the prayer of the righteous.
(PROVERBS 15:29)

Isaabel walked into the courtyard. The evening air was a welcome escape from the steamy cooking room. The guests had eaten, and her sisters now sat at the table, but she was not hungry.

She entered the stable and stroked Curly's neck. The donkey grunted. "Shhh. You don't want to give me away, do you?" Isaabel scolded.

A voice spoke behind her. "Are you hiding from someone?"

Startled, Isaabel gasped and whirled around. A stocky man stood before her with a mischievous grin on his face. His tightly curled hair framed his wide face.

She flushed. "I was just—"

The man held up his hand. "It's all right. I won't tell anyone you're out here alone with the animals."

Isaabel stifled a giggle.

The man smiled, his eyes kind. "I'm Sam. What's your name?"

"My name is Isaabel," she said quietly, glancing past him nervously.

"The others are still inside. I just came to check on the camels," he said.

Isaabel didn't know whether he was teasing or not.

"You weren't introduced to us, were you?" Sam asked, watching her closely.

She shook her head. "I was late returning from the market."

He chuckled. "Yes. We overheard that discussion. But the sister you were with came and served us."

Isaabel was surprised at his observance. "My mother has the older girls serve the guests. I stay in the cooking room."

Sam nodded slowly. "Your mother is wise."

Isaabel crinkled her brow in confusion.

Sam smiled at her expression. "My brothers are already fighting over their brides."

Isaabel found herself staring at him.

"It was nice to finally meet you." He turned and left the stable without another word. She continued to stroke Curly's neck a few minutes longer, wondering what Sam meant about his brothers fighting over brides.

Isaabel left the stable and entered the courtyard, shivering as a cool breeze swept past her. She had to return and busy herself with cleaning before her mother discovered her absence.

When she stepped into the narrow hallway, she heard voices coming from the front room. One was her father speaking. "The Lord has blessed me with five daughters, and until this moment, I didn't know why I couldn't procure marriage contracts for them."

Murmuring rose among the men. Someone said, "We know this is a unique situation, but it is the Lord's will."

"Tell me more about Zoram. Did he leave Jerusalem of his own free will?" Ishmael asked.

"Yes," came the reply. "He swore an oath to us that he would remain faithful to our family and follow the Lord's commandments. He is a good man. Even if he hadn't worked firsthand with Laban and seen the crumbling regime for himself, he wouldn't have stayed in Jerusalem much longer."

A long pause followed. Then her father spoke again. "There is a mandate out for his arrest. The elders accuse him of killing Laban."

Murmuring arose. A clear voice spoke over the others. "As the Lord liveth, I can assure you that Zoram did not kill Laban."

Silence ensued for several moments.

"Very well," Ishmael said. "I will call my wife, and you may explain the proposition."

Isaabel sped down the hall and entered the cooking room. She was about to explain herself to her mother's glowering face when Ishmael entered the room.

"Bashemath, come with me," Ishmael said.

When Isaabel's parents left, her four sisters stared at her.

"What is going on?" Rebeka demanded.

Isaabel looked away.

Anah's eyes narrowed. "If you know something, Isa, you'd better tell us."

Isaabel bit her lip, hesitating. "I overheard them talking, but it didn't make much sense."

Rebeka crossed to her sister and gripped both her shoulders. Through gritted teeth she said, "Tell . . . us . . . now . . ."

"They spoke about the destruction of Jerusalem," Isaabel said.

"What else?" Anah prompted.

"Father asked about someone named Zoram and if he joined the family of his own free will."

Rebeka grunted. "That's nothing," she said.

Looking at her sisters, Isaabel said, "I also heard Father say 'marriage contract.'"

All the women gasped. "Do you think—" Anah began.

"That I'm going to marry one of Lehi's sons?" Rebeka finished.

Anah shook her head. "Not Lehi's sons. Their wealth far exceeds ours. If we combined all of our dowries, it wouldn't be enough to secure even one contract. Father is probably talking about their friend Zoram."

Rebeka spoke quietly, "But they aren't wealthy anymore."

Anah looked puzzled. "What do you mean?"

"Laban stole all their valuables," Isaabel said.

"What about their land?" Anah asked.

Rebeka scoffed. "They live in the *wilderness,* Anah."

"But—" Anah protested.

"Shhh. Someone's coming," Tamar interrupted.

* * *

Nephi bowed his head as they waited for Ishmael to return with his wife. He felt content from eating such a delicious supper of boiled eggs, ripe fruit, and chicken. It was a miracle that Ishmael was thus far receptive to their offer. He knew the Lord had softened the man's heart. His brothers argued quietly whether they should camp on Ishmael's property or return to their abandoned house to spend the night.

Ishmael and Bashemath entered the room, and all conversation stopped. Bashemath smiled at the men and sat at the far end of the table. Ishmael's eyes were serious and his manner grave.

"Thank you for being patient. I want my wife to hear your offer." Ishmael looked toward Laman.

Laman cleared his throat, his face flushed. "As you know, we're living in the wilderness with our father. We were commanded by the Lord to, uh, leave Jerusalem and . . ."

Smiling beneath his hand, Lemuel listened to his brother stumble through the words.

"Why don't you explain the details, Nephi?" Laman asked.

Lemuel stared at his older brother. Passing the responsibility to Nephi was inappropriate. If Laman had trouble, then he, as the next oldest brother, should take over—not Nephi. Lemuel threw a stern look in Laman's direction as Nephi rose.

Nephi scanned the faces. "The plates of brass we obtained from Laban contain the record of the Jews, prophecies of the holy prophets, and a genealogy of our fathers. Our father received two commandments concerning them. First, we are to preserve them. Second, we are to pass the records to our posterity. The Lord does not want us to journey to the promised land alone."

Looking around the table at his brothers, Nephi's gaze finally settled on Bashemath. "The Lord commanded us to return to Jerusalem and bring your family with us into the wilderness. My brothers and I have offered to marry your daughters and raise posterity unto the Lord."

Bashemath stared at Nephi, her eyes wide. She gripped Ishmael's arm. Slowly she released her hold and asked, "Each son of Lehi will marry one of my daughters?"

All heads nodded.

"I have *five* daughters," she said, her voice incredulous.

"A man named Zoram, who travels with our family, is yet unmarried," Nephi said.

Bashemath seemed to understand, but a look of fear crossed her face. "What about my sons and their families? We can't leave them behind," she said.

"We'll ask them to join us." Ishmael took her hand.

Bashemath's bewildered face softened slightly. "If the Lord commands this, it shall be so."

"Very well," Ishmael said and kissed his wife.

* * *

"Our family will join Lehi in the wilderness," Ishmael said.

Gasps echoed throughout the room. Isaabel and her sisters began to ask questions at once. Ishmael held up his hand for silence. "Before you ask questions, let me explain. We have been offered a marriage contract, not just for one daughter, but for all five of you. Lehi's four sons and their friend Zoram have requested that we join them in fulfilling the Lord's commandments." Ishmael smiled. "Your mother and I have accepted their proposal, and we will prepare to leave immediately."

Isaabel looked down at the table, the words her father spoke echoing through her mind. Her sisters hugged each other in joy. They were to be married at last. Hope flooded Isaabel's heart—was it too far-fetched to dream that she might be chosen for Nephi?

Her oldest brother, Raamah, asked, "Where are they going, Father?"

Ishmael shrugged. "I don't know exactly. The Lord has commanded Lehi to take his family and ours into the wilderness. He will lead us to a promised land that has been prepared for our posterity."

Raamah frowned and looked at Heth. Though they lived in their father's household, they were not obligated to follow him.

Ishmael saw the exchange between the brothers. "I want our family to stay together. I hope you will join us."

After the conversation had died down, Isaabel excused herself to bed but took a detour through the cooking room. She stepped outside the door and sat on a low bench in the side courtyard. Closing her eyes, she let out a long sigh. She had thought Nephi was lost to her forever, but now there might be a chance to be together, even if it meant traveling into the wilderness and living out of a tent to prove her devotion. What did Nephi think of her? Did he see her as a young, foolish girl? Would he want to marry someone more wise and serious such as Tamar?

Isaabel shook her head at her thoughts. She was a fool to think Nephi looked on her as a bride. He was his father's greatest support and would want a wife who had absolute faith. She needed more faith, she realized. She wanted to trust in the Lord as Nephi did.

Isaabel folded her hands together and bowed her head. "Please, Lord," she whispered. "Give me the strength to follow Thy commandments." She paused, then added, "And let me be the one whom Nephi chooses." She couldn't bear the thought of marrying one of his brothers and having to live side by side with Nephi married to one of her sisters.

"Are you all right?" a voice asked above her.

Isaabel raised her head quickly and stared at the towering figure before her. Her heart thudded in her ears. She had forgotten how tall Nephi was. He cocked his head to one side, waiting for her answer.

She lowered her eyes. "I'm just watching the stars."

Nephi sat next to her on the bench. "You know the maps in the sky?" he asked, his eyes bright even in the faint moonlight.

She tried to steady her breathing. "Only what my father has shown me."

Nephi glanced at her profile and wondered if she was as nervous as he. "Your father is a good and wise man," he said. "I'm grateful he has decided to join our family."

Isaabel stiffened. She felt uncomfortable with Nephi speaking so plainly.

"I never had a chance to thank you for helping my father in the marketplace," he said. "You disappeared so quickly."

She felt her face grow warm.

They were silent for a moment. Nephi searched for something to say that would conceal his nerves. "Your father told me it was you who overheard Gomer plotting to rob my father's estate," he said quietly.

Isaabel nodded and stole a glance at him.

"My family is grateful to you." He paused. "You look troubled. Perhaps you don't want to leave your home."

"I've only heard the news a short time ago." Isaabel smiled faintly. "There's so much to consider."

Nephi's gaze remained on her face. "I understand."

Isaabel felt her pulse quicken. Not only were his features handsome, but his manner was tender. "Did you have trouble leaving your home?" As soon as she said it, she wished she hadn't. "I'm sorry. I didn't mean to ask."

Nephi chuckled, grateful that she was speaking at last. "It's all right. I remember the day you came with your father to my home just as I was leaving." He found himself memorizing her features—her almond eyes, straight nose, and full lips. "I too was anxious about traveling into the wilderness."

She stared at him.

"It's true. I was even hesitant to follow the Lord. But I can't deny His hand in all that has come to pass, so I choose to follow His commandments," he said gently.

Isaabel nodded, a lump forming in her throat. "I want to follow the Lord too, but I'm afraid of what will happen to our family," she confessed.

"It won't be easy." Nephi smiled. "But the Lord will protect us."

Isaabel looked away, afraid that her lack of faith would show plainly on her face.

"Tell me what's wrong, Isaabel," Nephi implored.

Hearing Nephi speak her name sent a flood of warmth through her. But she shook her head in dismay, knowing she couldn't reveal her true feelings.

With a sigh Nephi leaned forward. He rested his chin against his palms and stared into the darkness. This was harder than he expected.

Isaabel watched as his broad shoulders pulled the cloth tight across his back. In the moonlight, his dark, wavy hair shone.

Suddenly, he straightened. "Sam told me he spoke with you in the courtyard this evening."

"He was very pleasant," she said, feeling rather light-headed knowing that Nephi had discussed her with his brother.

"Sam is a good man. The woman who marries him will be fortunate," he said.

Isaabel held her breath. Was Nephi suggesting that she was meant for Sam?

Nephi continued softly, "Out of my brothers, he's the only one who knows the intentions of my heart."

Isaabel exhaled and looked at him, their eyes locking. She didn't dare hope.

"My older brothers can be selfish. If they knew my choice for a bride, they would probably try to thwart my plans just for spite. Although," Nephi said, holding her gaze, "I couldn't blame them."

Isaabel felt as if her soul somehow connected with Nephi's soul, and a peaceful feeling spread throughout her limbs. Her heart fluttered, but she realized there was something else too—something that transcended all her worries and fears. She felt safe with Nephi, like she could trust him with her life.

She was surprised that he would speak so plainly of the marriage arrangements, and she gave in to her curiosity. "Have you made your choice?" Although it made her cheeks burn to ask the question, she wanted to hear his answer.

Nephi couldn't take his eyes from her. He hesitated, then rested his hand on hers.

Isaabel drew her breath in sharply. The warmth from his touch seemed to seep into her very being.

"My heart has chosen you, Isaabel," Nephi said in a thick voice, leaning toward her until she could feel his breath on her cheek. "Tell me you'll accept me for a husband."

Isaabel began to feel dizzy and squeezed her eyes shut. When she opened them, Nephi was still there. She wasn't dreaming. "I—" The words stuck in her throat. "There would be no greater honor."

A slow grin spread across Nephi's face as his eyes searched hers. He lifted his hand and lightly traced her cheek. "I will use every ounce of strength and influence to make sure you become mine."

A sound came from the other side of the yard and made both of them freeze.

Nephi lowered his hand and brushed her arm. "Pray for us, Isaabel. Pray that nothing will come between us."

The possibility of their encounter being discovered brought Isaabel to her senses. She instinctively moved away from him.

"I must go now," he said, rising.

Before she could respond, Nephi had disappeared into the darkness. Isaabel placed a hand over her pounding chest. Not only had Nephi held her hand and touched her cheek, but he had proclaimed his feelings for her. Several minutes passed before she could muster the strength to stand. She crept through the cooking room and into the hallway. The house was silent. Entering her bedroom, she saw her sisters sleeping.

Isaabel lay on the bed and stared at the ceiling. Her heart swelled with happiness. Nephi was going to request her hand in marriage. She slipped out of bed and knelt on the bare floor. Closing her eyes, she began to pray.

CHAPTER 15

The Lord is longsuffering, and of great mercy,
forgiving iniquity and transgression.
(NUMBERS 14:18)

Nephi entered the front courtyard at Ishmael's house. His brothers stood with Ishmael and Heth in animated discussion.

"Have you made up your minds as to where we are sleeping tonight?" Nephi asked.

Sam turned to answer. "We're waiting for Raamah to return from the debtor's house."

"He's not back?"

"The hour grows late," Ishmael interjected. "I'm concerned."

Just then, Raamah walked into the courtyard and stopped before them. "Reuel will not come. He says that his debts have been forgiven since your father departed from Jerusalem without explanation," he said breathlessly.

Laman's face grew scarlet as he mused over the situation. "Reuel should be grateful that our father has waited until now to collect. He is a coward."

Next to him, Lemuel pushed out his chest. "Laman's right. The man needs to be disciplined." He grabbed a staff next to the door and handed it to Laman.

"Wait," Nephi said. "Perhaps if we explain our plight to Reuel, his heart will be softened. There's no need to use force."

Laman turned and set his gaze on Nephi. "We don't have time to wait for the Lord, Nephi. We're already risking our lives and Ishmael's as it is." His grip tightened about his staff. "We will visit Reuel tonight and collect our father's dues."

"What if Laban's soldiers see you?" Ishmael asked, concern in his eyes.

Lemuel fingered the knife at his waist. "Then, like our brother Nephi, we'll put our life in God's hands—"

"Who's coming with us?" Laman interrupted.

Raamah moved toward him. "I will."

Ishmael started to protest, but Raamah silenced him. "These men are asking us to follow them into the wilderness, Father. It is only reasonable that our family receives the appropriate mohar."

"I'm coming too," Heth said.

Laman nodded, then turned toward his younger brothers. "Sam, you and Nephi remain here. If we are not back before dawn, come after us."

Ishmael stepped forward and placed a hand on Laman's shoulder. "May the Lord protect you."

The men moved across the courtyard. "Leave the camels. It's not far, and we'll attract less attention," Raamah instructed.

Following Raamah, the men walked through a series of dark alleys. The city of Jerusalem was in a deep slumber. Whenever footsteps approached, the men quickly moved into the shadows.

Soon, Raamah stopped before an elaborate gate. "The guard is asleep," he whispered to the others. "Follow me."

Lemuel noticed that the design of the gate was similar to Laban's, though smaller in scale. They eased their way through the opening and passed soundlessly through the shadows of the courtyard.

"It looks as if he's gone to bed," Raamah said, scanning the area for signs of life.

"Where are his sleeping quarters?" Laman asked, his voice a harsh whisper.

Raamah hesitated, then led them to the right. He motioned for Lemuel and Heth to remain where they were and told Laman to follow him. They peered into a high window. Then, turning his face toward the others, Raamah grinned. "This will be some surprise."

He whispered something to Laman, who nodded eagerly and motioned for the rest to follow.

It was over within a few seconds. The men burst into the room, and Laman pounced on Reuel, pinning his arms beneath him. With one muscular hand, he covered the man's mouth to keep him from crying out.

In the corner of the dim room, Raamah had captured a half-dressed woman, who struggled fiercely against him. "Quiet," Raamah hissed. "Or I'll take you for a slave."

Lemuel stifled a laugh, and the woman's movements ceased.

Pulling Reuel into a sitting position with his arms pinned, Laman said, "Lemuel, hold his legs."

Lemuel obliged.

Heth fumbled with a lantern, and soon the room was bathed in an orange glow.

Laman gritted his teeth and spoke in an urgent voice. "Reuel, we've come to collect our father's debt. You will pay in full, or else . . ." A small squeal erupted from the woman whom Raamah still held captive. "Or else, your home will light the night sky with hungry flames."

The man's eyes filled with panic as he nodded.

"Is that a yes?" Laman asked, threatening.

Another nod.

With a shove, Laman released the man onto the floor and kicked his backside.

Reuel gasped for air and scrambled to his feet. In a trembling voice he said, "I will pay my debt, but first, let my woman go."

"Your woman?" Raamah asked. "Does your wife know about this?"

Reuel paled. "Please," he said.

"When your debt is settled, you'll have the woman back."

Lemuel snickered. Heth cast him a harsh glance. He would not stand for the mistreatment of a woman, no matter what the circumstances.

With Reuel leading the way, securely flanked by Laman and Lemuel, the rest followed him through the back of the house. The woman stumbled along behind, still held by Raamah.

In a small room behind the cooking room, Reuel removed a rug from the floor. He opened the door in the ground and stepped back. "I owe your father one hundred camels. All of my treasure equals at least that."

"Lemuel, Heth, bring it up," Laman instructed.

They descended into the narrow room and hauled up two metal chests, each containing coins and silver and gold jewelry.

Lemuel opened the lids and grinned. "Beautiful."

"Thank you for doing your duty." Laman patted Reuel on the back. "All of your debts to my father are now settled."

Reuel nodded, perspiration flowing freely down his face.

"And," Laman added, "when we safely leave your place of residence, we'll let your woman go."

The woman opened her mouth, but Raamah covered it before she could scream.

The men left Reuel behind, staring after them in shock. They passed the still-sleeping guard at the gate and turned toward Ishmael's house. After several streets, they released the woman.

* * *

The sun was high in the sky when the caravan left Ishmael's property north of Jerusalem. Ishmael had spent two days bartering the mohar, procured from Reuel, for desert provisions. His two sons had taken almost the entire two days to decide whether or not they would join the family.

Nephi rode next to Ishmael at the front of the group. The sisters walked in the center of the procession. Raamah and Heth walked in the rear behind Laman and Lemuel's camels. Raamah's son rode perched on top of a baggage camel. His wife had died four years earlier when she delivered their son. Heth's daughter rode with his wife, Zillah, who was with their second child. Heth's face was etched into a frown as he worried about his wife. Zillah was not a strong woman—she had suffered greatly in the birth of their daughter—and she had not been feeling well lately.

The first night finally fell on the weary travelers. Bashemath directed the men where to place the makeshift tents. The three full-sized tents would not be used until they reached the Valley of Lemuel. Zillah knew how to set up a tent, but she was feeling ill and spent the evening sleeping.

Raamah and Heth scoffed at their sisters, who were struggling unsuccessfully with the tents, and Laman and Lemuel joined in the teasing. It was clear that the women had never spent a night in the desert before.

Nephi and Sam proceeded to help the women.

"Look at your brothers doing the women's work," Raamah said, laughing.

"Next they'll be cooking." Lemuel and Heth joined their laughter.

Nephi ignored the jests and showed the women how to spread the tent and hammer the stakes. His eyes briefly met Isaabel's, whose gaze reflected her gratitude.

When the tents were set up, Anah sighed heavily. She stomped over to the jeering men. Placing her hands on hips, she said, "If you idle toads will fetch the wood, you'll eat your supper sooner."

Laman grinned. "I like a woman who feeds her man," he said, eyes shining. Gales of laughter exploded around her.

Anah blushed scarlet and turned quickly away. She joined the women and refused to speak the rest of the evening.

* * *

The following day, Isaabel noticed that Anah and Puah were falling farther and farther behind in the lineup. Soon they were walking directly in front of Laman and Lemuel. She heard occasional laughter coming from them.

Isaabel cringed. She still thought about what the brothers were like when they had come to her house drunk. Their demeaning words had cut through her like a knife. Isaabel stole a glance toward her mother, but she was half asleep upon her camel.

Tamar hurried alongside Isaabel. "It looks like Anah and Puah are trying to take their minds off their blistered feet," she said.

Isaabel felt a sharp pang of complaint coming from her stomach. "I hope it doesn't cause trouble for us."

"What do you mean?" Tamar asked, looking alarmed.

Isaabel lowered her voice. "The brothers will be choosing their brides soon, right?"

Tamar nodded, her expression still bewildered.

"What if, say, Sam notices Puah paying attention to Lemuel? And Father wants Puah to marry Sam—"

"I see what you mean," Tamar cut in. She glanced over at Rebeka. "Whom do you think Father will give Rebeka to?"

"I don't know. Rebeka might have a bad temper at times, but she would never do anything inappropriate. I don't see her fitting with Laman or Lemuel."

"What about you, Isaabel? Whom would you pick?" Tamar teased.

Isaabel reddened. "Do you think we'll be given a choice?"

"I've heard of it happening before. Why not to us? Come on, Isa, tell me."

"Right after you."

Tamar laughed. "I haven't narrowed down the selection yet."

Suddenly, Isaabel couldn't contain her secret any longer. "Nephi told me he wants to marry me."

Tamar almost dropped the bundle she was carrying. She grabbed Isaabel's arm and pulled her to a stop, but Isaabel tugged forward. "You'll draw attention to us," she hissed.

"Nephi spoke to you?" Tamar asked.

For once, Isaabel was grateful that she was wearing her veil, not only to protect her from the blowing sand, but to hide her unquenchable smile.

"Oh, Tamar. He is so wonderful that sometimes I don't believe he's real."

"I can't believe you didn't tell me," Tamar said, poking Isaabel's side.

"It wasn't easy keeping it quiet. Nephi said that his older brothers have first choice, and they may request me if they know his intentions."

Tamar remained quiet for a short while. "Are his brothers really that malicious?"

"I hope not. All I know is that I have never prayed so earnestly in my life."

Tamar linked her arm through Isaabel's. "I'll add my prayers to yours, then."

* * *

Nephi awoke with a start. He heard arguing outside of his shelter. Rubbing his eyes, he sat up. By the angle of the sun, he knew he'd only slept a couple of hours.

Laman appeared at the opening of the tent. "We're leaving, Nephi."

"What do you mean?" Nephi asked, staring through blurry eyes.

But Laman had disappeared. Nephi roused Sam, who was sleeping next to him. "Laman and the others want to move forward," he said.

Sam yawned. "I thought we were traveling at night."

But Nephi wasn't listening. He had stepped out of the tent and heard Raamah shouting at Ishmael. Something wasn't right, he realized.

He rushed over to Ishmael just as Raamah stomped away. "What's happening?"

Ishmael grasped Nephi's arm, his voice urgent. "My sons want to return to Jerusalem. Heth's wife is ill and—"

Lemuel walked up to them. "You're outnumbered, Nephi. Heth and Raamah are coming with us, as well as Anah and Puah," he said.

Ishmael's grip tightened on Nephi's arm as he faced Lemuel. "My daughters are staying with us."

Nephi held up his hands. "Wait. What is all this about?"

"None of us want to live in the wilderness," Lemuel said. "We can follow God just as well in the city of Jerusalem. The desert is too harsh for the women. Heth's wife is ill. She is burning with the fever, and Heth fears she'll lose the child she is carrying."

Nephi looked to where the others were packing their camels. "You would abandon Father and Mother?" he whispered.

Lemuel hesitated and his eyes narrowed. "You're not in charge of us. We'll do as we see fit." He turned and walked to the others.

Ishmael put his hand on Nephi's arm again, but Nephi shook it off. "I'll take care of this," he said, his eyes blazing.

Nephi strode to where Laman and Lemuel stood, whispering together. "How can you be so stubborn and foolish that you need your younger brother to set an example?"

Laman and Lemuel turned and faced him. "*You* are the one who is blind, *little* brother," Laman said with a scowl.

Angry now, Nephi tried to keep his tone even. "How can you disobey the Lord? How can you forget everything He's done for us? Don't you remember the angel?"

Heth and Raamah joined Laman and Lemuel. They crossed their arms over their chests and glared at Nephi.

Nephi was not deterred. "The Lord will take care of us. We only need to have faith. Zillah's sickness will soon pass. And if we are faithful, we will reach the promised land—"

Laman snickered. "We'll be dead before we reach the promised land." He looked at the others. "We need to start for Jerusalem soon."

Nephi grabbed Laman's arm. "Jerusalem will be destroyed. They have rejected the prophets and put them in prison. Father waits for us to return," he cried. His voice rose until everyone in the camp stopped and listened. "If you return to Jerusalem, you will die too." Suddenly he paused, then spoke with authority, "The Spirit of the Lord has told me that if you return, you will be destroyed."

Laman's face turned scarlet and his mouth worked silently. He shook off Nephi's hand. "Liar!" he finally burst out.

Next to him, Lemuel clenched his fists and took deep breaths. Making the first move, Laman lunged at Nephi, knocking him to the ground. Lemuel joined him, and they pinned Nephi into the sand. "Where's the angel now?" Lemuel shouted.

Nephi cried out and brought his hands up to shield his face, but Laman hit him, knocking him unconscious.

"Someone bring us a cord," Laman growled.

Seconds later, Raamah appeared with a rope from a disassembled tent. Laman snatched it, and he and Lemuel bound Nephi's hands behind his back, cinching the rope tight.

Ishmael arrived on the scene and gasped in horror at the sight. "Stop it," he bellowed.

"Stand back, old man," Laman warned. The look of fury in his eyes caused Ishmael to retreat a few steps.

"Bring me another rope," Laman commanded Raamah harshly.

With the second rope, Laman and Lemuel tied Nephi's feet together and hoisted him off the ground. "We'll take him over there," Laman said, nodding toward a hill. "The wild animals will enjoy a feast when he dies of starvation."

Suddenly, Sam pounced on Laman from behind, causing him to release Nephi and stagger backward.

In one swift movement, Laman regained his balance and faced Sam. "Foolish brother. There is no angel to save you today." He delivered a fierce kick to Sam's stomach.

Sam fell into the sand, gripping his middle. "Don't move," Laman threatened, his face dripping with perspiration, "unless you want to join Nephi."

Releasing Nephi, Lemuel moved to Laman's side. "Let's bind him too," he said with a sneer.

Without hesitation, Raamah joined Lemuel, and they tied Sam's hands behind his back.

Sam furiously struggled against the men, but he was no match for them.

"Lemuel, guard Sam until we're ready to leave this forsaken desert," Laman instructed.

A smile crossed Lemuel's reddened face. "Pleasure."

"Let's go," Laman said to Raamah and Heth. They lifted Nephi and started walking away from camp.

"You can't get away with this," Sam yelled after them. Next to him, Lemuel kicked him, stopping Sam from calling after his brothers again.

Some time later, the men returned without Nephi.

* * *

Nephi closed his eyes. Grains of sand scraped against his eyelids, making them burn. He groaned and tried to roll onto his side. The cords dug into his flesh, and he winced in pain. He didn't know how long he'd been lying in the hot sand. "Laman," he called weakly. Silence surrounded him. He was too far away from the camp to hear anything.

"O Lord," he whispered, "according to my faith which is in Thee, wilt Thou deliver me from the hands of my brothers? Please give me strength that I may burst these bands with which I am bound."

Staggering to a standing position, he bent his neck and looked at the ankle bands—they had loosened. Nephi wiggled his arms and found those bands loosened too. "Thank you, Lord," he whispered. He worked his hands out of the cords and removed those that encircled his ankles.

Nephi rubbed his wrists and rotated his sore ankles. With slow steps at first, he started back in the direction of camp. Soon, he could see the family in the distance, gathered around the camels. Most of the shelters had been taken down. As he came nearer, he saw the women huddled together outside a makeshift tent. He paused as the sound of weeping reached his ears. His heart sank with sorrow. What had become of his family?

Standing apart from the women, Heth and Raamah were arguing with their father. A short distance from them, Lemuel sat near a figure lying in the sand. It was Sam, Nephi realized. Anger rose in his breast. His brothers had forgotten the Lord so easily.

Increasing his pace, Nephi spotted Laman, who was securing bundles onto a camel.

Laman didn't hear him approach and swung around at the sound of his voice.

"Why are the women weeping?" Nephi asked quietly.

Laman stared at Nephi, his mouth gaping.

"Why are the women—" Nephi began to repeat.

"I heard you the first time," Laman hissed, his eyes filling with instant anger. "Zillah lost her baby. We are abandoning this foolish journey."

Lemuel, having seen Nephi, approached the two. "I see that your ropes weren't tight enough."

"The Lord loosened my bands so that I can convince you to stay," Nephi said.

Throwing his head back, Lemuel burst into an ugly laughter. "Don't tell me. An angel untied them," he mocked.

Taking a halfstep back, Nephi shook his head.

Laman's eyes darkened. "Angel or no angel, *you* are no longer part of this family. *I* am the eldest son, and I have decided we are leaving." He moved menacingly toward

Nephi and spoke with loathing, "We have been given a terrible sign. With Zillah's misfortune, more are sure to follow. The wilderness offers only misery."

Nephi straightened his shoulders. "The Lord—" he began.

"There is no room for your self-righteousness," Laman interrupted. He moved swiftly and pounced on Nephi, bringing him to the ground. "Hold his feet," he shouted at Lemuel.

Lemuel dropped onto Nephi's feet and wrapped his sash around Nephi's ankles.

By now, Ishmael's family had noticed the interchange, and the weeping stopped.

As Heth and Raamah joined Laman and Lemuel, Sam started yelling.

"How did *he* get here?" Raamah asked, out of breath.

Laman, who was lying on top of Nephi's chest, grunted. "Give me your knife," he said.

With haste, Raamah handed over his knife.

Sam's shouts grew louder. He was inching his way over to the brothers. At one point, he tried to stand but fell over in the sand.

"*Now* you'll listen," Laman said through gritted teeth, holding the blade to Nephi's throat.

A scream erupted behind them. Laman flinched but held his position.

"Get off him!" Isaabel shrieked. She flung herself at Laman and began to beat his back. He shook her off easily.

"Isaabel!" Bashemath yelled, running toward them. She grabbed Isaabel and pulled her away.

But Isaabel broke free and clung to Laman's legs. "Please, let him go," she begged.

Bashemath joined her daughter's side on the ground, sobbing. "Have mercy on your brother," she cried.

"Isn't losing one life today enough?" Sam's voice cut through the women's cries.

"Silence him," Laman shouted menacingly.

Lemuel moved toward Sam.

"Wait." Heth stepped forward, face pale. "He's right. We've already lost one life today. Grant the women their wish, Laman. Spare Nephi's life."

Laman looked at Heth, his eyes blazing. "No one commands me what to do," he hissed. His grip tightened around Nephi.

Isaabel's sobs quieted, and her voice gained strength. "He has done nothing but follow the Lord's commandments."

"Leave Nephi in our hands. Return to Jerusalem if you wish, but spare your brother's life," Bashemath pleaded, wiping her eyes.

The seconds passed slowly. Everyone waited for Laman's reaction.

Finally, Laman slowly lowered his head and let out a long breath of air. He relaxed his hold on the knife and let it fall to the earth.

The relief was audible. Laman crawled off of Nephi and sunk to his knees. Lemuel followed.

Nephi turned over, blinking the sand out of his eyes. He stared at Heth in a daze. Then he loosened Lemuel's sash from his ankles and slowly stood, looking around at the family of Ishmael, gratitude in his eyes. Ishmael stepped forward and embraced him, then Bashemath threw herself on Nephi's shoulder and sobbed. Isaabel hung back, clinging to her sisters.

As he pulled away from Ishmael and Bashemath, Nephi sagged from exhaustion. His heart was heavy and filled with pain. He turned his eyes to Laman, who remained kneeling in the sand, his head bowed.

Suddenly, Laman dropped to the earth and lay prostrate before Nephi. He reached out to Nephi. "Forgive us. We have sinned against you," he cried.

Lemuel fell beside his brother and bowed his head. "Please, accept our apology."

Nephi sank to his knees and placed his hands on his brothers' shoulders, his breathing ragged. "I forgive you. But you must pray to the Lord and ask *His* forgiveness."

CHAPTER 16

And he shall put his hand upon the head of the burnt offering; and it shall be accepted for him to make atonement for him.

(LEVITICUS 1:4)

Isaabel drifted into a troubled slumber, tucked between Tamar and Puah. In her dreams she watched Laman attack Nephi again and again. But her screams were silent this time.

Then she saw the knife coming toward her.

Isaabel bolted upright in the quiet tent. She was soaking wet from her own fear. Looking at the sleeping forms next to her, she wished she could rest peacefully. Though it had been several days since Nephi was attacked by his brothers, she couldn't erase the image from her mind. She trembled to think of what would have happened had Heth not interfered.

Tamar stirred next to her. "Did you have another bad dream?" she asked, breaking into Isaabel's thoughts.

"Yes," Isaabel said quietly and lay down next to her sister. "I am afraid of what Laman and Lemuel will do next."

Tamar reached out her hand and touched Isaabel's moist brow. "They have repented of their wickedness. We all watched them beg for Nephi's forgiveness," she said softly.

Closing her eyes, Isaabel felt a lump form in her throat, but she refused to let Tamar see her cry. It was over, wasn't it? And Nephi's brothers had repaired their ways. Then why did her throat go dry when she came face-to-face with Laman or Lemuel?

Tamar's easy slumber filled the tent. Isaabel rose and quietly stole outside. She leaned against the heavy black goatskin walls and gazed upward. The sky was illuminated with thousands of stars. Pulling her garment tightly about her, Isaabel walked around the tent. A fire glowed near her parents' shelter. Her father sat hunched over it, warming his hands.

Isaabel moved quickly to her father's side. She smiled and crouched next to him.

"Can't sleep?" Ishmael asked quietly.

She shook her head and remained silent.

"You haven't been yourself, Isa. What's the matter?"

Staring into the flickering flames, she wondered if she should tell her father. After a few seconds, her eyes began to burn, and she blinked rapidly. "I am afraid for Nephi," she whispered.

Ishmael stroked his beard in thought. "Ah. I understand. I thought you might be more affected than the others. What happened the other day was difficult for everyone, but we must take courage and put our faith in the Lord."

"I know," Isaabel managed to say.

"Here comes Nephi now," Ishmael said.

She jerked her head up and saw a shadowed figure moving toward them. She grabbed Ishmael's arm to steady herself.

Ishmael chuckled softly. "I invited him to sit with me for a while," he said. "You'll be a pleasant surprise."

Nephi approached them and stopped when he saw Isaabel.

"It's only my daughter Isaabel," Ishmael said.

Nephi moved to Ishmael's free side and sat down across the fire from Isaabel. His gaze settled on her, his expression serious. "You're awake late."

Isaabel's face flamed. "I-I couldn't sleep," she stammered.

Nephi shifted and cleared his throat. "Thank you for your help the other day," he said quietly, diverting his gaze to the fire.

"Heth was the one—"

"No. You were the one," Nephi cut in. His eyes blazed into her. "Because *you* begged my brothers to stop, their hearts were softened."

She bit her lip and wished away the hammering of her heart.

Nephi continued in a low voice, "And your mother pled for my life as if I were her own son." His voice broke.

Ishmael patted him on the shoulder. "We do consider you our son, Nephi," he said.

Isaabel's eyes shone as she watched the exchange between her father and Nephi.

"When we reach my father's camp," Nephi said, "we'll offer a sacrifice of gratitude on behalf of your family."

Ishmael embraced Nephi. "So be it," he said. Then he turned to Isaabel. "You look tired. Maybe you should try to sleep."

She rose, not daring to hope that Nephi would follow.

Nephi rose too and quietly asked, "May I accompany her, sir?"

The corners of Ishmael's mouth tugged into a smile, and he nodded.

Away from the glow of the fire, Isaabel shivered as the wind stirred her clothing.

Quietly, Nephi said, "I haven't seen you smile for some time."

Isaabel stopped and turned. Her eyes met his. "There's nothing to smile about," she said more loudly than she intended. "Your brothers nearly killed you."

"Shhh," Nephi said, looking beyond her to the women's tent. "Someone may hear us." He took her hand and turned her palm over, staring intently at the curves of her fingers. "I've forgiven them, and you must do the same."

Isaabel caught her breath at his touch. She felt her throat swell and knew that she couldn't bear it if anything were to happen to him. "But what if they become angry again?" she asked, letting him slowly trace her fingers.

Nephi brought his gaze to hers. "They might. Their anger will grow if they continue to complain." He squeezed her hand. "Remember when I asked you to pray for us?"

She nodded silently, losing herself in his eyes.

"The Lord is the only One who can protect us. You must have faith," he said.

"I have faith in *you*," Isaabel whispered, feeling her heart start its slow hammer.

Nephi grinned. He wanted to take her in his arms, but he knew he had to wait. "That's a start," he said. He released her hand reluctantly. "Hurry back to your tent and rest your beautiful eyes."

* * *

Lehi noticed the camels growing restless. He shielded his eyes with his hand and looked at the sky. It was late afternoon. Zoram was fishing, and Sariah and the girls were beating the tent rugs. All was silent except for the quiet gurgle of the river.

Lehi's heart warmed with hope. Perhaps his sons would return today with Ishmael's family and his prayers would be answered. He walked to the camels and patted one on its neck. He decided to ride it to the mouth of the canyon. Climbing upon the animal's back, he said, "Let's see what's causing you to stir."

When he reached the canyon wall, he paused and gazed at the massive ridge. A pebble tumbled its way down the face of the cliff. His camel flinched at the sound. "Come on," Lehi commanded.

Several minutes later, Lehi halted the camel. Someone was approaching. He strained to hear any conversation or activity. Then, two camels came into view. Lehi recognized Nephi immediately. Next to him rode Ishmael.

"Aiyah," Lehi said, spurring his camel forward. The camel lumbered to meet the oncoming procession. His grin was wide as he greeted the travelers. "Alleluyahu, you have arrived at last."

Nephi smiled. "How's Mother?"

"Her health is strong. She's prayed fervently for your safe journey," Lehi said. He turned to Ishmael, and his eyes widened. The man before him was only a shell of the man he knew in Jerusalem. His face had grown gaunt, and his once ample chest slumped beneath his loose clothing. Lehi climbed off his camel and helped Ishmael do the same. "Welcome, Ishmael. I have greatly anticipated this reunion."

Ishmael spread his arms. "My wife and I welcome your offer."

Lehi embraced his cousin. "Nephi will show you the way. I'll wait here and greet the others."

Nephi and Ishmael passed, and soon Sam appeared around the bend, followed by the women and children. Lehi greeted each in turn. He frowned when he saw those who brought up the rear. Laman and Lemuel rode with Ishmael's two sons. They rode with an air of confidence, close to disdain.

"Father," Laman said. "You have come to meet us."

"How was the journey?" Lehi embraced them after they descended from their camels.

Lemuel smiled. "As you can see, Ishmael's family was happy to join us."

Lehi looked at Raamah and Heth. "I'm sure your father is happy to have his sons along too."

They both nodded. Lehi noticed a flicker of uncertainty in Raamah's eyes.

When Lehi and the last of the group arrived at camp, they were met with a flurry of kisses and embraces. Sariah and Bashemath stood in each other's arms, tearfully speaking. Dinah and Elisheba played merrily with Raamah's and Heth's children.

Lehi raised his arms in the air, and all fell silent. "We welcome the family of Ishmael. We are grateful for their safe passage and the return of our sons. Let us prepare to offer a sacrifice of thanksgiving," he said. Everyone nodded.

The women gathered together and began to prepare the meal. The men unloaded the camels and led them to the stream to drink.

Ishmael and Bashemath drew Lehi aside. "We need to speak privately," Ishmael said.

"Of course," Lehi said, leading them to his tent.

Once inside, Ishmael rubbed his hands together nervously. "Maybe your wife should hear this too."

Lehi agreed and stepped outside the tent. He motioned for Sariah to join him. When all four were seated within, Ishmael began. "There was a problem on the trail," he said.

Concern crossed Lehi's face. "What happened?"

"Heth's wife, Zillah, became ill. Because of this, Raamah, Heth, Laman, and Lemuel decided to return to Jerusalem," Ishmael said quietly.

Sariah looked at Bashemath, who was staring at her hands. Lehi stroked his beard, his eyes full of sorrow, waiting for Ishmael to continue.

"When Nephi discovered their plans, he tried to convince them to stay. Two of my daughters, Anah and Puah, were also determined to leave. Laman and Lemuel didn't like Nephi telling them what to do. They bound him and carried him off to be devoured by wild animals," Ishmael said.

Sariah gasped as she reached for Lehi's hand. Lehi's eyes filled with pain.

In a low voice, Ishmael continued, "During Nephi's absence, Zillah miscarried her baby. At that point, I knew there was no hope of my sons staying. But, by the power of the Spirit, Nephi loosened his bands and returned to the camp." His voice trembled. "He spoke again to Laman and Lemuel, who became more angry. They threw Nephi to the ground, and Laman held a knife to Nephi's throat."

Crying out, Sariah clutched Lehi's arm.

Bashemath's eyes filled with tears, and she spoke in a shaking voice, "Our daughter Isaabel flung herself at them and pleaded for Nephi's life. I joined her pleas, but only after Heth interfered did Laman release the knife."

Sariah quietly wept at the news.

In a strained voice, Lehi said, "We are sorry about Zillah, and we are indebted to you for our son's life."

Raising her tearstained face, Sariah said, "We thought we were saving you from the destruction of Jerusalem, but you saved our son's life from his own brothers and lost a grandchild in the process."

Bashemath reached over and embraced Sariah. "Zillah was already having complications, so we don't blame anyone for her misfortune." She pulled away and smiled at Lehi. "We think of Nephi as a son, and we would protect him with our own lives."

Lehi nodded gratefully and cleared his throat. "What happened when Laman dropped the knife?"

Ishmael said, "Laman and Lemuel were filled with remorse and fell to their knees, begging for Nephi's forgiveness. Nephi told them to pray to the Lord and ask His forgiveness."

"Very well," Lehi said, his heart heavy. He rose to his feet. "A grievous sin has been committed and we shall prepare a burnt offering immediately."

* * *

Tamar yanked a comb through Isaabel's knotted hair. "We should wash our hair tonight when it gets dark," she said.

"Last night, the men sat by the fire until late," Isaabel said, wrinkling her nose.

"Camping is inconvenient, isn't it?" Tamar laughed. "Maybe we could suggest all the men leave for a day so the women can take heated baths."

"Sariah bathes in her tent," Isaabel said.

Tamar stopped combing. "She does?"

"I asked for her the other day, and Dinah told me her mother was bathing. No one was near the river or the sea, so I assumed she was in her tent," Isaabel said.

"Let's ask her if we can wash there too," Tamar said.

Hesitating, Isaabel said, "Won't she think we're vain and—"

"Come on, Isa," Tamar said, tugging her sister to her feet.

Outside Sariah's tent, Isaabel paused, but Tamar called out, "Sariah, are you in there?"

A small head poked out of the flap, then disappeared. "Mother, it's Ishmael's daughters," Dinah said from within.

Sariah appeared with a smile. "Welcome," she said, holding open the goatskin door for the girls to enter.

Inside, Isaabel stared at her surroundings. The oblong tent was divided into sections with curtains. In the first section, intricately woven mats lay upon the ground so that no sand was visible. Near the entrance, a fire pit was laid with fresh wood.

"Sit down," Sariah instructed.

Tamar and Isaabel knelt. "I didn't know a tent could be so beautiful," Isaabel said.

Sariah tilted her head, amusement in her expression. "The plainness on the outside doesn't reflect the beauty on the inside. There are more elaborate tents than this among the desert travelers, but we don't wish to draw attention to ourselves."

Tamar's eyes glimmered. "We heard you have a private bath," she said.

Isaabel was shocked at her sister's boldness.

Sariah chuckled. "Would you like to wash privately?"

Both sisters nodded.

Sariah rose and said, "Follow me." She led the way through the curtained sections until they reached a small room filled with steam.

A large pit had been dug and piled with glowing embers. Several clay pots filled with water surrounded the embers. Steam rose from the pots and warmed the air. The ground was covered with loosely woven mats.

Sariah lifted a copper ladle out of a pot. "Stand here and pour the water over your body. The water seeps through the mats into the ground." She pointed to the tent wall. "You may hang your clothes on those lashed sticks. Here is a cloth to dry yourself when you're finished. And you may use this on your hair," she said, handing over a small jar.

A voice giggled behind them. Isaabel turned to see Dinah and Elisheba standing in the entryway.

"Finish your chores, girls," Sariah said patiently. The girls left, and Sariah turned to face Isaabel. "You bathe first, and Tamar will keep watch."

Sariah left the room, leaving Tamar and Isaabel alone.

"She probably thinks we're foolish," Isaabel whispered.

Tamar gave a conspiratorial wink. "Hurry, before the others notice we're missing."

Isaabel quickly removed her outer garment and tunic. It felt strange to stand unclothed in the darkened steamy room. She lifted a ladle of fragrant water and touched the surface. The liquid was warm. She poured the water over her shoulder and closed her eyes as it cascaded down her skin.

"Hurry," came Tamar's whisper from the entrance.

Isaabel poured another ladleful of water down her back, then over her head. She opened the jar Sariah had given her and smelled the contents. The aroma of honey reached her nose. She poured out a few drops, not wanting to waste the precious luxury, and worked them into her hair. Three more ladles of water and she was finished.

Grabbing the linen square, Isaabel patted herself dry, shivering. She dressed quickly and called to Tamar.

While Tamar bathed, Isaabel ran her fingers through her wet hair, trying to separate the strands. She heard a movement behind her, and when she turned, she discovered Dinah.

Isaabel brought her hand to her chest. "You startled me."

Dinah's eyes twinkled. "Mother wants to speak with you. She told me to keep watch."

Isaabel hesitated. "Are you sure?"

Smiling, Dinah pointed in the direction that led to the front of the tent.

Isaabel walked slowly through the maze of curtains and came upon Sariah bent over the fire pit by the front entrance.

"There you are," Sariah said.

Isaabel smiled nervously and approached her. "Dinah said you wanted to speak with me?"

Sariah straightened and took Isaabel's hands. "I want to thank you for saving my son's life."

Isaabel's mouth fell open. "I didn't—"

"Your parents told us everything," Sariah said, her eyes moist. "You are a gift to our family."

Isaabel took a step back, her own emotions beginning to surface.

Sariah looked at her with remorse. "I'm sorry. Remembering has upset you."

Glancing away, Isaabel bit her lip.

"Sit with me," Sariah said.

Isaabel settled across from her and took a deep breath. "I am afraid of what Laman and Lemuel and my brothers might do next," she said quietly.

"I know," Sariah said. "Sometimes I'm afraid too, but I pray every night for my family, particularly my older sons. The Lord has blessed us thus far, and we must obey His commandments. When one or two don't obey, everyone suffers." She touched Isaabel's hand. "I know that you have a pure heart, something Nephi will need in a wife."

Isaabel's face reddened. "But—"

"I've seen your feelings in your eyes. Nephi has made his intentions known to me, and I will do what I can to bring you two together. But you must pray that nothing will come between you," Sariah said.

Isaabel felt tears pricking her eyes. "That's what Nephi told me."

"Then have faith, child."

Isaabel looked at Sariah, her face so pure and sweet. Sariah must be enduring all of the same hardships the rest of the family was, but Isaabel had never heard her complain. "How do you do it, Sariah? How do you stay so faithful?"

Sariah smiled gently and reached over, taking Isaabel's hand. "I too have struggled in my faith. It has been a growing process and not something that has come simply. I haven't seen the visions that my husband has, yet I believe in him with all my heart."

Feeling overwhelmed, Isaabel nodded. She wondered if she could ever be as devoted as Sariah.

"Keep praying, and you will discover that the Lord is truly mindful of us," Sariah said.

CHAPTER 17

For the Lord giveth wisdom:
out of his mouth cometh knowledge and understanding.
(PROVERBS 2:6)

"Lehi has called the families together," Ishmael told Bashemath.

She gripped his arm in apprehension. "Are we moving on?"

Ishmael patted her hand. "I don't know. Gather the girls, and we'll meet at the fire."

Half an hour passed before both families assembled. Lehi stood in the center with Sariah sitting at his feet and waited for everyone to arrive. Laman, Lemuel, Raamah, and Heth sat clustered together in intimate conversation. Bashemath clung to Ishmael and motioned for her daughters to join her. Heth's wife, Zillah, was sick with fever and remained in her tent. Dinah and Elisheba, having formed a recent attachment to Isaabel, each held one of her hands. Isaabel smiled at the doting girls and found a place where they could all sit together.

Sam and Zoram arrived and stood on the outskirts of the circle. Lehi caught Sam's eye. "Where's Nephi?"

"He stopped in the tent for something," Sam said.

Nephi appeared suddenly. "I'm here, Father." Lehi motioned for him to come to the center of the circle. He stepped around the crowded bodies and accepted a scroll of papyrus and a stylus from Lehi and then knelt beside his mother.

Letting out a long breath, Nephi looked at the face of each family member. When he had heard his father's call, he had gone into the tent and offered a prayer for understanding. He also prayed for his brothers to listen and obey Lehi's counsel.

Dinah waved at him and grinned. He smiled back and looked at the person next to her. His roaming gaze halted when he saw Isaabel. He hadn't realized she was so friendly with his sisters. The moment their eyes met, Isaabel looked away. Nephi noticed something different about her. His gaze traveled to her hands, each of which held one of his sisters' hands. Her fingernails were clean.

"Thank you for gathering together," Lehi began.

Nephi straightened and concentrated on his father's words, his stylus poised.

"I have dreamed a dream," Lehi said, looking at Ishmael, hoping that his words would be accepted by Ishmael's family. "Or, in other words, I have seen a vision."

Ishmael put his arm around his wife.

"In my dream, I saw a dark and dreary wilderness."

The family was silent.

"A man dressed in a white robe came to me and asked me to follow him," Lehi said.

Nephi felt the hairs on his arms rise.

"After spending many hours in the darkness, stumbling through the wasteland, I prayed to the Lord to have mercy on me. After I had prayed to the Lord, I saw a large and spacious field. In the center of the field was a tree, whose fruit was desirable to make one happy."

Nephi glanced up from his writing and noticed Lehi swaying above him. His skin warmed as his father continued. "After eating the sweet fruit, my soul was filled with joy such that I wanted nothing more than for my family to join me. A river ran near the tree. Sariah, Sam, and Nephi stood at its head. They had been following me in the dream."

With a steady hand, Nephi continued to write the words that fell from his father's lips. "I called to them. They joined me and ate of the fruit. Then I saw Laman and Lemuel and called to them as well. But they would not come," Lehi said.

Nephi silently wondered about the meaning of his father's dream. His mind raced as Lehi spoke of a rod of iron and a strait and narrow path. His father's dream had filled with people—numberless concourses of people coming toward the tree. A mist of darkness came, and many fell away from the rod of iron and became lost.

Lehi lifted his arms into the air. "I looked to the other side of the river and saw a great and spacious building rising high above the earth. It was filled with people, both old and young, male and female. They were dressed in exceedingly fine clothing, and they were mocking and pointing their fingers toward those who had come and were eating the fruit."

He continued to speak of those who fell away into forbidden paths, those who drowned in the depths of the fountain, and the great multitude who entered the strange building.

Nephi glanced at Ishmael and his wife. Their eyes were wide with wonder as they watched Lehi speak. Nephi's gaze moved to Zoram, who was watching Lehi in rapture, open tears streaming down his face. Then Nephi realized his father had lowered his arms and stood, surveying his family.

"Because of the things which I have seen, I have reason to rejoice in the Lord because of Sam and Nephi, for I have reason to suppose that they—and also many of their posterity—will be saved."

All eyes turned to Sam, who reddened, and then to Nephi. Nephi's eyes were drawn back to Isaabel, whose mouth formed a faint smile.

Lehi's gaze shifted to Laman and Lemuel. The older brothers stared at the ground, not moving or speaking.

"Laman and Lemuel never partook of the fruit," he said quietly. His voice trembled as he spoke. "I fear exceedingly for my oldest sons and worry that they will be cast off from the presence of the Lord."

A quiet sob broke free next to Nephi. He placed his hand over his mother's.

Lehi stepped toward Laman and Lemuel and held their gaze. "My sons, hearken to the Lord and perhaps He will be merciful and not cast you off. Keep the commandments and partake of the fruit," he implored with quiet urgency.

Nephi squeezed his mother's hand and wiped tears from his own eyes.

* * *

Staring at the ceiling of the tent, Nephi's mind raced through the words his father had spoken, making sleep impossible. He sighed and climbed out of his bedroll. Walking to the tent entrance, he stoked the fire that smoldered within the walls, then stretched his arms out and warmed his hands against the tired flames. It was amazing to him that Laman and Lemuel could sleep so soundly, especially after being told their souls were in danger.

He yawned and let his watering eyes travel the length of the tent. He paused when they reached the hollowed alcove created around Laban's brass plates. Behind the plates was Laban's sword. In the faint glow of the firelight, Nephi crept to the hiding place. Holding his breath, he lugged the plates of brass forward and reached behind them.

When his fingers reached the cold metal sheath, he hesitated. Almost as if in a daze, Nephi withdrew the sword. He held the heavy instrument in his hands and stared at the gold hilt. Closing his eyes, he remembered the moment he first saw the weapon. Beneath his touch, the metal warmed as if it had a life of its own, reminding him of the horror.

Someone stirred behind him. Nephi quickly replaced the sword and pushed the brass plates into their original position. He crossed to the fire and reclined before it, soaking up the warmth. It was many hours before he finally fell into a fitful slumber.

* * *

Nephi awoke coughing. He realized he must have fallen asleep next to the fire—the wafting smoke filled his lungs. Sitting up, he looked through the morning gloom and discovered his brothers still sleeping.

Zoram entered the tent. "Not much sleep last night?"

Nephi shook his head and yawned.

"I don't think your father slept either," Zoram said.

"Where is he?" Nephi asked, rubbing his sore neck.

"He's eating breakfast, and his eyes carry long shadows." He crouched beside Nephi and lowered his voice. "When your father spoke last night, I felt my chest burn as never before."

Nephi smiled knowingly.

"My throat constricted, and I knew I wouldn't be able to utter a sound even if I wanted to. Every word your father spoke seemed to pulse through my being," Zoram whispered. "I have never felt like that before."

"The Holy Spirit was testifying to you," Nephi said quietly.

Zoram stroked his cropped beard. "I think you are right, Nephi. My chest is still burning, and I feel like I could run faster than a wild animal," he said, his eyes bright.

Nephi chuckled. "Wait until after breakfast."

A loud yawn reached them. "Did I hear the word *breakfast?*" Sam sat up, his curly hair matted against his scalp.

Nephi shushed him loudly. "Take care not to wake the sleeping giants."

One of his brothers groaned.

Sam, Zoram, and Nephi left the tent together and settled around the fire. Lehi was nowhere to be seen. Sariah and Bashemath greeted the men and served them cooked fish. They ate ravenously. "Where is Father?" Sam asked his mother.

Sariah's face betrayed her worry. "He was just here. I hope he's catching some sleep. He mumbled all night."

Nephi looked at his mother. Dark circles had formed underneath her eyes. Her mouth was thin and drawn, emphasizing her wrinkles.

"Are Laman and Lemuel still sleeping?" she asked.

Nephi nodded and noticed that her hands shook.

"Let's catch fish for the midday meal," Zoram said, standing.

Nephi glanced at Zoram. "I'll catch up with you in a minute."

When Sam and Zoram had left, Nephi turned to his mother. "Are you still upset about Father's dream?" he asked.

"Yes," Sariah said, tears forming in her eyes.

Bashemath looked from mother to son and rose to leave.

"You can stay," Sariah said. But Bashemath waved off the invitation and walked away.

Sariah turned to Nephi. "My burden is heavy, but I have put my faith in the Lord. Laman and Lemuel know what's right, and I pray they will follow the Lord's commandments."

Nephi was happy to see his mother's strength still intact. He leaned over and kissed her cheek. "Perhaps the new baby and our weddings will bring you joy."

"I am grateful to feel strong." Sariah smiled. "Bashemath has wonderful ideas and is willing to help with all of the preparations."

A voice behind them boomed. "Who's getting married?"

Nephi turned and saw Lemuel approaching. "Mother has four weddings to plan," he said.

Lemuel bent and kissed Sariah's cheek. "So she has. Though I counted five daughters of Ishmael." His eyes twinkled.

"Yes," Sariah said. "Zoram will have a bride too."

Nephi watched Lemuel as he ate. Though Lemuel's manner was light, Nephi knew that inside he was affected by their father's dream. Nephi hoped their father's words had softened his brother's heart.

"Is there any left?" Laman had appeared.

"Yes," Sariah answered and dished out the cooked fish for her oldest son.

"Thank you," Laman said. He looked at the silent group. "We aren't sulking about last night, are we?"

Nephi raised his eyes and met Laman's gaze.

"Father's dreams always cast a gloom over the family. Maybe next time he could keep the not-so-nice ones to himself," Laman said.

Nephi shook his head. Sariah stood and excused herself, leaving an awkward silence.

"What did I say?" Laman asked when Sariah had gone, spreading his hands helplessly.

Lemuel laughed and tossed a piece of fish at his brother. Then his eyes widened. "Father's coming," he said.

Turning, Nephi watched his father approach them slowly.

Lehi stood before his sons and sighed heavily. "When you are finished with your morning meal, join me in the tent. Bring Sam with you."

The brothers consented, and Lehi left.

Not wanting to hear his brothers' complaints, Nephi excused himself and went to find Sam.

* * *

Nephi gathered the parchment and sat next to the tent entrance where the light was stronger. Laman and Lemuel settled onto their sides, propped up by their elbows. They expected another long tirade. Sam entered the tent, smelling of fish. He opened his mouth to ask a question but then shut it when he realized no one was speaking.

Lehi studied Laman and Lemuel until they looked away. "I have seen the destruction of Jerusalem," he said. "Many shall be carried away captive to Babylon. In due time, they shall be brought out of captivity and return to their land of inheritance."

"Sounds familiar," Lemuel said under his breath.

Lehi's voice rose. "In six hundred years, the Lord will raise a prophet among the Jews who will be the Savior of the world."

Nephi wrote the words *Savior of the world*. His father continued to speak about the prophets who had testified of the Redeemer and how all mankind could rise from their lost and fallen state only through the Messiah. Nephi glanced at Laman and Lemuel. Their eyes were half closed, and Laman stifled a yawn.

"A prophet will prepare the way of the Lord," Lehi said. "He will baptize with water in Bethabara, and he will baptize the Messiah with water. The gospel will be preached among the Jews and they will dwindle in unbelief." Lehi's eyes pierced through his oldest son. "When the Messiah is slain by His own people, He shall rise from the dead and make himself known to the Gentiles."

Nephi stopped writing and stared at his father. Tears pricked his eyes as he thought about the hardness of the hearts of those who would kill their own Savior. But he had seen his brothers turn on their own family members, and suddenly the death of the Savior didn't seem so unbelievable.

Nephi blinked and continued to write.

Lehi's voice fell into a rhythm. "The house of Israel will be compared to an olive tree whose branches will be broken off and scattered upon the face of the earth. They shall be gathered again after the Gentiles receive the fulness of the gospel and come to know the true Messiah."

After Lehi had finished speaking, the tent remained quiet for several minutes. Nephi constructed the last few sentences, then put down his writing stylus.

Laman sat up, bleary eyed. He nudged Lemuel from his stupor. "We'll see about the camels," he said. Lemuel rose to his feet, and the two brothers departed.

When Sam left to continue fishing, Lehi motioned for Nephi to join him. He scanned the written scrolls and nodded his approval.

Nephi saw the shadows underneath his father's eyes. "You should rest."

Lehi concurred and went into the sleeping section of the tent.

Left alone, Nephi reread the words his father had spoken by the power of the Holy Ghost. Then he turned to the vision Lehi had recited the night before. Nephi's heart beat deeply as he reviewed the words. He wanted to see the things his father had seen.

"If thou shalt seek the Lord thy God, thou shalt find Him, if thou seek Him with all thy heart and with all thy soul," Nephi whispered the words of Moses to himself. He rose and left the tent. His heart swelled with the desire to know for himself. Once outside of the camp, he began to hike the steep cleft in the granite mountain above him.

Alone at last, he fell to his knees and closed his eyes.

CHAPTER 18

If any of you lack wisdom, let him ask of God,
that giveth to all men liberally, and upbraideth not;
and it shall be given him.

(JAMES 1:5)

Nephi's heart lurched. He stood on top of a high mountain. He turned and scanned the unfamiliar horizon—there was no sun and no moon. The peach sky illuminated the golden earth beneath his feet.

His skin was warm and his body light. A soft voice spoke behind him. "Behold, what desirest thou?"

Nephi turned but saw no one. He sank to his knees and said, "I desire to behold the things which my father saw."

The voice spoke again. "Believest thou that thy father saw the tree of which he hath spoken?"

"Yes," Nephi said and opened his eyes. A man appeared before him. "Thou knowest I believe all the words of my father," he said quietly.

The Spirit half-sang in a loud voice. "Hosanna to the Lord, the most high God, for He is God over all the earth, yea even above all. And blessed art thou, Nephi, because thou believest in the Son of the most high God. Wherefore, thou shalt behold the things which thou hast desired."

Nephi bowed his head.

"Look." The Spirit pointed with his arm, and Nephi followed the motion.

A tree stood before him, blindingly white. It was the tree his father had seen in his dream. He gazed at its elegant white branches and intricate leaves.

The Spirit said again, "What desirest thou?"

Nephi didn't hesitate. "To know the meaning of the tree."

"Look!" the Spirit said again.

Nephi turned toward the human form, but He was gone. He slowly rose to his feet and gazed at the darkening clouds covering the sky. Below him, the valley began to lighten. Golden buildings came into view, and Nephi recognized the city of Jerusalem. He stared at the outer wall, the buildings within, and the temple. The temple was different, as if it had been transformed. His eyes moved southward, and he saw Bethlehem.

Great numbers of people were traveling to Bethlehem. Nephi looked northward, and another town rose around him. It was Nazareth. Farms surrounded the unwalled village that was filled with small square houses clustered together on the side of a hill. In front of him knelt a woman, dressed in white, her back to him. He walked around her and crouched to see her face.

The woman, who was young—very young—lifted her eyes heavenward, and Nephi saw that she was beautiful. Her skin was bronze, her eyes dark and luminous. She raised her hands and clasped them together. The young woman's rose-colored lips worked in supplicating prayer. She was wearing the white scarf of a virgin.

Nephi followed her gaze upward and saw the darkness divide. An angel descended from the parting heavens and stood before him. "Nephi, what beholdest thou?"

He looked again at the young woman. Her hands had dropped to her side, and her head was bowed in humility. "A virgin, most beautiful and fair above all other virgins."

"Knowest thou the condescension of God?" the angel asked.

Nephi shook his head. "I know He loves His children, but I don't know the meaning of all things."

"Behold, the virgin whom thou seest is the mother of the Son of God, after the manner of the flesh," the angel explained.

Nephi gazed at the woman again. A bright light surrounded her so that he could no longer make out her form. Nephi squinted against the brightness, then looked at the angel.

"Look!" the angel said, pointing to the woman.

He turned and saw the virgin again, holding a child in her arms.

"Behold the Lamb of God, yea, even the Son of the Eternal Father! Knowest thou the meaning of the tree which thy father saw?" the angel asked.

Nephi felt his pulse quicken. He knew. "It is the love of God, which fills the hearts of men. It is the most desirable above all things."

"Yea, and the most joyous to the soul." The angel pointed to the valley below. "Look."

Nephi's head was light with joy as he thought about the love that God had for everyone. He followed the angel's instruction and gazed downward and saw the Son of God walking among the people. He was clothed in a simple garment of linen, His feet dusty from the dirt road. A woman came before Him and sank to her knees. She bowed her head, worshiping Him. Others followed her and knelt on the ground before the Messiah. Nephi realized that the rod of iron, which his father had seen, was the word of God, and that the fountain of living waters was the love of God.

"Look and behold the condescension of God!" the angel said, breaking through Nephi's thoughts.

Nephi blinked and saw a man standing in the middle of a river. His hair was dark and wavy, his eyes clear and full of love. He held out his palm, and Nephi saw another man walk into the water. It was the Redeemer. The Son of God joined the prophet, and they clasped each other's arms. The prophet raised his right hand to the square and spoke a simple prayer, then immersed the Redeemer into the water.

Nephi watched as the heavens opened and the Holy Ghost descended upon the Redeemer in the form of a dove. Nephi felt his chest burn as he watched the Messiah step out of the water. Following the baptism, the Messiah went among the people and ministered to them. Nephi stared in amazement at the multitudes that gathered to hear the Redeemer, sitting at His feet. Then the multitudes drifted and the Messiah was cast from them.

As the Redeemer faded from the multitudes, Nephi noticed twelve men who followed Him, but a bright light surrounded them before their faces were revealed.

"Look!" the angel said, spreading his arms upward.

Nephi followed the angel's gaze and saw the heavens open again. More angels descended, and they went among the people, teaching them.

"Look!"

The Lamb of God was among the people again, healing the sick and casting out devils. Nephi's heart lurched in amazement. The divine miracles were performed right before his eyes.

"Look," came the whisper.

He turned in the direction of the angel and saw the Lamb of God standing in a bare cell in the bottom of a house. Outside this prison, the people chanted, "Crucify Him. Crucify Him."

Nephi shrank in horror. His hands grew clammy as he watched the mobs condemn their own Savior.

The Messiah was released to the mob, and they placed a cross upon His back. He staggered through the streets of Jerusalem until He reached a place called Calvary. Nephi watched the soldiers nail the Lamb of God to the cross and raise Him up between two thieves.

Nephi clutched his chest and groaned. The Son of God had been treated like a common thief. Overhead the sky darkened, and a mist rose around the temple. A heavy sorrow settled into Nephi's soul. The Redeemer's voice rent through the stillness. "Eli, Eli, lama sabachthani?" Nephi shuddered as he watched the soldiers offer the Son of God vinegar to drink. In the tranquil dark, the Redeemer's last words reached Nephi. "Father, into Thy hands I commend my spirit."

The Lamb of God bowed His head and released His last breath, yielding up the ghost.

Nephi sank to his knees and wept.

* * *

Some time later, Nephi opened his eyes. The sky above him glowed. He rolled stiffly onto his side and realized he was still on the mountaintop. He felt dizzy with grief. Slowly rising to his feet, he saw an enormous building before him— the one his father had dreamed about. It was filled with multitudes of people.

A voice spoke, "Behold the world and its wisdom; Yea, behold the house of Israel has gathered together to fight against the twelve apostles of the Lamb."

As Nephi turned and saw the angel, a deafening noise exploded around him. The building began to crumble and the people screamed. Nephi watched the walls collapse and dust billow from the ruins. Then there was an awful silence.

"Thus shall be the destruction of all nations, kindreds, tongues, and people that shall fight against the twelve apostles of the Lamb," the angel said quietly.

Nephi nodded, his throat dry.

"Look and behold thy posterity, and also the posterity of thy brethren," the angel said.

Nephi's eyes widened. The land of promise spread before him, vast cities and farms populated with numerous people. Then Nephi noticed an army forming. It advanced city by city, slaughtering men, women, and children. Another army rose, and another. His stomach churned at the awful sight.

A mist rose before him, covering the great cities. Above him lightning and thunder crackled through the heavens. The earth vibrated beneath his feet, and he fell to his knees. Nephi watched the earth split apart and mountains tumble to the ground. Cities sank into the earth and fires spread across the land.

Nephi buried his head in his hands and trembled as the earth shook with destruction. After several minutes, he noticed that the ground had stopped shaking. He raised his head and saw that the vapor of darkness had left the promised land. The people who were still alive gathered together.

The sky brightened above Nephi, and he looked up. The clouds parted and the Lamb of God descended to the land of promise. Nephi's heart leapt. The Savior had been resurrected. Hope had been restored to Nephi's being. The multitudes bowed before the Lamb of God and gazed upon His wounds. One by one, the Redeemer called forth twelve men, whom He ordained.

"Behold the twelve disciples of the Lamb, who are chosen to minister unto thy posterity," the angel whispered.

Nephi stood and watched as four generations of people passed away. The angel spoke again. "The fountain of filthy water thy father saw represents the depths of hell. The mists of darkness are the temptations of the devil that rise up to blind the eyes and harden the hearts of men that they wander off the path and lose sight of the love of God. And the large and spacious building is constructed of their pride and the vain imaginations of their hearts."

Nephi's heart grew heavy as he watched his people lose their faith in God and sink into wickedness. Armies formed again. The posterity of his brothers fought against his own posterity, defeating and annihilating them. He closed his eyes against the image of death, and soon everything went black around him.

* * *

Isaabel filled her vessel with the clear water from the stream. It was nearly dark, but she wanted to replace the water she'd used in Sariah's tent. She lugged the goatskin over her shoulder and trudged through the sand.

As she walked, Isaabel thought about Lehi's speech the night before. Nephi and Sam and their posterity would live righteously and be saved. Out of breath, Isaabel sat on the ground and rested. She wondered what all the things in Lehi's dream meant.

"Are you hurt?" a voice spoke behind her.

Isaabel turned and saw Laman standing above her. She scrambled to her feet and grabbed the goatskin bag.

Laman put his hand over hers. "Let me carry it for you."

Her eyes widened, and Isaabel clasped the bag closer. She shook her head. "No, thank you. My mother will be cross if I don't finish my work."

"Nonsense," Laman said, his eyes gleaming. "It's late."

Isaabel dropped her gaze, but held the bag tightly.

"You've not changed since leaving Jerusalem. You're still stubborn," Laman said, laughing.

Isaabel's face went red, and she was grateful for the darkness. But she was afraid of being alone with Laman. He stood close—too close.

Laman smiled, his teeth glinting in the moonlight. "Why did none of your other sisters plead for Nephi's life?"

She took a step back, but Laman grabbed her arm. "You are young, but I like your passion—a passion that only a husband could contain."

Wincing at his touch, Isaabel stammered, "M-my mother is waiting—"

Laman drew her to him and pressed his mouth against her ear. "I know my brother wants you for himself. But since I am the oldest, I will choose first," he hissed.

A falling rock sounded behind them. Laman released Isaabel and gazed at the cliff above him. A figure was descending the rocky face. "Nephi?" Laman called.

Isaabel stared at the man above her and swallowed hard. If it were Nephi, he must not see her alone with Laman. She hefted the goatskin onto her shoulder and backed away.

A spray of rocks and dirt showered onto Laman and Isaabel. "Watch out up there," Laman shouted.

Isaabel turned and hurried toward camp. Her hands were shaking, and her legs felt weak. She didn't want to hear what Laman would say to Nephi.

* * *

Laman stared at Sam in the moonlight. "What do you mean, Nephi's missing?" he asked.

Concern showed plainly in Sam's eyes. "He left this morning and never returned. I hiked to one of his favorite places, but he wasn't there."

"Maybe he's back in the camp," Laman suggested.

"You might be right," Sam conceded. "Let's go."

The brothers walked slowly through the sand. "Who were you talking to?" Sam asked.

Laman grinned. "Isaabel."

Sam felt a jolt of anxiety run through him. "What was she doing out here?"

"Fetching water. Or maybe she was looking for Nephi too," Laman said, chuckling. "And that's why she didn't want me to help her."

Sam tried not to ask surprised. "Help her?"

"I offered to carry the water back to camp, but she refused."

Sam hid a knowing smile. "Women can be stubborn."

Laman snorted and increased his pace. He was curious to see if Nephi had returned. Being the eldest brother, he would be put in charge of searching for him, not something he looked forward to.

When Sam and Laman reached camp, Lehi was pacing before his tent. As soon as he spotted his sons, he rushed over. "Any sign of Nephi?"

Sam shook his head.

"Were you looking too, Laman?" Lehi asked.

Laman glanced at Sam, then sighed. "No. I was returning to camp when I met Sam. I didn't know Nephi was missing."

Worry seemed to etch itself even deeper into Lehi's brow. "It's not like him to leave without letting someone know."

"Did anyone see him leave?" Laman asked.

Sam and Lehi shook their heads.

Zoram joined the group. "It's too dark now to make any progress. We'll just have to pray for his safe return."

As soon as he could, Laman walked away from the group. He found Lemuel stoking the fire. "Did you know Nephi was missing?"

Lemuel looked up. "He's probably somewhere in the mountains praying for our lost souls."

"And since we have so many sins to be forgiven of, he lost track of the time." Laman snickered at his own reply.

Lemuel chuckled, then stood and stretched. "Let's go inside the tent. I need to rest."

Laman followed his brother, and they spread out on their mats. "Everyone in the family is watching us," he said.

Lemuel rolled over and faced him. "What do you mean?"

"Since father told the entire family that we wouldn't eat the fruit in his dream, it's as if we're outcasts," Laman said.

"If I had a dream about a fruit tree, I don't think anyone would care. But if Father does, then suddenly it has something to do with our eternal salvation," Lemuel said, lazily drawing circles on the mat with his fingers.

Laman sighed. "I wonder what it will be like."

"What?" Lemuel asked.

"When we die and float to heaven," Laman said quietly.

Lemuel stared at his brother, then snorted. "You aren't serious, are you? We don't float to heaven."

Laman propped himself up on one elbow. "Our bodies don't, but what about our spirits?"

Lemuel frowned in confusion.

"And what did Father mean when he spoke about the house of Israel being like olive tree branches?" he asked. He lay back on the mat and exhaled.

Lemuel sat up, his expression serious. "If you really want to know, I think the olive tree represents our family, and the branches are all of our children.

Laman slugged him. "Since you know everything, tell me what the rod of iron meant."

"If you hold onto the rod of iron, you won't get lost," Lemuel offered.

"So then why did all those people let go if they knew they would get lost?" Laman asked.

Lemuel sighed with frustration. "Why are you so interested? You haven't cared to interpret Father's dreams before."

Laman lifted a shoulder. "There's nothing else to think about in this dreary wilderness."

"No, that's not it." Lemuel looked at his brother with narrow eyes. "A certain young woman came rushing back to camp just before you appeared. Did you have anything to do with her flushed face?"

Laman masked his face in innocence. "I don't know what you're talking about." But his eyes betrayed him.

"Ah-ha. You are trying to impress Isaabel," Lemuel whispered. "Father made us look bad in front of everyone and now you are hoping to counter it."

Laman rose to his feet, his eyes blazing. "Don't tell me what I hope," he hissed.

A movement at the front of the tent startled both of them. Sam appeared in the entryway.

CHAPTER 19

*And in a day when the children of men shall esteem
my words as naught and take many of them from the book which
thou shalt write, behold, I will raise up another like unto thee.*

(MOSES 1:41)

Isaabel called into Sariah's tent, and Dinah appeared immediately. Isaabel smiled. "I've brought water for your mother."

Dinah grabbed Isaabel's hand, pulling her inside the shelter.

"Come in," Sariah spoke from the far side of the tent.

Isaabel crossed to Sariah, her goatskin bag in tow. "I've brought fresh water for your bath."

Sariah's face erupted with pleasure. "How kind. I didn't expect you to fetch my water."

"I know," Isaabel said, "but I wanted to thank you for your kindness."

Sariah laid a hand upon Isaabel's shoulder. "You're welcome to come anytime and—"

"Mother," said Elisheba, entering the tent. She hesitated when she saw the company.

"What is it?" Sariah asked.

"Nephi still hasn't returned."

Sariah folded her hands. "Let's pray for his safe return."

She and her daughters knelt on the ground. Isaabel followed their example and bowed her head. As Sariah prayed, Isaabel stole a glance at Nephi's sisters. They both had their heads bent and hands clasped together. Sariah's sweet supplication filled the tent, and Isaabel felt her eyes sting. Her own mother had never led her daughters in prayer. Isaabel's heart swelled as she felt warmth surround her from all sides.

"Amen," Sariah said.

Isaabel opened her eyes and smiled at her companions.

"Time for sleep, girls," Sariah said. Dinah and Elisheba groaned and left.

Isaabel heard them giggle once they reached the other side of the paneled wall of skins.

Sariah took Isaabel's hand and patted it. "Would you like some hot tea?"

She consented gratefully. She didn't want to leave the pleasant environment. When Sariah handed her a cup, Isaabel let out a long breath.

"Don't worry. Nephi will return soon," Sariah said.

Isaabel felt the heat rise in her neck. "I wasn't—" she began.

"I know you weren't," Sariah interrupted with a gentle smile. "You need to understand what kind of man Nephi is."

Isaabel fell silent.

"He often goes off by himself to pray," Sariah said.

Nodding, Isaabel bit her lip.

Sariah lowered her voice. "He's had visions like his father."

Isaabel nearly dropped the cup she held.

"He'll be a great leader some day." Sariah stared past Isaabel. "A mother knows these things in her heart."

Isaabel gripped the cup of tea in her trembling hand, watching the woman before her.

Sariah continued, as if speaking to herself. "My youngest son has become my strongest and most faithful. He will follow in my husband's footsteps and raise children unto the Lord. If it weren't for his pure heart, I wouldn't be able to endure the disobedience of Laman and Lemuel. But a mother never gives up hope."

After a few minutes of silence, Isaabel thanked Sariah for the tea and slipped out of the tent. She hurried to her own tent, where her sisters were preparing for bed, and managed to enter without creating any interest. Once inside her bedroll, she waited until all her sisters fell asleep before she woke Tamar.

"What is it?" Tamar asked through a yawn.

"Shhh," Isaabel said. "I want to tell you something important without the others hearing."

Tamar rose on an elbow and looked at her sister's shining face. "Go ahead, I'm awake now."

"I took some water to Sariah's tent tonight, and she told me that Nephi has visions like his father and he goes into the mountains to pray—"

"Slow down," Tamar whispered. "Why did you take water to Sariah?"

"Because I wanted to thank her for letting us use her bath," Isaabel explained.

Tamar rolled her eyes. "You fetched water in the dark?"

Isaabel moaned in agreement. "Don't worry, I won't do that again. Not after what Laman said . . ." She stopped, realizing what she'd just admitted.

"Laman? He spoke to you?" Tamar grabbed Isaabel's arm. "Tell me everything."

Isaabel let out a soft moan. "I sat down to rest, and Laman appeared. He offered to carry the water for me, but I refused. Then I thought I heard Nephi coming down the trail. But it couldn't have been Nephi. I don't know who it was—"

"Shhh. I think I hear someone outside," Tamar warned.

Isaabel fell silent and listened. Faint voices could be heard around the campfire. "Maybe Nephi's back," she said, hope in her voice.

Tamar and Isaabel remained mute for several minutes.

"Tell me about Nephi's visions," Tamar eventually whispered.

Isaabel moved closer to Tamar. "Sariah said that Nephi has spoken to the Lord and received instructions from Him."

"What kind of instructions?" Tamar asked.

Isaabel shrugged. "I don't know, but it can only mean one thing."

"What?" Tamar asked eagerly.

"It means I can't marry him now."

Tamar stared at her sister with disbelief, then burst into suppressed laughter. "You can't be serious."

Isaabel looked at Tamar, her eyes unnaturally bright. "Don't you see? If Nephi is having visions, then he is a prophet like Lehi."

Opening her hands, Tamar waited for further explanation.

Isaabel's eyes filled with tears, and she looked away. "I'm not worthy to be a prophet's wife," she said quietly.

* * *

Nephi's head pounded. As the darkness around him lessened, he slowly opened his eyes. The angel stood in the air before him, waiting. Nephi rose to his feet and stood in readiness.

"Look," the angel said.

His gaze followed the angel's outstretched hand and saw many nations and kingdoms stretched across the valley.

"These are the nations and kingdoms of the Gentiles," the angel explained.

Nephi watched the people gather to build towers and form large congregations.

A voice whispered beside him. "Behold the formation of a church which is most abominable above all other churches, which slays the saints of God and binds them down and yokes them with a yoke of iron, bringing them down into captivity."

Fingers of cold fear traced Nephi's skin. The devil had entered into the hearts of the people. A man and woman passed before him, laughing, their clothing made of fine-twined scarlet linen. The man wore a knee-length tunic, embroidered with silk threads. The woman raised her hand and touched the man's face. Rings glittered on her fingers, and gold necklaces shimmered around her neck. The emptiness in Nephi's stomach grew as he realized the woman was a harlot.

As the couple's laughter faded, Nephi saw a great ocean of water dividing the Gentiles from his brothers' posterity. Men with pale hair, dressed in dark, fitted clothing boarded a ship and traveled to the promised land. Nephi saw that the Gentiles had the Spirit of the Lord with them as they carried a book throughout the land.

"The book that thou beholdest is a record of the Jews, which contains the covenants of the Lord and many of the prophecies of the holy prophets. It is a record like the engravings which are upon the plates of brass," the angel said.

Nephi watched as the Gentiles took the book to many nations.

"Wherefore, thou seest that after the book has been through the hands of the great and abominable church, there are many plain and precious things taken away from the book, which is the book of the Lamb of God," the angel declared.

Nephi wondered how the people would learn God's true commandments.

The angel answered Nephi's unspoken question. "The Lord God will not suffer that the Gentiles shall forever remain in that awful state of blindness."

He stared at the angel. Other books appeared before him.

"These last records, which thou hast seen among the Gentiles, shall confirm the truth of the first, which are of the twelve apostles of the Lamb, and shall make known the plain and precious things which have been taken away from them. They shall make known unto all kindreds, tongues, and people that the Lamb of God is the Son of the Eternal Father and the Savior of the world, and that all men must come unto Him or they cannot be saved," the angel said in a soft, reverent voice.

Nephi swallowed the lump in his throat.

The angel continued. "If the Gentiles listen to the Lamb of God and soften their hearts, they will be included in the house of Israel. The righteous Gentiles will be blessed and delivered from the abominable church. Rememberest thou the covenants of the Father unto the house of Israel?" the angel asked.

"Yes," Nephi said.

"Look, and behold that great and abominable church, which is the mother of abominations, whose founder is the devil."

He followed the angel's gaze and saw an assembly of people, who carried wickedness in their hearts, rise before him.

"Behold there are save two churches only: the one is the church of the Lamb of God and the other is the church of the devil," the angel said.

Nephi furrowed his brow. The hearts of the people determined which church they belonged to. Nephi watched as the harlot of the earth sat upon many waters. The great cities and their riches, gold, precious stones, and pearls reigned in dominion over all the earth. The fine linen, silver, precious wood, iron, and marble held dominion over the souls of people.

Astounded, Nephi stared as multitudes gathered together to fight against the Lamb of God. The power of God descended upon the saints of the covenant people of the Lord, and they were armed with righteousness and with the power of God in great glory.

Wars began, and the wrath of God was poured out upon those who held the great and abominable church in their hearts.

"Behold, the wrath of God is upon the mother of harlots. And behold, thou seest all these things. When the day comes that the wrath of God is poured out upon the wicked, then the work of the Father will commence, and His covenants will be fulfilled," the angel said quietly. "Behold one of the twelve apostles of the Lamb."

Drawing a deep breath, Nephi turned. A man appeared before him, dressed in a white robe. His black hair reached his shoulders, falling in gentle curls. Dark eyebrows arched above his heavy-lashed eyes. The man sat at a table, his head bent in concentration, and in his hand he held a writing instrument.

"Behold, this is John, who shall write the remainder of these things and also many things which have been. He shall also write concerning the end of the world."

Nephi watched as John wrote in long, sure strokes.

The sky grew dim and the earth faded below him. Nephi reached toward the angel, but no one was there. Mists swirled around his ankles, and as they faded, Nephi beheld a new civilization. His eyes widened as he watched events unfold around him.

* * *

Sweat trickled along Nephi's forehead into his eyebrows. A cool breeze dried the perspiration on his face and stirred his hair. He opened his eyes. The stars above him glittered innocently in the night sky.

Nephi let out a long sigh. Were these the eternities? Turning his head, he saw the moon, steady and bright. He raised his exhausted arms and pushed himself into a sitting position. The ground beneath him was dull and dry. He picked up a jagged rock and turned it over. It was solid.

His vision was finished.

Nephi winced at the throbbing in his temples. He drew his knees to his chest and dropped his head onto them. His heart pounded, and his breathing became ragged as he remembered the destruction of his people. The wars, the slaughter of multitudes, the great and abominable church . . .

He groaned and rubbed his eyes. The breeze around him made his flesh rise in bumps. He clutched his chest and cried out, "O Lord, give me strength."

Salty tears fell on his knees and dripped onto the dirt. The earth accepted his sorrow calmly. Had his father, too, seen the future? Did he know what would become of his posterity? Nephi buried his face in his knees. What would he tell his father? What would Laman and Lemuel think? Or Sam? His mother? Isaabel?

At last, Nephi fell into an exhausted sleep.

CHAPTER 20

To him that overcometh will I give to eat of the tree of life,
which is in the midst of the paradise of God.
(REVELATION 2:7)

When he awoke later, Nephi didn't know how much
time had passed since he had first climbed the rocky cleft,
but he knew he must return to camp. Grabbing his staff, he
rose, the muscles in his back and legs protesting.

Nephi moved forward and braced himself against the
first unsteady step. With each step he grew stronger, and
soon he had descended the mountain. By moonlight he
followed the path leading back to the campsite.

He noticed the thin trail of smoke rising in the night air.
The campfire had been recently extinguished. He scanned
the quiet tents and decided to tell his father he had
returned. Lifting the entrance flap of his parents' tent, he
peered through the darkness. His mother sat up and rose to
greet him.

"You've returned," she said, wetting his cheek with kisses.

He clung to her.

When Sariah pulled away, she gazed into her son's eyes.
"Are you all right?"

"Yes," he said, his voice heavy.

Lehi stirred from his sleep. "Nephi?" He rose and embraced his son.

The tears came fast as Nephi held onto his father. "I've had a vision, Father."

"It is as I had expected," Lehi said with calmness. "Sit and tell us."

Nephi sat before his parents in the dim light. In a broken voice he recounted all that he had seen. Sariah gripped his hand and sobbed openly when he told of the destruction of their people. Lehi tried to comfort his wife but was overcome with emotion himself.

When Nephi finished, his parents clung to him for several moments. "You have been shown these things for a reason, Nephi," Lehi said in an uneven voice. "As hard as the burden of knowledge can be, you will be strengthened by it." Sariah gripped Lehi's hand and squeezed. "We are your parents," Lehi said, "and we will help you carry this burden."

Some time later, Nephi left his parents' tent and made his way to his own. As he approached, he heard voices coming from inside. He paused outside and listened for a moment. His brothers were arguing. Nephi's shoulders sagged. He had hoped to rest his weary mind before facing them.

Sam's voice rose above the others just as Nephi entered. "Father only wants you to love God as he does." Sam stopped speaking when he spotted Nephi. He crossed and embraced his brother. "You're safe."

Nephi removed his outer garment. "You weren't waiting for me, were you?"

"Everyone's been looking for you," Lemuel said.

Nephi's eyes filled with surprise. "I didn't see anyone."

Laman laughed. "Perhaps your eyes were closed."

A shadow crossed Nephi's face. "Actually, my eyes were opened."

"What do you mean?" Sam asked, watching Nephi carefully.

Nephi sat down. "Let me rest, then I'll explain." He removed his sandals from his aching feet. "Could you bring me a drink?"

When Nephi had drunk his fill, he looked at Laman and Lemuel. "You were talking about Father?"

Laman's eyes clouded. "We don't understand what Father meant when he spoke about the natural branches of the olive tree or about the Gentiles."

Nephi closed his eyes for a moment and sighed. "Have you prayed to understand the things which Father saw?"

Laman scoffed. "We didn't think the Lord would speak to the disobedient sons."

"Not all of us can spend hours in the mountains praying," Lemuel said harshly. "Someone has to feed the family."

Nephi felt anger rising in his chest. He was physically exhausted from his vision and devastated by some of the things he had seen. Any semblance of patience for his brothers' hard-heartedness had fled.

He stood, anger fueling his strength. His eyes blazed as his voice rose. "How can you continually reject the commandments of the Lord? Why do you hold on to your pride when you know you will perish?"

Laman's eyes widened, and Lemuel raised his hand as if to ward off the words.

Nephi towered over his brothers, his mouth twitching. "Don't you remember what the Lord said? If you will open your hearts and ask Him in faith and keep His commandments, these things will be made known to you."

Laman and Lemuel glanced at each other, but remained silent.

Nephi sighed as he crouched before them and held their gaze. "Father's vision compares the house of Israel to an olive tree. Our family is like a branch that has been broken off from the house of Israel. When Father spoke of the grafting in of the natural branches through the fulness of the Gentiles, he was referring to our posterity in the latter days. When our descendents have dwindled in unbelief and many generations have passed since the birth of the Messiah, then the fulness of the gospel will be brought to the Gentiles. The Gentiles will bring it to the remnant of our posterity."

Rising, Nephi began pacing before his brothers. Sam moved out of Nephi's path and sat, listening intently.

"The remnant of our posterity will know that they are of the house of Israel. They will learn about their forefathers and about the gospel of their Redeemer. They will be included in the house of Israel and will be grafted in, being a natural branch of the olive tree, into the true olive tree." Nephi paused and gazed at his astounded brothers.

He lowered his voice. "And that is what Father meant when he said the fulness of the gospel will come by way of the Gentiles."

Sam glanced at Laman and Lemuel as Nephi continued to speak. Their heads were lowered. Lemuel traced a circular pattern with his finger on his mat, and Laman remained perfectly still. Sam looked at Nephi again and listened to him speak of the Jews who would reject the Messiah and the covenant the Lord made to Abraham. Nephi then quoted Isaiah, who prophesied about the restoration of the house of Israel and the gathering of the covenant people.

When Nephi fell silent, Laman raised his head and looked about the room. His eyes focused on Nephi. "What does the tree stand for that Father saw in his dream?"

"It was a representation of the tree of life," Nephi replied.

Laman nodded, and Lemuel cleared his throat before asking, "What does the rod of iron mean? The one that led to the tree?"

"The rod of iron represents the word of God, and whoever obeys the word of God and holds fast to it will not perish. They will not be overpowered by the temptations or fiery darts of the adversary," Nephi said.

Nephi knelt before his brothers and placed a hand on Laman's and Lemuel's shoulders. "Listen to the word of God and always keep His commandments," he begged earnestly.

Laman and Lemuel both consented, their eyes moist.

"You know how much Father loves you, and you see how it pains Mother when you complain," Nephi said quietly.

The brothers remained still. After a few moments, Laman asked softly, "What does the river of water mean?"

Nephi dropped his hands and rocked back on his heels. "The water represents filthiness, though Father didn't see the filth during his vision. The river separates the wicked from the tree of life and the saints of God. It also represents an awful hell for those who do not repent of their sins."

Laman furrowed his brow in concentration. After a moment he asked, "Does hell refer to the torment of the body in the days of probation or the final state of the soul after death?"

Pausing, Nephi said, "Both. The day will come when we'll be judged by both our spiritual and our temporal works on the earth." He rose to his feet and began to pace again. "No unclean thing may enter into the kingdom of God. So, a place has been prepared for those who are filthy."

Laman swallowed hard. "So that's why Father was so upset when we didn't partake of the fruit of the tree of life?"

"The fruit is the most precious and desirable above all other things. It is the greatest of all the gifts of God." Nephi had stopped pacing.

With those words, a reverent hush fell over the tent.

A few moments later, Lemuel sighed and looked at Nephi. "You have told us more than we can bear."

Laman nodded in agreement.

Exhausted, Nephi sank to the floor, his energy spent. "I know I've spoken of difficult things, especially against the wicked," he said slowly. He frowned with concern. "But the righteous will be lifted up at the last day."

Nephi's eyes met Sam's for a moment. Then he gazed at Laman and Lemuel. "My brothers," he said, his voice barely above a whisper. "If you are righteous—listen to the truth, and walk uprightly before God—then you have no need to complain that I have spoken hard things."

Sam looked at Laman and Lemuel, whose faces had softened.

"Keep the commandments of the Lord with all diligence that you may be saved at the last day," Nephi pleaded again.

Laman and Lemuel both lowered their heads. "We'll try," Laman said humbly.

Lemuel moved into a kneeling position. "Let's pray together."

Nephi's heart swelled with joy. The four brothers knelt together in a circle and bowed their heads. Nephi offered a prayer, and when it was over, they all embraced.

* * *

A fly droned above Isaabel. When it landed on her cheek, she haphazardly swatted it with her hand, missing it. The insect buzzed away to find a calmer perch.

"Nephi's back," Tamar whispered behind her.

Isaabel turned slowly, squinting into the glare of the sun. Nephi stood outside of his tent talking to Sam.

"Tonight is the council," Tamar said, settling next to her.

Isaabel looked at her sister. "What council?"

"When Lehi and Father determine the marriage matches."

"So soon?"

Tamar smiled. "We've been here a month."

Isaabel flushed and lowered her head to concentrate on her embroidery work, knowing Tamar wasn't fooled.

Minutes later, out of the corner of her eye, Isaabel watched Nephi as he walked toward the river.

"Where do you think he went yesterday?" Isaabel asked.

"Ah-ha! You *are* interested." Tamar smiled triumphantly, nudging her.

Isaabel glared at her sister. "You're always trying to embarrass me."

Laughing, Tamar said, "Aren't you curious to know where Nephi was?"

"Do you know?" Isaabel asked.

Tamar leaned back and folded her arms. "I have my source of information."

Pushing the needle into the embroidery cloth, Isaabel asked, "And what does the source say?"

"Nephi had another vision," Tamar said in a low voice.

Isaabel dropped the needle into her lap and stared at her sister. "About what?"

Tamar lifted a shoulder. "My source said to my other source that it was like Lehi's dream."

"Then it wasn't something new," Isaabel said quietly, picking up the embroidery piece again. She bit her lip to contain her tumbling emotions.

Tamar playfully pinched her sister's arm. "How can you be so serene? Your future husband is having visions like a prophet, and you just—"

"How can you call him my future husband? I told you I can't marry him," Isaabel said, her face scarlet.

Tamar crossed her arms. "Why do you keep saying that? What are you going to do—watch one of your sisters marry him?"

Keeping her head lowered, Isaabel remained silent for several moments. When she looked at Tamar again, her face was pale. "I love him so much, Tamar, but I am afraid—afraid that I don't deserve the honor of being Nephi's wife. Look at Sariah. She's so pure and full of faith, just like a prophet's wife should be."

Tamar shook her head. "Sometimes I don't understand you, Isa. Do you think Sariah was born with faith? She had to learn like the rest of us."

"What if Laman asks for me?" Isaabel whispered, tears forming in her eyes.

Tamar gripped her sister's arm. "Nephi has told you that he wants to marry you—put your faith in that."

"Shhh! Here come the others," Isaabel interrupted. She picked up the half-finished embroidery and bent over in concentration.

Rebeka, Anah, and Puah approached the two sisters.

"Aren't you finished with that piece yet, Isa?" Anah asked.

Isaabel continued stitching nonchalantly, jamming the needle through the fabric. "What's the hurry?"

Puah laughed. "She's right, Anah."

Anah and Puah sat next to Isaabel and Tamar. "Have you told Father whom you want to marry yet?" Anah asked.

Rebeka gasped above them. "How can you say such a thing?"

"Rebeka is frightened she'll be given one of the 'disobedient' brothers," Anah said with a chuckle.

Puah giggled next to her.

Groaning, Rebeka turned her back on her sisters.

Puah nudged Isaabel. "I think a man with a little rebellion is much more interesting, don't you?"

Isaabel looked at Rebeka. "Why can't you speak with Father?"

She turned, her face red with anger. "It would disrespect his authority."

Isaabel glanced at her other sisters, who clearly held a different view. "Why can't *we* tell Father whom we've chosen? Doesn't he have the final say anyway?"

"You're right. We could meet with our parents and tell them whom we hope to marry," Tamar said.

Rebeka sighed with exasperation and shook her head. "You'll be disciplined for being so bold."

Anah's eyes danced. "Why not? Let's decide among ourselves whom we would choose—if we're given a choice—and present it to Mother. Then she could approach Father for us."

Everyone nodded except for Rebeka.

"All right, Rebeka. You choose first," Anah said.

Rebeka scowled at her sisters and turned away.

Anah smiled. "Then I'll choose . . . I think I'll marry Laman. You know, someone who's handsome and knows his mind."

Puah clapped her hands together. "Then I'll choose Lemuel."

Rebeka turned her head slightly and watched her sisters out of the corner of her eye.

"I guess I'll take Sam." Tamar joined in the game, nudging Isaabel.

Isaabel bit her lip and smiled slowly. "That leaves Nephi for me."

Rebeka turned to face her sisters and placed her hands on her hips. "What about me?" she asked, jutting her chin out.

"You can have Zoram," Anah announced with a pleased grin.

Rebeka opened her mouth to protest, then closed it again. She looked at Anah in amazement. "Perhaps that would be best," she said, a trace of a smile playing on her lips. "Zoram is older than Lehi's sons, and he is a good man . . ."

Puah's eyes twinkled. "If you can stand his incessant talking."

The sisters broke out in laughter.

Rebeka rolled her eyes and stomped away.

* * *

Ishmael stared at his wife. "Our daughters desired this arrangement themselves?"

Bashemath wrung her hands together. "Anah told me that they had all agreed."

"Hmm. It is interesting, although I have to consider Lehi's offer first," he said.

Bashemath smiled, her expression accentuating her aged skin. "Of course. It was just a suggestion." She lowered her voice. "I think they are worried about Rebeka."

"Rebeka?" Ishmael frowned. "Why? She should be the most grateful, after all we've been through with Sabtah—"

"She is grateful. But you know how strict she is with herself. She would never dare go against any law or tradition. So perhaps Laman wouldn't be an ideal match for her anyway."

"And this plan would solve that problem," Ishmael said, tugging at his beard.

Bashemath hesitated, wondering if he was convinced. "Laman is not the most, uh, traditional brother. I think it would cause contention in their marriage."

His eyes widened, then his face melted into a smile. Ishmael stepped forward and pulled his wife into an embrace. "You may be right, Bashemath." He chuckled and kissed her on the forehead. "Our headstrong eldest daughter would fare better with a husband who can abide her self-righteousness."

Bashemath relaxed into her husband's arms. Relief spread through her as she silently prayed for a successful outcome to the meeting. Then another concern surfaced. "You've grown so thin, Ishmael."

Ishmael drew away and looked at his wife's gently lined face. "I feel better than I did in Jerusalem. Don't worry about me. Are there any other details that I should know about?"

She shook her head, then stopped. "I think there is something between Isaabel and Nephi."

"Anyone can see that." Ishmael put his arm around his wife. "Coming into the wilderness has been a great blessing for our family."

* * *

Tamar practically pounced on top of Isaabel, who was filling a bag with river water.

Isaabel braced herself and steadied the goatskin bag underneath the current. "Watch out." She threw a glare at her older sister.

Tamar laughed. "Sorry. I was running too fast to stop in time."

"Why were you running?" Isaabel asked.

"Mother told Father our plan, and he thought it might work," Tamar burst out.

Isaabel brought the goatskin bag out of the water, deftly tying the opening. "Even Rebeka marrying Zoram?" She held her composure, not daring to smile.

Beaming, Tamar nodded. "Even you marrying Nephi."

The corners of Isaabel's mouth tugged upward, then a shadow crossed her face.

"Now what's wrong, Isa?" Tamar asked.

"Nothing," she said. "I'd better get this water back to camp." Isaabel stood and hefted the water over her shoulder. As she walked the familiar path, she remembered the last time she had taken the same steps—when Laman had offered to carry her water.

CHAPTER 21

Forsake her not, and she shall preserve thee: love her,
and she shall keep thee.

(PROVERBS 4:6)

Nephi crouched in the shaded alcove, cooling himself. He had just finished spreading out cleaned animal skins to dry. Leaning against a jagged rock, he chewed on a piece of wild grass. His eyes roamed over the narrow valley where the rest of the family worked at their daily tasks. Sam should return soon with the water. They would spend the rest of the day on their high perch, turning the skins every hour.

A faint cry sounded below him. Nephi walked to the outer ledge and peered over the side. Someone was lying in the sand, struggling to rise. Nephi zigzagged his way down the mountainside until he reached the person. He came face-to-face with Isaabel.

"Are you all right?"

Isaabel's eyes were filled with pain. "My foot twisted, and I—"

"Sit down. Let me see if it's injured." Nephi supported Isaabel's elbow and guided her to a boulder. He knelt and carefully removed her sandal.

She winced at his touch.

Nephi looked up. "Did that hurt?"

Isaabel nodded, slightly closing her eyes.

"Sorry," he said. He gently pressed his fingers against her foot, feeling for any jutting bones.

Isaabel bit the inside of her cheek to keep the tears from flowing.

"Sam should be coming with water," Nephi said, gazing up at the sky. "We need to move you out of the sun." Before Isaabel could protest, Nephi gathered her in his arms and began carrying her up the steep slope. "There's an alcove just above us where the shade is cool," Nephi said.

Isaabel held her breath, hoping to lessen Nephi's burden.

When they reached the alcove, Nephi set her down gently and found a rock to rest her foot upon. "You can breathe now."

Isaabel stared at him, then smiled. "I wasn't holding my breath—"

"I've carried heavier things than you," Nephi interrupted with a grin.

Her face grew red, and Nephi laughed. "What are you doing up here by yourself?" Isaabel's throat went dry, and she looked to the ground.

He sat beside her and waited.

Finally Isaabel swallowed and said, "I was looking for a place to pray."

Nephi looked at her in disbelief. "All the way out here?" A warm smile tugged at the corners of his mouth.

Embarrassed, Isaabel glanced at him through her dark eyelashes. "I've heard that it's the best place to get answers to prayers."

Nephi's gaze held hers. "I think you're right," he said softly. "What are you praying for?"

She looked away, afraid of Nephi seeing her distress.

Nephi waited for a moment, then asked, "Will you tell me?"

Isaabel blinked back her tears. "I pray that my father will choose the best husband for me tonight."

"Then I will pray with you."

She lowered her gaze again.

Noticing the troubled look on her face, Nephi asked, "Are you worried the Lord won't answer your prayers?"

She hesitated for a moment. "What if someone else prays for something different than I?"

"I don't understand."

Finally, Isaabel couldn't hold back any longer. "Laman told me that he would be the first to choose a bride."

Nephi stared at her, letting the words sink in. "Did he ask you to marry him?"

Isaabel shook her head, feeling confused. She didn't know how much influence Laman had, but she felt scared.

"Do you want to marry him?" Nephi asked.

Isaabel gasped. "No. I want to marry you—" She covered her mouth and flamed red.

He burst out laughing. "I'm glad to hear that."

She buried her face in her hands, not sure whether to laugh or cry.

Nephi gently pried her hands away from her face and held them in his. "Isaabel, look at me."

She raised her eyes to meet his, feeling mortified.

"You already have my heart. I'm glad to know that I have yours."

Isaabel felt her face grow hot. She pulled her hands away and nervously clutched them in her lap.

"Do you remember that day in the market?" Nephi asked quietly.

She nodded. "When your father was hurt?"

"You came out of the crowd like a rescuing angel," he said.

A smile played on Isaabel's lips. "I just wanted to help."

"No one else cared," Nephi said. "You helped my father, risking your own safety in a dangerous crowd. It was then that I knew I wanted to marry you."

Isaabel met his gaze, amazed at his words.

"And when my father was commanded to leave Jerusalem, I only had one regret—leaving you."

Isaabel caught her breath. "Oh, Nephi, how can I bear not knowing the outcome of the marriages?"

A shadow crossed Nephi's face, and he leaned against the rock wall with a sigh. "Sometimes it is better not knowing the future."

Footsteps sounded below them.

"Nephi?" a deep voice called out.

Nephi rose to his feet and stepped out of the alcove. "I'm over here, Sam."

"I thought you'd left," Sam said, dropping the water-filled goatskin to the ground.

"We have a guest," Nephi said.

"Who?"

Nephi stepped aside. "See for yourself."

Sam peered around the corner into the alcove. Isaabel waved sheepishly at him.

"She twisted her foot while climbing the mountain," Nephi said behind Sam.

Sam crept into the alcove and looked at Isaabel's foot with concern. "Can you move it?"

"A little," she said. "But it's still throbbing."

Sam backed out of the alcove and turned to Nephi. "How will we get her down the mountain?"

"I'll carry her," Nephi concluded.

Glancing back at Isaabel, he said, "It's a long distance back to camp."

Nephi's eyes twinkled. "I can manage."

"The others will be worried."

Nephi clapped his brother on the shoulder. "Will you return and tell her mother what's happened? When I've finished turning the skins, we'll make our way back to camp."

"But how are we going to get the skins down?" Sam asked.

"We'll bring them tomorrow," Nephi said simply.

Sam opened his mouth to protest, but Isaabel cut in. "If we could find a long stick for me to lean on, I could find my own way back," she began.

Nephi shook his head. "You're not going anywhere alone."

"I'll be fine," she insisted, wiggling her foot a little.

"Let me fetch a stick," Sam said. A moment later he returned with a sturdy, if gnarled, stick.

Isaabel smiled bravely and rose gingerly to her feet. She placed her sore foot on the ground and flinched. "I think I can make it."

But Nephi was already shaking his head. "It's too far."

Isaabel fell silent. She couldn't complain too much about the prospect of Nephi carrying her in his arms—if it was necessary, of course.

Sam and Nephi left Isaabel to rest and stepped into the stark sunlight.

"How long has she been here?" Sam asked quietly.

"Not long." Nephi glanced at the sky. "She was looking for a place to pray."

"Oh," Sam said.

Nephi turned and faced him. "Has Laman told you anything about whom he wishes to marry?"

Sam hesitated, his eyes clouding over.

Nephi nudged him. "Tell me what you know."

"Last night, I overheard Laman and Lemuel arguing about Isaabel."

"What did they say?" Nephi asked.

"I'm not sure. I heard them mention her name, and when I stepped inside the tent, they stopped talking," Sam said.

Looking behind him, Nephi lowered his voice. "Laman also spoke to Isaabel about marriage."

"He has intentions for her?"

"I don't know," Nephi said. "But I need to find out soon."

Sam agreed. "When I return to camp, I'll try to discover his plans."

* * *

When Sam left, Nephi checked on Isaabel again. Her eyes were closed, but when he started to leave, she opened them.

"Were you sleeping?" he asked.

She shook her head and smiled.

"Are you hungry?" Nephi asked.

Isaabel had never felt better. "I'm fine."

Nephi knelt beside her and unwrapped a cloth. He drew out a meager loaf of bread and broke it in half, handing a portion to Isaabel.

She pressed it back into his hands. "You're the one who needs strength."

Nephi refused to take it. "Eat. It will be a few hours before we return to camp."

Isaabel took the bread and held it in her lap. Nephi bit a chunk out of his half and began to chew. When he finished, he took a drink from the goatskin bag and handed it to her. Isaabel brought the liquid to her lips, feeling immediate relief as she drank.

"Can I get you anything?" Nephi asked.

Isaabel felt pleased that Nephi was so thoughtful. "No, I'm all right."

"I hope Sam makes it back to camp soon," Nephi said, hesitating, "so that your family won't worry."

"As your family worried about you last night?"

"I guess I was gone for a long time," Nephi admitted.

"Everyone was looking for you."

Nephi stared at the ground with troubled eyes.

"What happened?" Isaabel asked, hardly daring to believe that he would tell her.

Nephi raised his gaze. "I had a vision."

Isaabel waited, feeling her heartbeat quicken. Nephi's next words sent shivers down her back.

"It was wonderful and awful at the same time."

"What do you mean?" she asked, her voice barely audible.

Nephi stood. "I'll share it with you someday, but now you should rest."

He looked at her for a moment, as if he wanted to change his mind. Then he turned and stepped out of the alcove.

* * *

"We're almost there," Nephi said.

Isaabel silently rejoiced. Nephi's heavy breathing made her heart sink. She knew he must be exhausted, though he had stopped only once to rest. "I can try to walk now," she offered.

Nephi shook his head, drops of sweat landing on Isaabel's arm.

Isaabel watched the drops dissipate in the heat. She turned her head and scanned the terrain before them. They were on a particularly rocky section, and she feared Nephi would stumble and hurt his own ankle.

"There's someone coming," Nephi said.

She squinted, but she couldn't see anyone. A few minutes later, Sam came into view. "I've brought a camel. It's waiting at the base."

"All right," Nephi said and continued walking.

"Do you want me to carry her?" Sam asked.

"No," Nephi replied. "Did you tell her family?"

"I told Ishmael, and he suggested I bring a camel to meet you."

When they reached the base of the mountain, Nephi and Sam helped Isaabel climb onto the camel.

"Did you find out about Laman?" Nephi asked Sam quietly as they led Isaabel's camel.

"No," Sam said. "Laman, Lemuel, and Zoram were gone. But Father has called a family council for tonight before he meets with Ishmael."

Nephi nodded and remained silent the rest of the way to camp.

Bashemath rushed out of her tent to meet her daughter, with Tamar trailing behind.

"I'm all right, Mother," Isaabel protested. Nephi and Sam helped her climb off the camel, and she hobbled to her tent, supported by Bashemath and Tamar. She took a final backward glance at Nephi, but found that he had started walking toward the stream.

✦ CHAPTER 22 ✦

Nevertheless neither is the man without the woman,
neither the woman without the man, in the Lord.
(1 CORINTHIANS 11:11)

Sariah sat next to Lehi, their sons gathered before them. Lehi touched his wife's hand briefly, then began. "I've called this council to discuss the marriage contracts which I will submit to Ishmael tonight."

Everyone waited in anticipation.

"As you know, Ishmael has five daughters, and we have four sons," Lehi said, looking at Sariah. "Zoram will also have a wife."

Sariah nodded, smiling at her sons and Zoram.

"Marriage is a holy and binding contract, and we will not subject the daughters of Ishmael to debate. Thus, I would like each of you to prayerfully consider who might be the best choice for you. I will meet with you individually after the evening meal and consider your requests. As the eldest son, Laman will be first."

Laman flashed a smile at his brothers.

* * *

Have you considered your choice?" Lehi asked when he and Laman were alone.

Laman's anxious eyes betrayed his serious face. "I don't wish to cause any of my brothers sorrow," he said, "but if you are going to give Zoram the youngest daughter, I think you are mistaken."

Lehi brought his hand to his chin. "Who would you suggest for Zoram?"

"Rebeka," Laman said. "I could not abide her. Besides, Zoram is older than I."

Lehi seemed to consider the suggestion.

"I have a preference," Laman continued, his eyes glittering, "but I will not say it until the others have made theirs known."

"Does it matter whom the others choose, if you have first choice?" Lehi asked.

Laman nodded. "Of course it matters. But I'll wait until the end."

"All right, send Lemuel in."

Laman left to call his brother, and Lehi closed his eyes in thought. He wondered if Laman was sincere in his apparent concern. Lemuel appeared in the entryway, his eyes expectant.

"Come in, son," Lehi said.

Sitting across from his father, Lemuel fidgeted nervously. "Uh, my choice may seem out of order. But I would prefer Puah."

Lehi wrote the name on the scroll in front of him. Puah was the third daughter.

"I'll consider your request. You may send Sam in."

Sam entered the room and quietly told his father that he would choose Tamar, but would be happy with any outcome.

When Sam had gone, Lehi looked at the list before him—if he took Rebeka for Zoram, Puah for Lemuel, and Tamar for Sam, it would leave Anah and Isaabel for Laman and Nephi.

Nephi entered the tent and strode over to his father. "What did Laman say?" he asked.

Lehi's face grew serious. "It is confidential."

"Tell me, please." Nephi stared at his father, his eyes glowing.

Lehi sighed. "He wanted to choose last."

Nephi paced the room. "Laman is trying to undercut me," he said quietly.

"What do you mean?" Lehi asked, frowning.

"He knows I have feelings for Isaabel."

"And you think he'll choose her for spite?"

Nephi stopped and looked at his father. "Last night, Laman and Lemuel were so humble that I renewed my hope in them."

Lehi nodded, but kept silent.

"But I cannot leave my marriage to chance. I wish to make Isaabel my wife, but I will not write her name on your list." He hesitated. "Father, you must follow the Lord's will." Nephi left the tent.

Lehi stared after his son. He was amazed that Nephi would refrain from choosing his bride because he feared losing her.

A movement at the tent's entrance caught his eye. Laman had entered the room. "Have all my brothers made their choices?" he asked.

Lehi rose to his feet. "All except Nephi, who asked me to put it in the Lord's hands."

A shadow passed over Laman's face. He paused, then bowed his head. "That is my wish too, Father."

* * *

Sariah waited until all her sons were gone before she entered the tent. She stopped just inside the entryway, lingering until Lehi finished praying.

"Lehi," she said. "Have you prepared the contracts?"

He shook his head, his eyes troubled. "Something is going on between Laman and Nephi."

"What do you mean?" Sariah asked.

"Nephi made his intentions clear to me, but he refuses to name a bride for fear that Laman will override him."

Sariah chose her words carefully. "Isaabel is beautiful and no doubt has caught Laman's attention, but she is meant for Nephi."

Lehi looked at his wife in surprise. "You know about this?"

She couldn't help the smile that played on her lips. "I'm their mother, and I am also a woman. Even if you offer Laman for Isaabel, I think Ishmael would turn you down."

"You've spoken to Bashemath about this?"

"Some things don't need to be said." Sariah's eye caught the written words on the scroll before Lehi. "What does it say?"

Lehi sighed. "Lemuel chose Puah, and Sam chose Tamar. Laman suggested pairing Rebeka with Zoram."

Sariah calculated on her fingers, then said, "That leaves Anah for Laman and Isaabel for Nephi."

"You may be right," Lehi said.

Sariah leaned over and kissed his cheek. "All you can do is offer. Ishmael has the final say."

Lehi closed his eyes, enjoying the tender caress from his wife. That his sons' marriages would be as happy as his own would be all that he could ask for. "Thank you, Sariah."

* * *

Ishmael stared at Lehi. "I've always known you to be a man of God, but this is amazing," he said, gazing at the scroll before him.

"Do you approve?" Lehi asked.

Ishmael raised his moist eyes to Lehi's face. "I had arrived at the same conclusion."

It was as if a weight had been lifted from Lehi's shoulders. "We think alike," he said.

Ishmael took another sip of the hot tea Sariah had served. The silver cup was delicately engraved. He had never seen the silver tea set before and assumed it was only used on special occasions. The names before him seemed to blend in harmony. "These are your sons' first choices?" he asked.

Lehi hesitated. "Two of them refused to choose."

"They didn't have a preference?" Ishmael asked, raising his eyebrows.

Lehi shifted in his position and picked up a warm teacup. The vapors rose, warming his face. "They put their faith in the Lord," he finally said.

"Then we'll hear no complaining," Ishmael said. "What about your daughters? Will they be pleased with the outcome?"

Ishmael chuckled. "Actually, they are the ones who made the suggestions."

Leaning back, Lehi surveyed his companion, a man who willingly followed him into the wilderness, a man who valued his daughters' opinions. Lehi smiled. He was honored to have such a friend.

Ishmael pulled the contracts toward him and signed his name on the five documents. Then he embraced Lehi and kissed him on each cheek.

"May God bless our children," Lehi said.

"Amen."

* * *

Tamar squeezed Isaabel's hand. "It can't be much longer now."

Closing her eyes, Isaabel again offered a prayer. Then she looked around the circle at her sisters. They had long stopped talking and now sat in silent reflection, the firelight dancing across their faces. Even Zillah had joined the circle and waited patiently with her sisters-in-law. Bashemath stood guard at the tent door, watching for Ishmael to exit Lehi's tent.

"He's coming," Bashemath suddenly said. She clapped her hands together and choked back her emotion. "And he looks happy."

Squeals erupted around the circle, and Isaabel grabbed Tamar's arm. "I don't think I can stand it," she said.

Tamar agreed nervously.

Ishmael entered the tent with a smile on his face. He looked at his daughters. "I thought you'd be asleep." Groans greeted him. He crossed to an opening in the circle and knelt. In his hand he carried five scrolls.

Bashemath hurried to her husband's side and knelt beside him. Her eyes watered as she looked at the marriage contracts. "Open them," she said earnestly.

"I will read Rebeka's first," Ishmael said.

Rebeka gripped her hands together and stared at her father.

He looked at his oldest daughter. "Zoram will take you for his wife."

Gasps echoed throughout the room, and Rebeka smiled.

"Are you pleased, daughter?" Ishmael asked.

Rebeka flew at her father and embraced him. Ishmael smiled and gently pried her away. "Your sisters are waiting for their news."

She wiped her eyes and took her place again.

"Anah," Ishmael said, turning to his second daughter.

Her eyes shined in reply.

"Laman will be your husband."

A slow grin spread over Anah's face, and she turned and embraced Puah.

Ishmael chuckled. "And Puah, you will marry Lemuel."

An excited cry broke from Puah, and she ran to her father. She planted a kiss on his cheek. "Oh, thank you."

Isaabel's heart hammered. Only two remained.

Gazing upon his fourth daughter, Ishmael said, "Tamar, Sam will be your husband."

Tamar smiled and embraced Isaabel. "Only Nephi is left," she whispered.

Isaabel fought the burning tears and looked at her father, who hesitated before he spoke. "And my little Isa is to have a husband of her own too . . . Nephi."

Isaabel felt her heart skip a beat. She sensed Tamar's arms around her, but she could no longer feel the ground beneath her. *Nephi,* her mind whispered. Had her father really spoken his name? She rose and embraced him. Her prayers had been answered.

Ishmael pulled away first and spoke above the chatter. "The erusin will take place tonight." Surprised looks met him.

"The hour is late . . ." Bashemath began.

Holding up his hand for silence, Ishmael continued, "The men are already waiting for us in Lehi's tent."

The blood pumped furiously through Isaabel's veins. *Tonight?* She felt someone grab her hand. Together, she and

Tamar followed the others out of the tent. With each step, Isaabel felt more peculiar, as if her head was no longer attached to her body and her feet were skimming the sand.

Eventually, she realized that Tamar was speaking to her. "Lower your veil," she was saying in an urgent whisper. With unsteady hands, Isaabel covered her face and stepped into Lehi's tent.

The warmth of the tent surprised her. But perhaps it should be warm, with a roaring fire near the door and five men waiting for their betrothed. The thought almost made her knees buckle. Once again, she was grateful for Tamar's support next to her.

Isaabel stole a glance at the men, who stood across from them. Zoram's broad smile seemed to engulf Rebeka. Isaabel was sure Rebeka was returning that smile from beneath her veil. Laman and Lemuel stood together, engaged in furtive conversation. Sam's face was slightly redder than usual. He stole occasional glances at the women, in Tamar's direction. Isaabel felt Tamar shift beside her and let out a soft sigh.

For a desperate instant, Isaabel didn't see Nephi. Then she discovered him standing in the corner with Lehi, his head bent in concentration, examining something in his hands. When he raised his head and spotted her, Isaabel quickly lowered her eyes, feeling the heat rise from her neck. Even beneath the veil, she couldn't bring herself to meet his stare.

Ishmael stepped forward and greeted Lehi enthusiastically. "Each marriage offer has been accepted graciously."

Lehi beamed, clasping Ishmael by the hand. "Then let us begin."

The men formed a semicircle. In turn, Ishmael brought each of his daughters to stand before her betrothed. Isaabel stopped in front of Nephi and held her breath. She felt a sudden urge to reach out and touch him, to see if this was really happening or if she was living in a dream. She was thankful that this ceremony didn't require her to speak.

Lehi began his instructions in a low voice, and before she knew it, Nephi had taken her hand and slipped a ring onto her finger. Her skin tingled below the weight of the gold, one of the treasures that had been obtained on a dark night's visit to Reuel's estate. Nephi's voice slipped through her veil like a soft breeze. "Behold you, Isaabel, daughter of Ishmael, are consecrated unto me, Nephi, son of Lehi, with this ring according to the law of Moses and Israel."

* * *

Isaabel shivered in the dark. It had been hours since she had climbed into bed, but sleep eluded her. Tamar slept peacefully next to her. Isaabel envied her sisters and their dreams. Fidgeting with the gold ring that weighed on her finger, she thought about when Nephi had placed it on her hand. It was too loose now, but she knew that with bearing children and the physical changes that would bring, her fingers would grow stout. She sighed heavily and rose. Drawing her wrap around her shoulders, Isaabel stepped over the sleeping forms. Slipping through the tent opening, she sat next to the outside wall. The stars above shone steadily over the quiet camp.

As the night deepened, Isaabel's worries grew. She didn't know how to be a wife, especially to a man like Nephi. He was so sure of himself and faithful and . . .

A hacking cough interrupted her thoughts. A figure exited her parents' tent. It was her father.

"I thought I heard something," he said, drawing close to his daughter.

Isaabel tucked her legs beneath her. "I couldn't sleep."

Ishmael sat down and cleared his throat. "Ah. There is much to think about. Tell me what's on your mind, Isa."

She hesitated. "Nephi is so strong and sure—"

"You are strong too," Ishmael cut in. "Of all my daughters, you are the one who will most complement Nephi."

"I don't want to disappoint him."

Ishmael turned his daughter's face toward him and placed both hands on her cheeks. "Don't you understand? Nephi didn't choose you."

Her face fell. "He didn't? Whom did he choose?"

"He chose the Lord."

Isaabel lowered her gaze, her cheeks burning.

"Nephi loves you, but he left his choice of bride to the Lord. He would never go against the Lord's will," Ishmael said, taking his daughter's hand. "You must understand that your marriage has been sanctioned by God."

She raised her head, her eyes shining.

"That is why, Isa, you can show your joy. You will learn how to be a wife and mother in time, but for now you can rejoice in the Lord's blessing of giving you a righteous husband."

Isaabel embraced her father.

Ishmael held his daughter against him tightly. Her young body was so fragile, yet her will was strong. He knew she would face many hardships in her married life, but he knew she would always be cherished by her husband. A stray tear found its way onto Ishmael's cheek. "I'm returning to the tent," he found himself saying rather gruffly. "I didn't want my coughing to wake your mother, but I think it has subsided now."

"I'll stay out here a little longer," Isaabel said, noting the emotion in her father's voice.

When her father had gone, Isaabel gazed at the vast sky and sighed. She no longer had to fear, she realized. The Lord had answered her prayers, and she needed to have faith in that answer. Footsteps coming from the right startled her. She pulled the mantle over her exposed head and drew her knees to her chest. She hoped she wouldn't be noticed.

The figure came closer, and Isaabel realized it was Nephi. He stopped when he saw her sitting outside the tent. "Isaabel?" he asked quietly.

Isaabel began to rise, and Nephi reached out a hand and helped her to her feet.

"Is everything all right?" he asked, still holding her hand, fingering her betrothal ring.

Unsure of her voice, Isaabel nodded.

"And are you pleased with our betrothal?"

She smiled. "My prayers have been answered," she managed to say.

Nephi grinned and wrapped his arms around her, pulling her close.

Isaabel was too surprised to react, since no man other than her father had ever embraced her before. Every part of her body seemed to stiffen, yet at the same time an incredible warmth spread through her limbs, making her feel dizzy. Soon she found herself relaxing against his broad chest. After all, they were betrothed, she told herself. The mantle fell away from her hair, revealing the gleaming waves.

"Soon we'll have a tent of our own," Nephi whispered. "There will be no more lonely wanderings in the night."

She pulled away, afraid that someone would discover their embrace. She looked at him. "Were you wandering?"

Nephi released his hold, and a shadow darkened his brow. "I took a walk to think about all the things the Lord has shown me."

"In your vision?" Isaabel prompted.

His expression lightened. "Most of all, I had to thank God for giving me you." He touched the hair cascading over her shoulders. "Your hair is just as I imagined it to be."

Isaabel swallowed nervously, her heart hammering. She tried to ignore the fire his touch brought to her skin. "Tell me about the vision that troubles you."

Nephi dropped his hand and gazed at her. "An angel appeared to me and showed me all of the things my father had seen in his dream."

She remained quiet, waiting for Nephi to continue.

"I beheld the Messiah's mother," Nephi half-whispered, then hesitated. "In the vision, I saw the Messiah minister to the people in Jerusalem."

Isaabel watched Nephi's blazing eyes. His skin seemed to glow as he spoke, and his voice, though low, was full of power.

"The Lamb of God was lifted upon a cross and slain for the sins of the world."

Shuddering, Isaabel pulled her mantle tightly about her.

Nephi's eyes burned into hers. "Then I saw the land of promise and multitudes of people—our posterity." He took one of Isaabel's hands into his and told her of the wars and destruction.

She stared at him, too astonished to reply.

Then his voice fell to a whisper. "Cities were sunk and burned with fire . . ." Nephi looked past Isaabel as if he were seeing the vision again. His voice was barely audible. "When the vapor of darkness left the land, the heavens opened, and the Lamb of God descended out of heaven. He showed himself to the people who hadn't been destroyed. Twelve men were ordained as disciples of the Lamb . . . Then four righteous generations passed away."

Nephi stopped talking and hung his head. He sank to his knees, still holding Isaabel's hand. She followed and knelt facing him.

"Our people fell into wickedness and great pride. The posterity of my brothers battled against our posterity and overpowered them." Nephi shook his head and whispered, "Our family's people became a dark and loathsome people, committing all manner of wickedness."

"Shhh," Isaabel said. She leaned close to Nephi and cautiously touched his face. She gazed into his pain-filled eyes. "You don't have to carry this burden alone," she whispered.

His head dropped onto her shoulder, and he soaked her tunic with his tears. Isaabel stroked the back of his neck until his breathing evened.

CHAPTER 23

For this cause shall a man leave his father and mother,
and cleave to his wife; And they twain shall be one flesh:
so then they are no more twain, but one flesh.
(MARK 10: 7–8)

The tent buzzed with excitement. Isaabel groaned and buried her head, covering her ears. Her body felt like lead, and her limbs ached. She hadn't left Nephi until the sky had begun to lighten.

"Get up, Isa," Tamar said, shaking her shoulder.

Isaabel moaned. "I'm so tired."

"Mother wants everything carried out so we can dismantle the tent."

Isaabel's eyes shot open. "What?"

"I thought that would wake you." Tamar laughed.

Sitting up, Isaabel stared at her sister. "Are we moving on?"

"No, we're creating smaller tents to share with our husbands."

Looking about frantically, Isaabel asked, "Now?"

Tamar nodded. "Yes. We're to be married tonight."

Isaabel's mouth fell open. "I thought it would be at least a few weeks away."

"Apparently Lehi told our father it would be best to hold the marriage ceremonies immediately."

"But there is so much to prepare," Isaabel said. Still she felt the irrepressible anticipation grow within her.

Tamar winked. "Lehi probably doesn't want any of his sons changing their minds." She turned and said over her shoulder, "And by the looks of what time you came to bed last night, the sooner the better."

Isaabel started to protest, but Tamar had left the tent laughing. Isaabel rose to her feet and dressed. She wrapped her arms around herself, feeling the nervous excitement in her chest. She exited the tent and made her way to the stream, where Anah and Puah washed the morning cookware.

"You're awake," Anah teased.

Isaabel ignored the comment and dipped her feet into the cold water.

"Were you dreaming about Nephi?" Puah asked.

She scowled at her sisters but remained silent. She splashed the refreshing water on her face.

Anah laughed. "Tamar and Rebeka are weaving the garlands. Mother said when they're finished, she wants to speak to each of us about our wifely duties to our husbands."

Puah started to giggle.

Isaabel reddened. "I'll go and help them." She turned with relief and left her sisters.

With a grin, Tamar watched Isaabel approach. "You've decided to join the living today."

Isaabel ignored the comment and sat in the shade next to Tamar and Rebeka. She began to weave the palms scattered before her. "How many are left to make?"

"Six," Rebeka replied.

In the distance, Isaabel could see her parents spreading out a large canopy. "I didn't know Mother brought a huppah."

Tamar nodded. "She's been saving it for a long time and didn't want to leave it behind."

"Mother is waving to us," Rebeka said. She stood and waved back. "Let's go and meet her."

Isaabel rose with her sisters. When they arrived at camp, Bashemath was flustered. "I can't find the ceremonial ring."

* * *

Sariah embraced her youngest son. "I'm so happy you will marry Isaabel."

Nephi held her tightly. "I'm pleased the Lord has seen fit to make it so."

"You continue to astound me, Nephi." Sariah pulled away and clicked her tongue. "Tonight all of my sons will be joined in marriage."

A slight smile crossed Nephi's lips. "I'm surprised we are marrying in such haste."

Sariah lowered her voice. "Your father thought it would be best, so there is no tension between you and Laman."

"Laman? What do you mean? Has he complained?"

"No," Sariah said, shaking her head. "But it may only be a matter of time. Your father knows how you feel about Isaabel, and he couldn't help but notice Laman's interest."

"I will not stand for another man coveting my wife. I must speak with Laman immediately."

Fear leapt into Sariah's eyes. "Nephi, the betrothal has taken place and the contracts have been drawn. Laman will learn to live with his lot."

Nephi stared at his mother. "It's not so simple. This family will break apart if we don't willingly obey the word of God."

* * *

Laman threw a rotted bunch of dates into the swirling water below him. Beside him, Lemuel raised his head from his resting position. "What did you do that for?"

"Does it matter?" Laman grunted. "There's nothing else to do out here." He scanned the desolate horizon.

"We can share our tents with our wives," Lemuel said, smiling.

"Ha. Then what? Have children in the desert and watch them die from starvation?"

Lemuel sat up and stared at Laman. "We'll reach the promised land before children are born."

Laman turned to his brother, his eyes burning. "Yesterday I might have agreed with you. But now . . . now I don't know what to believe."

"What do you mean?"

"Listen," Laman said in a harsh whisper. "Father and Nephi both have the same visions, they support each other in everything, and now Nephi is given Isaabel to wife."

"But Father said the Lord guided him," Lemuel said, frowning.

"Exactly. Father is leading us into the wilderness so that he can establish his own colony and run it how he pleases. And our younger brother Nephi will succeed him."

Lemuel leaned back, thoughtfully chewing on a piece of dried grass. "Do you think they planned to have Ishmael's family come all along?"

Laman scoffed in agreement. "I think Nephi was interested in Isaabel long before we left Jerusalem and he pleaded for Father to invent a vision to bring the family here."

"Do you think Ishmael is a part of the scheme too?" Lemuel asked.

Laman shrugged. "I'm not sure yet. But I plan to enjoy our weddings, and I'll take Anah with me when I leave the camp."

"When are you leaving?"

"I haven't decided. But I'm glad Nephi got Isaabel. She is too young to keep up with my plans," Laman said.

"Don't leave without me," Lemuel said.

"I won't. It's going to be hard. But we'll make it back to Jerusalem, even if we have to beg our way," Laman said.

Lemuel shot up. "Someone's coming."

Moments later, Nephi appeared on the trail below them.

"What brings you here?" Laman asked as he rose to meet Nephi.

Nephi looked hard at his older brother. "I don't want any misunderstandings between us about our marriage contracts."

Laman raised his eyebrows in feigned surprise. "Aren't you happy with your bride?"

"You knew she was my first choice, but I left it up to the Lord."

"So you did." Laman smirked. "And I left mine up to Father." He clapped Nephi on the shoulder. "Congratulations, brother. I hope your wife will please you as I know mine will please me." He glanced at Lemuel. "We must go help our parents with the wedding preparations. Good-bye, Nephi."

Nephi stared at his brothers' descending backs. He had not expected Laman's complete acceptance.

* * *

The canopy stretched between four poles, and the canvas roof flapped in the gentle breeze. A most unusual wedding was about to take place—the marriage of five couples.

Zoram, Laman, Lemuel, Sam, and Nephi stood at the front, wearing their ceremonial prayer shawls, waiting for their brides. Lehi stood in front of the bridegrooms, doubling as a witness and as the priest.

Elisheba presided over the wine and the five cups that would be used in the ceremony, and Dinah guarded the washing bowl.

Heth's wife, Zillah, began to play the psaltery, the melody floating among the waiting family members and up through the walls of the canyon.

Murmuring arose as Rebeka, ceremonially washed and dressed, exited her parents' tent, escorted by Ishmael and Bashemath. A white veil covered her face, and she walked with her head bowed. Being the eldest daughter, she wore more jewelry from the mohar than her sisters. Two gold necklaces framed her neck, two earrings dangled from each ear, three silver anklets encircled her legs, and a single nose ring adorned her face. Ishmael smiled at everyone, and Bashemath sniffed and wiped her eyes. When Rebeka stood across from Zoram, her parents left to escort their next daughter.

Anah wore a scarlet dress with a white veil. She held her head high and walked purposefully toward Laman. He grinned and bowed deeply when she stood across from him.

Minutes later, Puah emerged. Her bridal dress was of dark blue. She walked slowly, as if keeping time with the melody. She joined Lemuel, a quiet smile playing on his lips.

Tamar appeared with deliberate steps. Her dress of magenta dye swirled about her ankles. After leading their fourth daughter in front of a beaming Sam, Ishmael and Bashemath returned to their tent for the fifth time.

Inside, Isaabel knelt upon the ground, her head bowed.

"Why are you kneeling in your wedding clothes?" Bashemath asked. "Everyone is waiting."

Ishmael hushed his wife, and she fell quiet as she realized her daughter was praying.

A short time later, Isaabel opened her eyes and stood, brushing off her pale linen dress.

Ishmael took her hands in his. "You look beautiful," he said quietly.

Swallowing the lump in her throat, Isaabel smiled and pulled her veil over her face.

Bashemath stared at the veil. "Did you embroider this?"

She nodded.

Her mother lifted the hem of the veil and fingered the intricate stitching. "I had no idea you could embellish this well," she said, almost to herself.

With a smile, Isaabel linked her arm through her father's. She closed her eyes for a moment and inhaled deeply.

"Ready?" Ishmael asked.

The three stepped out of the tent into the waiting sunset.

With the appearance of Isaabel, the final bride-to-be led to the huppah, the family broke out in song. When Isaabel reached Nephi, she lowered her eyes. Even through her veil she could feel the warmth of his gaze. He reached out his hands and took hers.

Lehi stood before the five couples and began the *kiddushin.* He smiled at each one, love and concern in his eyes. Lehi moved to Zoram and Rebeka first and spoke the ceremonial marriage words. Both agreed to take each other as husband and wife.

Each couple in turn was joined together in marriage.

When Lehi finally reached Nephi and Isaabel, his voice was husky with emotion. He placed his hands on their shoulders and said, "Nephi, will you take Isaabel to wife according to the law of Moses and of Israel?"

"Yes, I will," Nephi said resolutely.

Isaabel met his gaze and willed her heart to slow its fierce beating.

"Isaabel, will you take Nephi as your husband according to the law of Moses and of Israel?" Lehi asked.

"Yes," Isaabel said, her voice strange to her ears.

Nephi squeezed her hands.

Elisheba approached the couple and held out the cup of wine. Nephi sipped from it first, then passed it to Isaabel, who took a sip from the cup and returned it to Elisheba.

Lehi brought out the ceremonial ring and gave it to Nephi, who placed it on Isaabel's finger. "Behold, thou art consecrated unto me with this ring according to the law of Moses," Nephi said.

Isaabel smiled at him with shining eyes.

"From the beginning, God created male and female," Lehi said.

Isaabel walked around Nephi, circling him seven times. When she stopped, Nephi lifted her veil and placed its hem on his shoulder. Nephi then removed his prayer shawl and placed it upon Isaabel's shoulders.

"What God hath joined together, let no man put asunder," Lehi said.

Bashemath and Sariah stepped forward and placed a palm garland on the bride's and groom's heads. Dinah brought the bowl of blessed water, and Nephi and Isaabel dipped their hands into it.

Ishmael moved in front of the couple and read the marriage contract, which they both signed. Lehi took a step back and bowed his head. Then he raised his voice to the Lord and offered a prayer in behalf of the married couples, blessing them with the *sheva berachot:* "Bless the fruit of the vine, which brings joy and sanctification. We praise Thee, who created this earth. We are thankful for human life," Lehi said. "We ask Thy blessing on the brides and grooms. Bless them with children. And bless them with companionship and joy."

When Lehi finished, he turned to the other family members. "The words of Jacob have been fulfilled today who said, 'And let my name be named on them, and the name of my fathers Abraham and Isaac. And let them grow into a multitude in the midst of the earth.'"

The family members bowed their heads and murmured, "Amen."

Lehi turned his face upward and raised his arms. "Praise to God, the Almighty, for today our cup runs over."

The family members cheered, and the married couples embraced. Zillah began to play a joyous tune, and the family joined together in song. A large circle formed and the dancing began. Bashemath and Sariah hurried away to prepare the feast.

Nephi released Isaabel from his embrace and gazed into her glowing eyes. "I love you," he said quietly.

She smiled and wrapped her arms about his neck, nearly pulling him over. "I love you too."

Pulling away, Nephi kissed his new wife soundly. Applause from the surrounding family members broke them apart. Isaabel's face flared crimson, but she couldn't deny her happiness.

Nephi held out his hand and smiled. Together they joined the dancing.

⊶❦ CHAPTER 24 ❦⊷

*Therefore they had this miracle, and also many other miracles
wrought by the power of God, day by day.*

(ALMA 37:40)

Nephi awoke early. The morning light was still a promise
in the horizon beyond the sleeping camp. He had not yet
grown used to waking up next to Isaabel. He gazed at her
peaceful face in wonder. The lines of worry had melted from
her features since they had married. Though it had only been
a few weeks since they had become husband and wife, Nephi
felt they had been together an eternity. He wondered how he
had ever lived without her by his side.

Isaabel's eyes fluttered open, and she smiled. "I told you
not to watch me when I'm sleeping."

He smiled and kissed her. "Forgive me."

"Always," Isaabel said, nestling into his embrace.

"Nephi," a voice spoke from outside their tent.

Isaabel muffled a groan, and Nephi called, "I'll be right
there, Father." He turned to Isaabel. "Be back soon," he said,
kissing the top of her head.

She shook her head. "No, you won't." But her eyes twinkled. Each morning, Nephi met with his father before the

others in the rest of the camp awoke. At first the routine was disconcerting, but soon Isaabel came to respect the close relationship between father and son.

Nephi reluctantly left his warm bed and stepped out of the tent to greet his father, but Lehi was already walking toward Sariah's tent. Nephi frowned with concern. Usually they built the breakfast fire and warmed themselves while they talked. In his heart, Nephi knew that something had happened.

Following his father, Nephi stepped into the tent and squinted in the darkness.

"Over here," Lehi said quietly. He sat hunched over Sariah where she lay moaning on her mat.

"Mother?" Nephi asked. He crossed to Sariah and knelt beside her. "What's wrong?"

Lehi's voice was filled with concern. "She has a fever and has felt labor pains."

"Isn't it too early?" Nephi asked.

The anguish on Lehi's face was answer enough.

"Should I fetch Bashemath?"

"No. We'll give her a blessing," Lehi said.

Nephi closed his eyes and bowed his head.

Lehi fell silent for a few moments and then began. "Sariah, we bless you with strength and health to carry this baby until it is the proper time to deliver it. We bless your body to rid itself of the fever, and we bless the labor pains to diminish."

Nephi heard his mother's breathing deepen as she relaxed.

"If it is God's will, the child you carry will be born healthy and strong," Lehi said.

When Lehi finished the blessing, Sariah grabbed his hand and placed it upon her protruding stomach. "He moved."

Joy crossed Lehi's face.

"I felt the baby move as you spoke," Sariah said, tears welling in her eyes. "The baby will be strong."

Lehi leaned over and kissed Sariah's forehead.

She rose to her elbows. "I should get up. I have much to do."

Lehi placed a hand on her shoulder. "You need to rest."

With gentle persuasion, Sariah lay back in her covers. Lehi rose to leave, and Nephi followed his father to the entrance of the tent.

"How long has she been sick?" Nephi asked.

"She awoke in the middle of the night with a fever, but the pains didn't start until an hour ago."

Nephi nodded. "She probably just needs to rest for a few days."

"That's something I can't give her right now," Lehi said with a sigh.

"What do you mean?" Nephi asked.

"The voice of the Lord spoke to me last night and commanded us to continue our journey into the wilderness today."

Nephi spread his hands wide. "Today? But Mother is sick."

Lehi opened the tent flap and motioned Nephi to follow him. Lehi picked up a bundle that lay on the ground and removed the wrap, revealing a brass ball. He placed it on the ground before them. Nephi crouched down and inspected the curious instrument. "Where did this come from?"

"I found it near the door of the tent this morning," Lehi said.

Nephi bent closer to examine the two spindles enclosed within the ball. "What is it for?"

"The Lord sent it to guide us in the direction we must travel. It serves as a liahona, although I've never seen one quite like this."

Nephi squinted at the curious object, then glanced at the horizon. "It's pointing in a south-southeastern direction." He ran his fingers carefully over the smooth brass.

Lehi crouched next to his son. "Go and wake Ishmael and tell him I need to speak to him. I'll tend to Mother until your return."

Nephi rose. He stopped at his tent on the way to find Ishmael. Isaabel had fallen back asleep.

He tapped Isaabel's shoulder lightly and watched her eyes slowly open. A smile lit her face. "I was just dreaming about—" She stopped when she saw the look of concern on Nephi's face. "What's wrong?"

"My mother is ill."

Isaabel rose and pulled her mantle on. "I will tend to her."

"No, Father is there," Nephi said, restraining her. "We must prepare to leave camp. The Lord told my father we are to continue our travel into the wilderness today."

Isaabel removed his hand from her arm, her gaze steady. "I will tend to your mother. My sisters can load our tent."

Nephi stared after his wife as she left. He shook his head and made his own exit. *Perhaps Isaabel was right,* he thought as he walked to Ishmael's tent.

* * *

Isaabel bent over Sariah and murmured soothing words to her. Sariah opened her eyes briefly and then shut them again. "You rest, and we'll take care of everything," Isaabel said.

Sariah grasped Isaabel's hand. "I felt the baby move."

Dinah entered the room and handed Isaabel a wet cloth. She placed it gently over Sariah's forehead.

"Will you pray for me?" Sariah asked.

Impressed with the unrelenting faith of her mother-in-law, Isaabel bowed her head and offered a simple prayer. When she finished, she looked up and saw Lehi standing in the entryway.

Isaabel blushed. Lehi crossed to the women and knelt beside them. He kissed Isaabel's cheek and said, "Thank you for your prayer, Isaabel."

Sariah smiled at Lehi. "I'm ready to help pack."

"I don't want you to move until the camels are loaded."

Sariah sighed with acceptance.

Turning to Isaabel, Lehi said, "Stay with her until we are ready to leave. Your company gives her comfort."

She nodded, and Lehi rose to leave. She could hear the commotion outside and wondered how her sisters had reacted to the news. During the first weeks after the marriages, there had been only happiness. But the past few days, some of the old complaints began to surface. Yet Nephi had been so dedicated in his beliefs that he had easily squelched them.

Sariah took Isaabel's hand again. "You must gather your things."

"It's all right," Isaabel said. "Nephi will see that it gets done."

Elisheba entered the room. "All the bedding is rolled, and the cooking things are assembled. Do you want anything to eat before we load?"

Sariah started to shake her head, but Isaabel interrupted. "Bring your mother some tea. She needs the nourishment."

When Sariah had swallowed a few mouthfuls, slight color returned to her cheeks. She reached behind her and brought out a trinket box, inlaid with detailed carvings. "I want you and Nephi to watch over this for me."

Isaabel stared at the box, then took it in her hands. It was surprisingly heavy. "Shouldn't one of your daughters do this?"

"You don't understand," Sariah said. "Inside are the only valuables I have left in this world. They are handed down from my mother, and I intended to present the jewelry to my daughters on their wedding days. But we are moving further into the wilderness now, and I don't know how we will eat."

Isaabel traced the intricate design on the box. "You want to sell your precious things for food?"

Sariah lowered her voice. "Arabia is a harsh place, and some tribes are brutal people. If my jewels can save the life of my sons or the virtue of my daughters, I am willing to part with them."

Isaabel's eyes widened at Sariah's candid words.

"We can't take this," Isaabel said quietly.

"I trust you and Nephi to watch over the treasure. You'll know when to put it to use," Sariah said. "I want you to keep this spare key."

Isaabel accepted the key reluctantly.

* * *

Sariah's tent was the last to be taken down and loaded onto the camels. Isaabel supported her mother-in-law until Nephi came to help her on the camel.

Nephi turned to Isaabel. "You were right, Isa."

"About what?" she asked.

"About watching over Mother." Nephi kissed her.

Isaabel took a step back. "Nephi, not in front of the others." She was still not used to his public affections.

Nephi laughed and pulled her close. "We're married now."

"I know, but—"

He kissed her again.

Sariah spoke above them. "Nephi, your father's waiting."

Nephi glanced at his mother and nodded. Smiling, she gazed down at him. Isaabel followed Nephi to their camel, her cheeks still blazing.

* * *

Isaabel walked beside Tamar. They followed behind Sariah and her daughters. Lehi and Ishmael were at the helm, with the other men riding in the rear.

"Did you see the brass ball?" Tamar asked.

Isaabel glanced at Tamar. "What are you talking about?"

"When Lehi left his tent this morning, there was a brass ball with two spindles sitting on the ground. He said it is from the Lord and will direct the way we should go."

"How curious." She pursed her lips.

Tamar watched her sister for a moment. After a few moments she said, "Nephi seems a lot different since you've married."

"What do you mean?"

"He's more lighthearted," Tamar explained. Nephi's serious demeanor had softened, and even Sam had noticed the difference. Tamar thought Nephi had always seemed older than his years, but now lightness was in his step and his smile came easy. Laman and Lemuel had even softened their attitudes and spent more time working with the others.

Isaabel nodded slowly. "Everyone is in high spirits right now. But I'm worried about Sariah. She was very ill last night, and although she is doing better, this traveling can't be good for the baby she carries."

"You have helped her a lot lately," Tamar commented.

Isaabel shrugged. "No more than her own daughters."

Tamar watched Isaabel quietly. She knew that Sariah's spiritual strength had drawn Isaabel to their mother-in-law. And, perhaps, Isaabel felt an added kinship since her husband was also a visionary man.

* * *

Lehi pulled his camel to a stop and surveyed the land-scape. They had been traveling for four days in a southeast direction from the Valley of Lemuel. The caravan had crossed the River Laman and left the shores of the Red Sea. Now they had reached a small valley surrounded by the Al-Sarat mountain range. They called the valley Shazer after its many clumps of trees.

Gazing eastward, Lehi scanned the rising mountains, then turned his gaze west toward the Red Sea. The land beneath his feet consisted of stark sand, but Lehi knew the mountains held promise for food.

Lehi lodged his staff into the earth and called to Nephi. "We'll dig our well here."

As the women unloaded the provisions and began to set up tents, Nephi and the men started to dig.

Sitting on a mat, Sariah watched the women work. They would not allow her to help and insisted that she rest at every possible opportunity. The labor pains had diminished and were replaced by tiny feet kicking her womb. As the child inside her grew, Sariah felt more at peace. She had become gradually accustomed to the desert life, and her faith waxed stronger because of it.

Sariah found herself grateful for the simple things of the wilderness. The day before, they had encountered a Bedouin tribe who had shared their dried locusts with them. Since locust season only came once every several years, they were considered a delicacy among the desert dwellers.

Lehi crossed to Sariah and placed the Liahona onto the mat beside her. Sariah smiled and gazed at the curious director. The spindles continued to point southeast, the direction in which they would travel. Sariah sighed with relief. The family would rest while the men hunted for food. It would be a welcome treat.

"Mother," a voice spoke quietly above her.

Sariah looked up and saw Isaabel.

"Your tent is ready."

Isaabel helped Sariah to her feet, and they walked to the tent together. Isaabel hovered over her mother-in-law and saw to her comforts.

"Isaabel, you must tend to Nephi. He will be leaving tomorrow to hunt for several days," Sariah said. "Call Elisheba. She will finish in here."

She smiled and left.

When Isaabel approached the other women, she asked, "Where is Elisheba?"

Dinah looked around, then shrugged. "She's probably caring for Raamah's son."

Isaabel scanned the working camp. The men were digging the well and Nephi labored in the middle of the group. Her heart swelled with pride as she watched him work. His face dripped with perspiration as he concentrated on the task. In contrast, Laman and Lemuel dug at half Nephi's pace. Then she noticed Raamah standing off to the side, apparently on a break. He was staring into the distance. Isaabel followed his gaze and turned to see what he looked at.

Elisheba was several hundred paces away, playing a game with Raamah's four-year-old son. Isaabel felt a jolt run through her. Until now, she had never realized that Elisheba was just a year younger than herself, and Raamah was an unmarried man. Isaabel swallowed the lump in her throat and looked again at her eldest brother. He had never spoken of the death of his wife, Leah. But the pain had been evident in his eyes when his son asked about her.

Isaabel realized that Raamah was the only unmarried man in the family now. Seeing all of them married must have been difficult, she realized. Raamah's son saw his father watching him and stopped his playing. He ran over and hugged Raamah, Elisheba trailing behind.

* * *

"How long will you be gone?" Isaabel whispered, stretching next to Nephi.

Nephi smiled. "Why are you always whispering in our tent? No one can hear us."

Still keeping her voice to a whisper, Isaabel said, "The other tents are close by."

"Not that close," Nephi said, his eyes twinkling. He raised his voice. "I don't think it will take more than three or four days to catch enough food. Especially since all the brothers are going."

She pushed at him playfully. "You don't need to announce it to everyone."

Nephi grinned. "Ask me another question."

"Only if you promise to keep quiet."

Nephi closed his mouth, waiting.

Isaabel nestled her head against his chest. "Do you think Raamah is lonely without a wife?"

Nephi hesitated. "He has his son to keep him busy. Maybe once we reach the promised land, he'll want to remarry."

"Or," Isaabel said slowly, "maybe he'll marry Elisheba."

Nephi laughed out loud. "Elisheba? She's just a child."

"Shhh," Isaabel said, looking mortified. "Someone will hear us." She paused. "Elisheba is only a year younger than I."

Nephi lifted his head and looked at Isaabel. "Really? She seems so much younger." He leaned back and stroked his chin. "The desert has caused us all to age more quickly."

They remained silent for several minutes. "What about your brothers?" Isaabel asked. "Do you think they'll become angry with you again?"

"Sometimes I think they won't," Nephi said, stiffening. "But other times . . . they can be unpredictable."

"Sam and Zoram are always faithful, aren't they?"

Nephi agreed.

"And my brothers?" Isaabel asked.

"I'm not sure," Nephi said with a shrug. "Heth wants to be everyone's friend. But Raamah, I don't know. He is a quiet man, brooding most of the time. Maybe another marriage would be good for him."

* * *

The days crept slowly by as Isaabel and her sisters waited for their husbands to return. They ate sparingly and rested during the hottest part of the afternoon. Sariah recovered but spent most of the daylight hours in her tent. Lehi and Ishmael pored over the brass plates together, studying and discussing the ancient writings.

The air was unusually humid one afternoon. Isaabel lay inside her tent alone, her body bathed in sweat. She was half asleep when she heard shouting from the distance. She quickly pulled her mantle over her moist hair and scurried out of her tent. The men were returning. The women gathered together and watched the approaching camels with joy.

Carcasses of wild gazelles and oryx were strewn across the camels. Isaabel clapped her hands together. Nephi looked tired, but well. She had worried about how his brothers would treat him. All the men were smiling as they climbed off the camels and greeted the women.

A fire was started immediately, and the men cleaned the carcasses. The women busied themselves preparing a feast, as far as the limited resources would allow.

After everyone had eaten, Lehi stood before the group. "We will leave in the morning. Sariah has recovered, and we have food for several days. We should not delay."

Zoram cleared his throat and stood. "May I say something?" Lehi sat down.

"Rebeka informed me upon our return that she is with child."

Sariah and Bashemath, who sat together, cried out. Ishmael and Lehi embraced Zoram with fervent congratulations.

Isaabel stared at Rebeka, whose scarlet face broke into a grin. The women flocked to Rebeka, kissing and hugging her. The men patted Zoram on the back and made jokes about the lack of wine.

Hanging back, Isaabel watched the celebration. Nephi joined her and took her hand. "What's wrong? Aren't you happy for your sister?"

Squeezing his hand, Isaabel swallowed hard. Then she crossed to Rebeka and embraced her. When she returned to her place, she sat with a sigh. She wondered how Rebeka could know for certain. It had only been just over a month since their marriages. She would have to ask Tamar about the signs. Isaabel smiled at Nephi when he looked at her, but the seed of fear in her stomach had sprouted. What if the scant food wasn't sufficient to nourish Rebeka? What if she lost her baby? What if she died in childbirth like Leah?

But tonight, no one carried any worries, and Isaabel eventually joined in their gaiety.

══✣ CHAPTER 25 ✣══

For the Lord thy God is a merciful God;
he will not forsake thee, neither destroy thee.
(DEUTERONOMY 4:31)

The families spent many days traveling in a south-southeast direction. With the guidance given by the Liahona, they were able to travel through the more fertile parts of the land and hunt along the way. As they neared the base of the Asir Mountains, Lehi instructed the family to set up camp.

Although the air was relatively cooler in the mountain valley, the daytime heat had made it nearly unbearable to travel. It had been two days since they'd eaten fresh meat, and the men began preparing for another hunt.

After Lehi watched his sons organize the camels and provisions, he walked over to where Ishmael sat on a rug outside of his tent.

In his hands, Ishmael rubbed the bows with olive oil. He shook his head sadly when he saw Lehi approach. "It's no use—the bows can't be repaired."

Lehi squatted next to Ishmael. "How could the spring of the bows be lost?"

Ishmael pulled back his turban, revealing his sweat-drenched hair. "It's the humidity, my friend. I'm surprised the rust hasn't eaten more of the steel bow than it has."

Nodding thoughtfully, Lehi said, "At least Nephi's bow is still intact."

Ishmael's shoulders sagged. "His bow is our last hope. Let's send him and the others in the morning. The next day, we'll be out of food."

Lehi rose and left Ishmael. He soon found Nephi and gave him the news.

"We're planning to leave at first light," Nephi said. "I'll tell the others to bring their slings. Maybe they'll spot some grouse."

The following morning, Nephi woke before dawn. He kissed Isaabel's sleeping face and crept out of the tent. He scanned the bleak plains of rocks, stopping to eye the mountains rising above him. It would take most of the morning to climb high enough to hunt.

Lehi met the men by the camels and offered a prayer in their behalf. "Take the last of our meat for the journey."

Nephi shook his head in protest, but Laman grabbed the bundle. "We'll need to keep our strength. The others can survive on dates and mereesy until our return."

The brothers set off into the warmth of the rising sun. Once they reached the foot of the mountains, they split into two groups. Nephi, Heth, and Sam traveled south; Laman, Lemuel, and Raamah headed north. Zoram had remained at camp.

An hour passed before Sam spotted a gazelle. "Stop. Look up there," he said.

Nephi, Sam, and Heth climbed off their camels and began the ascent. With little cover, they moved slowly and quietly. Soon Sam and Heth fell behind, knowing that their slings would only scare the animal. Nephi stopped fifty paces from the gazelle. Its ears quivered as it raised its head. Seeing no danger, it bent and began to tug at the mounain grass.

Pulling the bow into position, Nephi took aim. With a dead-center target, he released the arrow. Just as the arrow ejected, Nephi stumbled backward, overextending the bow. The sound of snapping metal reverberated through the canyons. The gazelle turned with a jerk and tore up the rocky face of the mountain. Nephi had missed. In his hands he held not one, but two pieces of steel.

Looking down at his broken bow, Nephi's head began to swim. Disbelief clouded his mind, and he pushed the jagged steel ends together. But there was no way to repair it—he had broken the bow. His shoulders sagged, and he released the smooth metal. Just as it dropped, Sam and Heth came into view.

"What happened?" Sam asked, approaching Nephi.

Nephi stared at the twisted metal on the ground.

Heth gasped and sank to the earth. He grabbed the broken bow and gaped at the two pieces.

The three men wordlessly descended the mountain and climbed onto their camels. With the sun beating upon their backs, they rode to where they had left the others. Night fell before Laman, Lemuel, and Raamah returned, their weary heads bobbing in tandem as they rode closer.

"Nothing?" Sam asked quietly.

"Nothing." Laman scanned the men before him. "Where's your catch?"

Nephi stepped forward and held up the broken bow. The moonlight bounced off the steel, mocking its former strength.

Laman's jaw fell open. Lemuel groaned, and Raamah ran his fingers through his hair.

"We'll hunt for grouse and hare in the morning," Nephi said sullenly.

Laman climbed off his camel and took the bow from
Nephi. After he examined it, he threw the pieces onto the
ground. He stared at Nephi. "What happened?"

Nephi grimaced. "I stumbled just as I took aim—"

Laman interrupted. "Do you know what this means?"

"The Lord will—" Nephi began.

Laman spat. "Save it for Isaabel," he shouted. He turned
and walked away.

The men unloaded their bedding without a word and fell
into a foreboding sleep.

* * *

"They're coming," Isaabel said softly.

Tamar sat listlessly beside her.

It had been three days, and they had been subsisting on
dates alone. The cramping in Isaabel's stomach relaxed, if
only for a moment. *It would feel good to sleep on a full
stomach again,* she thought. But as the men approached,
Isaabel's heart lurched. Something was wrong. There were no
carcasses displayed like prizes on the front of their camels.
The men's faces were tight and drawn. Laman reached the
camp first and climbed off his camel.

Anah rushed over and embraced him. Laman shoved her
away and strode to Isaabel, stopping before her. Isaabel took
a step back and clutched her mantle under her chin. Laman's
eyes seemed to scorch her skin. "Nephi has ruined us."

Isaabel gasped, and Laman pushed past her. She watched
as Nephi descended from his camel and brought out his
steel bow.

The family moaned when they saw the broken weapon.
Sariah cried out and buried her face in Lehi's shoulder. Lehi
cast his eyes heavenward and began to mouth the words to a

prayer. Bashemath broke down and ran into her tent, followed by several of her daughters.

Isaabel stood still, unable to move. There was no food.

* * *

The somber faces stared into the dancing flames. Nephi swallowed at the immovable lump in his throat. His father wouldn't speak to him, and even Isaabel was at a loss for words. The perspiration of hunger formed on everyone's brow, and Nephi knew he was to blame.

Nephi stood before the family, but they had lost interest in anything but their own survival. "We can return to the mountains tomorrow and look again for food."

No one spoke.

"The Lord will provide for us. We must have faith," Nephi said louder.

Ishmael sat on a rock, too weak to stand any longer.

Raamah rose and left the circle.

Staring after him, Nephi said, "If we give up now, we will surely perish."

"Finally you admit it," Laman said, rising to his feet. "We're all going to die out here. The only food left is the camels. When they are gone, we will be trapped. The Lord had nothing to do with this journey, Nephi. Tell the truth."

Nephi stared at Laman in bewilderment.

"There is no promised land, is there?" Lemuel rose beside his brother.

"Tell them, Father," Nephi said, looking at Lehi.

But Lehi just hung his head.

"Father?" Nephi asked, his voice cracking.

He raised his head and stared at the ashen faces of his family members. "The Lord knows that we need nourishment to continue our journey." Lehi shook his head sadly. "I don't know why He has forsaken us. We've done everything we've been asked to do . . ."

"Father," Nephi said with disbelief. "A way will be provided."

Lehi remained silent. Without the bow, they would be forced to eat their camels. Then they would be stranded in this forsaken land. Sariah choked back a sob. Even Sam hung his head.

Nephi looked at the surrounding family members. One by one, each left the campfire and retreated to their tents.

* * *

The orange embers had long since lost their glow when Nephi left the empty circle. He stood outside the tent he shared with Isaabel. Finally, he crept into the opening and lay down.

"Nephi?" Isaabel touched his arm.

The hairs on Nephi's arms straightened at her touch.

"I was afraid you weren't coming."

He turned and looked at her, barely making out her profile in the dim light. "Have you given up too, Isa?"

Isaabel touched his face. "Never."

He shut his eyes. The tears came hot and fast.

"Nephi?"

He took a deep breath. "Yes?"

"Can't you make another bow?" Isaabel asked.

Silence filled the tent, and then Nephi sat up. "I can try," he whispered. "Thank you." He rose and left.

In the light of the moon, Nephi made his way to the firewood stack. After inspecting several pieces of Atim olive wood, he found one that was longer than his arm. He began to carve by memory the shape of his broken bow. The wood chips fell away from his knife as if he were slicing cheese.

"Can you still use this?" a voice asked quietly.

Nephi turned to see Isaabel standing behind him. She held the bowstring she had removed from the broken steel frame. Isaabel wrapped her arms around his shoulders. "I knew you'd find a way."

Nephi nodded, his throat too tight to speak. When he finished carving the wooden bow, Isaabel fastened the string to the notches.

"Now for an arrow," Nephi said. Isaabel produced a suitable stick, and Nephi whittled the wood into an arrow.

"It's finished," Nephi said, rising. He examined his effort in the growing dawn.

Isaabel yawned and smiled. Nephi took her hand and walked her back to the tent. "Get some sleep. I'll be back soon."

* * *

"Where should I go to obtain food?" Nephi asked.

Lehi rubbed his eyes and stared at Nephi. He rose slowly to his feet and inspected the wooden bow and arrow that Nephi held. "You made this?" he asked, his voice incredulous. Turning the bow over, he ran his hands along the smooth arches. Lehi looked up at Nephi, his eyes moist. "It's beautiful. I never thought . . ." His shoulder's sagged, and he bowed his head.

Nephi put his hand on his father's shoulder. "Father, where should I go to obtain food?" he said again softly.

"I'll inquire of the Lord," Lehi said hoarsely.

Nephi stepped out of the tent and waited. The camp was just beginning to stir. He heard a child cry and felt his own hunger pains intensify. A few minutes later, Nephi heard his father's ragged call. He entered the tent and found Lehi kneeling upon the ground, his face contorted.

Kneeling beside him, Nephi took his father's hands. "What happened?"

"The Lord has truly chastened me because of my murmuring," Lehi said quietly, his eyes filling with tears. "He wants the family to gather and look at the Liahona."

Nephi helped his father to his feet, and they exited the tent together. When everyone had gathered, Lehi brought forth the Liahona. He held it in his hands and stared at the spindles. Then he began to tremble. Laman took the ball and saw the words inscribed within the spindles. His eyes widened, and his hands shook.

Lemuel seized the Liahona and gaped at the words, "It says—" His voice faltered, and he dropped the instrument in the sand.

Nephi knelt and turned the director face up. He read the words grimly and took a deep breath. "The Lord has chastened us." He looked at the apprehensive faces surrounding him. "The Lord will only guide and bless us according to our faith and diligence."

Bending over the ball, Ishmael read the words silently. *Ye have no food because of the hardness of your own hearts.*

Sam stared at the spindles. "The words are changing."

A gasp spread through the family members.

Lehi fell to his knees before the Liahona and read the inscription out loud. "Nephi must travel to the top of the mountain to obtain food." Lehi squinted into the rising sun and pointed. "The one that towers above the others."

Everyone turned and looked. Nephi rose and took up his wooden bow. He strode to the camels and, without a word, tied two of them together. Isaabel picked up her skirts and ran after him.

Nephi stopped when he felt her hand on his arm.

"Take these, Nephi," Isaabel said softly, handing him a parcel of dried dates.

He looked at the scraps of food, then back at his wife. "This is your portion for today."

Isaabel fought the tremble that rose in her throat. "You'll need it more than I."

For a moment, Nephi was at loss for words. He then embraced Isaabel. "Pray for me," he whispered.

She choked back a cry. Swallowing hard, she tried to smile.

Nephi mounted the lead camel and set off into the rising terrain with renewed hope in his heart.

✦ CHAPTER 26 ✦

Behold, I have graven thee upon the palms of my hands.
(ISAIAH 49:16)

The mid-morning rays glared down upon Nephi's hunched shoulders. He kept his gaze lowered, protecting his eyes from the swirling sand. The wind had only picked up a few moments before, but already it was gathering strength. Fine particles of sand settled on his cracked lips, causing his mouth to long for sweet water, but he knew he must pace himself and not allow his appetite to grow greedy. The food and water he carried would not sustain him for long as it was.

The rhythmic motion of the lurching camel set Nephi's stomach on fire. It was one thing to be hungry, but to have to ride upon a camel with such emptiness was torture. Nephi leaned forward, finding that it somewhat eased the pain in his stomach.

The peak rose before him, magnificent yet foreboding in its stature. It was here the Liahona had directed him. It was here his fate would be sealed. He must find food, or the entire family would perish.

Nephi removed a date from the parcel Isaabel had so carefully wrapped. A tear escaped his eye as he thought about

his dear wife who had given him the last of her food. The
hope in her eyes was written on his heart. The dry, sweet
flavor startled his senses. With renewed energy, he urged the
camels forward. He had neared the upper base of the mountain, and from there he would have to travel by foot. Scanning
the terrain, he spotted an alcove that would provide shade for
the camels. Nearby were scrub bushes, indicating the presence
of water below the sandy surface. It was as good a place as any.

"Good boy," Nephi said softly, stroking his camel's neck.
He climbed off the beast and led both camels to the alcove.
Hesitating for an instant, Nephi decided to leave the two
animals tied together. Perhaps they would be less likely to
wander off.

Nephi surveyed the sky. Only a short time remained
before dusk. He would not make it to the top of the mountain
before dark, which meant that he would not be able to hunt
until morning. But the mountain would shelter him from the
wind and make the climb easier.

He turned to the camels. "I'll be back," he said. They
merely blinked their layered lashes in reply.

The first part of the climb proved to be the toughest.
Nephi's stomach protested at the physical exertion, and twice
he stopped to empty its minimal contents. Yet he pressed on.
His body grew accustomed to the effort, and soon he found
that his muscles responded in kind.

As the sun set and the air cooled, Nephi was provided
much-needed relief. Even as the light grew too dim to see
clearly, he knew he couldn't stop yet. The terrain became too
steep to walk upright, and Nephi crawled the remaining
distance to the top, feeling his way in the dark. When he
crested the final peak, a blast of cold wind struck his face. The
heavens stretched out before him like a black rug, with glittering stars intricately woven into the threads.

Exhausted, he inched back down from the peak, finding a niche that gave some protection from the wind. He removed the bedroll from his back and fell asleep immediately.

* * *

The sound of a falling pebble awoke Nephi, and he sat up slowly. The wind had died down, and the stars above glistened in the blessed silence. Dawn was more than an hour away. He held his breath. Another sound came from just above him—the sound of hoofed steps.

Nephi's pulse began to beat wildly. Without hesitation, he picked up his bow and arrow and stealthily moved up toward the peak. Silhouetted against the moonlight stood a wild goat. It was small, but it was food.

Positioning the arrow, Nephi pulled back the bow and took aim. The arrow struck the animal in the neck, felling it before it had a chance to run. He scrambled to the animal, keeping his body close to the ground. If there was one beast, there might be another. He grabbed its leg and dragged the still-warm body to his sleeping place. After withdrawing the arrow, he climbed the short distance to the top and waited. "I thank Thee, Lord," he mouthed.

Nephi stayed in his position until the sun crested the horizon. Just as the first warmth hit the top of his shoulders, a gazelle appeared on the far side of the plateau that separated him from the opposite end of the peak. Nephi watched the animal for a moment, then another gazelle appeared. *There must be a small herd on the other side of the peak,* he thought. He would have to skirt the plateau and try to single them out without raising alarm.

Ignoring his waning strength, Nephi made his way slowly around the summit, pausing behind boulders and hiding in crevices. Finally he was within striking range, but he had to wait until a gazelle moved away from the others. By now there were half a dozen beasts helping themselves to the sticky brush.

It wasn't long before one wandered away from the main group. Nephi took aim and released the arrow. The gazelle flinched as it was struck, then it started to run. Holding his breath, Nephi waited to see what the other animals would do. They bolted to the edge of the plateau and disappeared. After several minutes, the injured gazelle gave up, and Nephi retrieved his arrow.

Nephi dragged the gazelle back to his resting place and set it next to the goat. His legs quivered with exertion, his breathing labored. Yet he knew that there might still be a chance to kill another gazelle. He took a measured drink from his goatskin bag and made his way back to the plateau.

All was quiet on top.

He crossed to the other side and hid himself in a crevice. From that point, he could see that the gazelles had made their way down the other side of the mountain. Disappointment welled up inside him. The two beasts he had killed wouldn't sustain his family for long. A movement to his right startled him. He turned slowly and saw another gazelle. It was either too slow to keep up with the others or unaware of the danger that had befallen its comrade.

The gazelle lifted its head and seemed to gaze straight at Nephi, as if challenging him to take aim. "This is for you, Isaabel," Nephi whispered, assuming position.

The animal staggered and then fell, as if it knew there was no point in running and death was imminent.

Nephi leaned against the warm rock next to him and closed his eyes. "I thank Thee, Lord, for delivering these beasts into my hands." He began to weep openly. He had accomplished what he had set out to do. His family would live.

* * *

Isaabel pulled her cloak tightly around her thin frame. The sun was just setting on the third day. Nephi would not have enough water to sustain him for a fourth—this she knew—and the agony in her heart increased with each passing hour. The others remained in their tents, too weak to do much else, but Isaabel stood defiantly against the elements, waiting for her husband.

She stared at the mountain where Nephi had gone, willing it to give him back. "Bring him home," she whispered over and over. She licked her dry lips, bringing temporary moisture to them. Then the fear hit her—the fear of Nephi not returning, the fear of never eating again, the fear of death.

Isaabel's legs crumpled beneath her, and she sank into the rippled sand. She was too dehydrated to give up tears, but the sobs came anyway. "Please, God," she said. "Take me if Thou wilt, but bring Nephi home with food for the family." She rocked back and forth, knowing she couldn't last much longer.

She didn't have the strength to crawl back to her tent. Closing her eyes, she found herself drowsing in the sand, dreaming. The dreams filled her soul with longing. She saw her sister Tamar laughing while she shopped in the streets of Jerusalem. Her mother, with her stern face, planning the evening meal, making sure each detail was in place. Rebeka, fretting over the embroidery on the hem of her dress. Working in the fields were her brothers, Raamah and Heth, their limbs strong. She saw Anah and Puah, arm-in-arm, whispering together in delight about the latest betrothal. Then she saw her father, his lined face kind and gentle, taking her in his arms and comforting her.

A voice surrounded her, caressing her heart. It was Nephi's voice. The best part of her dream, she realized. She could feel his touch, so warm and so real, gently lifting her arm.

"Isaabel!"

She opened her eyes and tried to focus on the person above her. "Nephi?"

He lifted her into his arms and held her tight.

"Am I dreaming?" she cried out, gripping his neck.

"No," he said in a hoarse voice and kissed her, his tears falling onto her cheeks.

Isaabel pulled back and stared at his streaked face. "You're alive," she said, choking back a sob.

"And I've brought food for everyone."

Just then, a shout went up from the camp. Laman and Raamah had come out of their tents. "Nephi's back!" Laman yelled.

Heads popped out of tents, and cries sounded.

Isaabel turned and saw the two camels laden with carcasses. She brought her hands to her chest. "Oh, Nephi," she said, looking at him. "The Lord has answered our prayers."

Nephi grinned, his teeth white in contrast to his dirty complexion, but his eyes seemed to waver.

"Are you all right?" Isaabel asked.

"Now I am," he said, looking down at their entwined hands.

Isaabel followed his gaze and saw that his hands were stained with blood. Their rough, dry surfaces were cracked and blistered. She gently turned them over and brought them to her face.

Family members surrounded them, breaking them apart and hugging Nephi in joy. After the brief rejoicing, the men dragged the carcasses from the camels and began to work frantically.

Anah and Puah prepared the fire and threaded chunks of meat onto skewers. Everyone but Ishmael had gathered around the fire to watch the meat sizzle.

Isaabel laid out a rug for Nephi to lie upon near the fire. Raamah and Heth carried Ishmael out of his tent to see the spectacle. His face was pale and drawn, but a smile lit his eyes. From his resting place, he praised Nephi and thanked the Lord.

When the meat was nearly cooked, Lehi stood before the family and lifted his arms. "Praise the Lord," he said, his voice cracking. His arms dropped to his side and he hung his head, waiting for composure, but when it did not come he continued to speak with halting words.

"We have . . . been blessed with food . . . that Nephi has brought. The Lord . . . has been mindful of us . . . Let us dedicate this meal . . . to Him . . . and go forward in faith." He buried his face in his hands, his shoulders heaving.

The first cut of meat was delivered to Lehi, who took the first bite. A cheer rose up, and all began to devour their portions, tradition set aside.

Isaabel ate slowly, savoring each swallow that filled her stomach little by little. Nephi watched her eat, a gentle smile on his lips.

"Aren't you going to start?" she asked with surprise.

"I have dreamed of this moment." He reached for her hand.

"So have I," she said. She squeezed his hand gently for fear of causing him pain. "I know now that we are guided by a loving God who answers our prayers. Whatever may come, we will endure it together."

Nephi brought her hand to his lips. "Amen," he whispered.

⊹⟿❧ CHAPTER NOTES ❧⟿⊹

CHAPTER 1

Scriptures referenced: 1 Nephi 1:1, 5; 7:6

The Valley of Jehoshaphat, or the Kidron Valley, begins on the north of the old city and runs along the east. The Hinnom Valley starts west of the modern-day old city and curls around to the south.

Sukkot, the Feast of Booths or the Tabernacles, was celebrated from the fourteenth to the twenty-first of the month of Tishri, which fell in September or October (Brown and Holzapfel, 227; Exodus 13).

John L. Sorenson, in his essay "The Composition of Lehi's Family," estimates that Nephi would have been about sixteen years old when he began his account (*By Study and Also by Faith* [Salt Lake City: Deseret Book, and Provo, UT: FARMS, 1990], 2:176). He also places Ishmael's age at fifty-three or fifty-four (2:187).

Head coverings worn by men are depicted in Sennacherib's stone panel, which is based on the Assyrian attack on the Judahite city of Lachish a century before Nephi's time period (David Ussishkin, *The Conquest of Lachish by Sennacherib* [Tel Aviv: Sonia and Marco Nadler Institute of Archaeology of Tel Aviv University, 1982], 86–87).

Yigael Yadin explains that the *gamma* is a right-angle pattern derived from the Greek letter *gamma*. Gamma motifs appear only on women's garments (*Bar-Kokhba* [New York: Random House, 1971], 76).

It was considered a privilege for the women to serve supper to male guests. In this chapter, the two older daughters are asked to serve, being the most eligible for marriage.

CHAPTER 2

Scriptures referenced: 1 Nephi 1:4, 6–11, 13–14

Book of Mormon scholars believe that Lehi was first called to be a prophet in 598 B.C. at the commencement of Zedekiah's reign in the midst of religious and political upheavals (Brown, *Voices from the Dust: Book of Mormon Insights*, xi).

Papyrus is a material that may have been used during Lehi's time to write upon. According to observations made by S. Kent Brown in *From Jerusalem to Zarahemla*, it is unlikely that Lehi would have used permanent materials such as metal plates to make records before leaving Jerusalem (30–32).

Purple dye was obtained from the blood of a single white vein near a shellfish's throat. Shellfish were harvested off the coast of Phoenicia. Thus, only royalty could afford to wear purple-colored clothing. Traditionally, scarlet or bright red colors were more commonly found in men's clothing than women's (Yigael Yadin, *Masada IV, The Yigael Yadin Excavations 1963–1965: Final Reports* [Jerusalem: Israel Exploration Society, The Hebrew University of Jerusalem, 1994], 241). The pious Jews also wore *sisith,* or fringes, at the hem of their garments.

Ancient Hebrew women covered their hair in public, but not necessarily their faces. The only artistic rendering of women during this time period is found on Sennacherib's panel. A white mantle, or head covering, was worn indoors only. The color denotes faith in God.

CHAPTER 3

Scripture referenced: 1 Nephi 2:1

In this chapter, Jonas is a fictional character created for the purpose of furthering the story line. In 2 Nephi 5:6, it states that Nephi had at least two sisters. Although we do not know if they were born in Jerusalem or in the wilderness, I have placed them in Jerusalem.

According to J. W. Jack, the word sarim applies to "members of the official class, i.e. 'officers' acting under the king as his counselors and rulers" (qtd. in Nibley, *Lehi in the Desert,* 8–9).

Camille Fronk describes the items Lehi may have had in his home, according to remains from the more wealthy homes in Jerusalem. These items include beds, chairs, tables, oil lamps, clay vessels for storing food, etc. Decorations may have included pictorial and metal art, vases, carved ivory plaques, glass beads, and decorated pottery ("Desert Epiphany: Sariah and the Women in 1 Nephi," *Journal of Book of Mormon Studies* 9, no. 2 [2000]: 7–8). In Egypt, beds have been recovered from the tomb of Tutankhamen that consist of stretched wicker-work tied to a frame made out of reeds.

It may be presumed that Lehi's family used camels for their departure from Jerusalem (Fronk, 13). Nibley also illustrates that there is no doubt that Lehi's family were camel nomads (*Lehi in the Desert,* 54–56).

In *Discovering Lehi,* Lynn M. Hilton and Hope A. Hilton discuss the possible provisions taken into the wilderness by Lehi's family, including such items as tents, food, bedding, weapons, and cooking utensils (38–39). Black goat hair was spun into panels to make tents. The panels measure approximately two feet wide by the length of the tent (56).

CHAPTER 4

Scriptures referenced: 1 Nephi 2:2–4

Hilton and Hilton document that goatskin bags were the standard method of transporting liquids. The front legs and dorsal opening are sewn together with tongs, and the neck becomes the spout (*Discovering Lehi,* 40).

A woman's marriage trousseau would include silver and gold jewelry of earrings, nose rings, bracelets, and anklets. Even today, Middle Eastern women still wear these ornaments as status indicators throughout their lives (Raphael Patai, *Sex and Family in the Bible and Middle East* [New York: Doubleday, 1959], 57). Bedouin women wear all of their jewelry when they travel, except for what they keep in a locked box. Charles Doughty informs us that nomadic women typically possessed one locked box in which to hold medicines, combs, mirrors, and valuables. The key hangs from the back of her veil (*Travels in Arabia Deserta,* 1:268).

Ancient Hebrews did not keep their valuables in their houses. The jewelry they weren't wearing would be buried in their yards. While the scriptures say Lehi left all of his valuables, I theorize that Sariah brought along her inherited jewelry—something with great meaning. E. Neufeld clarifies that the gifts a woman received from her family upon her marriage remain her own property (*Ancient Hebrew Marriage Laws* [London: Longmans, Green, 1944], 239).

In this chapter, Lehi as the sheikh does not give verbal orders but leads by example (Nibley, *Lehi in the Desert,* 70–71). Antonin Jaussen reveals, "When the place of encampment is reached the *sheikh* puts his spear in the ground, and at once the tents are pitched." (qtd. in Nibley, *Lehi in the Desert,* 71.)

CHAPTER 5

Scripture referenced: 1 Nephi 2:5

According to S. Kent Brown, Lehi's family could have taken a number of routes out of Jerusalem. The route east then south is detailed in "New Light from Arabia on Lehi's Trail" from *Echoes and Evidences of the Book of Mormon* (Donald W. Parry, Daniel C. Peterson, John W. Welch, eds. [Provo, UT: FARMS, 2002], 57–59). I have chosen to place Lehi on this route because it's also one offered by the Hiltons (*Discovering Lehi*, 20). Lehi's family would have traveled approximately twenty to twenty-five miles per day. It is possible they could have reached the oasis Ein Gedi the first night.

Lynn and Hope Hilton also suggest that Lehi may have chosen to travel Wadi al 'Araba (instead of the King's Highway) along the west shore of the Dead Sea, to avoid Amon, Moab, Edom, Hebron, and Beer-sheba (*Discovering Lehi,* 20). The name *Araba* means "wilderness."

The Ascent of Ziz, or the Cliff of Ziz, was the last landmark before the wilderness (2 Chr. 20:16). It is also referred to as Salt Mountain in modern times (Hilton and Hilton, *Discovering Lehi,* 20). Eloth was also called Ezion-Geber (see 2 Chr. 20:36; 26:2). Today the town is called Aqaba.

Doughty explains that the nomadic lifestyle for women was full of responsibilities, i.e., setting up tents, taking them down, loading supplies onto camels, preparing meals, making clothing, guarding flocks, gathering firewood, churning butter, and collecting water. Breakfast consisted of *leban*—dates with sour milk—or, if a guest were present, dates in buttermilk with sweet butter (*Travels in Arabia Deserta,* 1:262).

A camel's lifespan averages forty years. Working camels are retired when they reach about twenty-five. Camel's milk, rather than goat's milk or sheep's milk, was considered the best kind of sustenance by the Bedouins (Doughty, *Travels in Arabia Deserta,* 1:370).

Al-hamdu-l-illah is a common Arabic expression and illustrates the speaker's well-wishes. It means "Thanks be to God."

CHAPTER 6

Scriptures referenced: 1 Nephi 2:6–7, 9–10

S. Kent Brown informs us that Lehi's family camped a three-day's journey south or southeast of Eloth, approximately seventy-five miles in distance ("New Light from Arabia on Lehi's Trail," *Echoes and Evidences from the Book of Mormon,* 60–61). George D. Potter gives us a detailed description of the land of Midian in which he discovered the possible site for the Valley of Lemuel in "A New Candidate in Arabia for the Valley of Lemuel" (*Journal of Book of Mormon Studies* 8, no.1 [1999]: 54–63).

Before Lehi's time, Aqaba was a chief city in the kingdom of Edom. King David captured this city (2 Sam. 8:14). King Solomon stationed his ship fleet in Aqaba (1 Kgs. 9:26), using the natural resources of copper and iron ores to his advantage (Hilton and Hilton, *Discovering Lehi,* 20).

The Hiltons describe the *adze* as a sharpened iron blade used to shape lumber (*Discovering Lehi*, 119). Hammers were a common tool in biblical times, as described in Psalm 74:6. As referenced by the Hiltons, Tim Serverin said, "All early texts make it abundantly clear that early Arab ships were not nailed together, but that their planks were sewn together with cord made from coconut husks" (qtd. in *Discovering Lehi*, 118).

In agreement with Mosaic law, an altar was constructed of unhewn stones (Ex. 20:24–25). With apparent disregard to the laws of sacrifice outlined in Deuteronomy 12, Lehi built an altar in the wilderness. David Rolph Seely explains that Lehi was in fact acting in accordance with the Mosaic requirement because the offering of a sacrifice was "allowed only outside of the radius of a three days' journey from the temple in Jerusalem" ("Lehi's Altar and Sacrifice in the Wilderness," *Journal of Book of Mormon Studies* 10, no.1 (2001): 69). The peace offering is described in Leviticus 3.

According to the Mosaic law, the sacrifice is eaten the same day on which it is offered, even if the participants have to feast into the night (see Lev. 22:30). For a more detailed description, read S. Kent Brown's commentary in *From Jerusalem to Zarahemla* (2).

The *sajc* is a short exhortation spoken with fervor, resembling a chant, in which two verses parallel each other (Nibley, *Lehi in the Desert*, 85–89).

A picture of the Valley of Lemuel can be found on the inside back cover of the *Journal of Book of Mormon Studies* 8, no.1 (1999).

CHAPTER 7

Scriptures referenced: 1 Nephi 2:16, 19–24

Women would not have been able to read during this era. Charles Doughty reveals that "most of the men are lettered, but not all; children learn only from their fathers" (*Travels in Arabia Deserta*, 1:186).

Nibley details Lehi's political power and influence in Jerusalem in *Lehi in the Desert* (11–12). In siding with Jeremiah, Lehi essentially became a traitor to his social class. Even Lehi's oldest sons turned against him (1 Ne. 2:13), just as the sarim had accused Jeremiah of treason (see 1 Ne. 7:14).

CHAPTER 8

Scriptures referenced: 1 Nephi 3:2–7, 15–20

CHAPTER 9

Scriptures referenced: 1 Nephi 3:24, 29, 31; 4:1–3, 5; Alma 10:3

Nibley tells us that every man in the Middle East carries a stick by which to assert authority over his inferiors. Therefore, it was typical for Laman and Lemuel to beat their younger brothers with a stick to show their angry dominion (*Lehi in the Desert,* 69–70).

CHAPTER 10

Scriptures referenced: 1 Nephi 4:13, 32–34

More than a dozen years before Lehi's call to be a prophet, King Josiah rid the kingdom of sacred tree worshiping and many heathen religious practices. But after Josiah's death, King Jehoiachin allowed them to creep back. Thus, during King Zedekiah's reign, immorality and unrighteousness were present again in full force, including idolatry (worshiping foreign deities such as *Aseherah*), hill-worship (sacred trees or groves), heathen religious practices (burning incense), all manner of immorality (sacred prostitution), and unrighteousness. Through Lehi's contemporary, Jeremiah, the Lord accuses the priests, princes, and elders of many corrupt and abominable practices (*Old Testament Student Manual: 1 Kings–Malachi* [Religion 302 Student Manual, 1982], 235–37).

The *marzeah* was not only a social institution, but also a religious one centering around funerary banquets. Jeremiah was forbidden to enter the *bet marzeah* (see Jer. 16:5), and Amos condemned the *marzeah* of Samaria because they were socioeconomic oppressors of the people (see Amos 6:4–7). Theodore J. Lewis acknowledges the connection of the *marzeah* banquets with funerary but thinks they were mainly occasions to justify heavy drinking (*Cults of the Dead in Ancient Israel and Ugarit* [Atlanta: Scholars Press, 1989], 82). Scholars such as John Sorenson suggest that Laban was out at night with the elders, participants of the *marzeah* group, and that the requirement of the brass plates at the meeting was plausible—they may have been honoring dead heroes or ancestors, etc.

Nibley describes the sword (*khanjar*) that Laban would have carried as being one of the famous Damascus blades with a hilt of pure gold (*Lehi in the Desert,* 107–108). He also informs us that an oath made among desert people is considered sacred. In order to be binding, an oath should be made by the life of something (103).

CHAPTER 11

Scriptures referenced: 1 Nephi 5:4–5, 8, 11–15, 18–19; Leviticus 1:4

Lehi's family engaged in several types of sinning that required a burnt offering. Laman and Lemuel had murmured about collecting the brass plates, beaten Nephi and Sam with a stick, and murmured after the angel appeared. Also, Sariah complained against her husband and questioned the Lord's commandments (Brown, *From Jerusalem to Zarahemla*, 3–6). Brown also theorizes that the burnt offering may have applied to Nephi as well. With the killing of Laban, Lehi's family would have found themselves in unfamiliar territory, and they wouldn't want to risk that this deed would somehow tarnish the family (*Voices from the Dust*, 9). As illustrated in the Book of Omni, we see what would have happened to Lehi's family if Laban had not been slain and the records taken into the wilderness. The people of Zarahemla left Jerusalem at the time of Zedekiah's capture, journeyed through the wilderness, and crossed the waters like Lehi's family, but they had brought no records and thus experienced many wars and the corruption of their language (Omni 1:15–17).

The Mosaic law specifies that turtledoves or pigeons should be used in burnt offerings, but wild ones were also acceptable (Jacob Milgrom, "Leviticus 1–16," *The Anchor Bible*, William Foxwell Albright and David Noel Freedman, eds. [New York: Doubleday, 1991], 762).

CHAPTER 12

Scripture referenced: 1 Nephi 5:20

CHAPTER 13

Scriptures referenced: 1 Nephi 7:1–2, 4

Mohar (or *moher*) is the custom of the groom giving his future parents-in-law a present or bride price ("Dowry," *Encyclopedia Judaica*, 185). The value of the gift varied according to the wealth of both families. Gifts may include jewels of silver and gold for the bride and precious things or money for the parents (Gen. 24:53). Gifts could also include land and water or springs (Josh. 15:18–19; Judg. 1:15; see also W. O. E. Osterley, "Jewish Marriage in Ancient and Modern Times," *Church Quarterly Review* 106 [1928]: 89–104).

CHAPTER 14

Scripture referenced: 1 Nephi 7:5

CHAPTER 15

Scriptures referenced: 1 Nephi 7:6, 8

Ishmael wouldn't have been wealthy enough to afford camels for everyone to ride. After baggage, the men and the children would have taken precedence. Healthy women would be the least likely to ride.

Hugh Nibley parallels Nephi's experiences with those described by the desert poet Rubah. He explains that an Arab who leaves one's enemy lying in the desert to be devoured by wild beasts was a common occurrence during this time and "no mere figure of speech" (*Lehi in the Desert*, 46). According to Nibley, Nephi's brothers could yield to a woman's entreaties without losing face. Nephi experienced a narrow escape since rivalries between sons of a sheikh commonly led to loss of life (70).

CHAPTER 16

Scriptures referenced: 1 Nephi 7:22; 8:2

Alleluyahu means "praise God" in Hebrew.

CHAPTER 17

Scriptures referenced: 1 Nephi 8–10; Deuteronomy 4:29

CHAPTER 18

Scriptures referenced: 1 Nephi 11–12; Matthew 27:46; Luke 23:21, 46

S. Kent Brown and Richard Neitzel Holzapfel describe Nazareth as being an insignificant village at the time of Christ. Only in later years, when Christianity became the principal religion, did Nazareth become a place of tourism (*Between the Testaments*, 243). Apparently Nephi was either familiar with the city of Nazareth and recognized it, or the angel told him the name of the city.

The translation for *Eli, Eli, lama sabachthani* is found in Matthew 27:46, "My God, my God, why hast thou forsaken me?"

CHAPTER 19

Scriptures referenced: 1 Nephi 13–14; Revelation 18:11–18

Bruce R. McConkie states that the great and abominable church includes any organizations designed to take men away from God ("Church of the Devil," *Mormon Doctrine* [Salt Lake City: Bookcraft, 1979], 137–139). For an in-depth study of the great and abominable church, read Stephen Robinson's thought-provoking article "Nephi's 'Great and Abominable Church'" in the *Journal of Book of Mormon Studies* 7, no.1 (1998): 34–39.

CHAPTER 20

Scriptures referenced: 1 Nephi 15; 16:2–5

Nephi's sharpness with his brothers was undoubtedly due to his spiritual fatigue and the devastation of seeing his own descendents slaughtered in his vision. Nephi continues to mourn, even years later, over the destruction of his people as illustrated in 2 Nephi 26:7, 10.

There are numerous biblical accounts of marriages arranged by parents (Gen. 21:21; 24; 28:2) and marriages occasionally arranged with the bride's consent (Gen. 24:5, 58). But there are also several accounts of romantic unions to be found (Gen. 29:20; Judg. 14:1; 1 Sam. 18:20; 2 Sam. 11:2–4; 1 Kings 2:17; 2 Chr. 11:21; see also "Marriage," *Encyclopedia Judaica*, 1027).

CHAPTER 21

Scripture referenced: 1 Nephi 16:6

CHAPTER 22

Scriptures referenced: 1 Nephi 16:7–8

Erusin was the first part of the marriage ceremony, in which the bride and the groom were betrothed. The man gave his future bride a ring or other valuable object in the presence of witnesses. In the presence of these same witnesses, the groom said, "Behold, you are consecrated unto me with this ring according to the law of Moses and Israel." Then prayers, or benedictions, were said over wine ("Marriage," *Encyclopedia Judaica,* 1031). According to Michael Fischer, the patterns of marriage customs are similar between the three major religious groups in the Middle East, namely, Islam, Zoroastrianism, and Judaism. He says that it "apparently stems from quite ancient times since similar terms can be found in the cuneiform texts of Mesopotamia" (*Women in the Muslim World* [Cambridge: Harvard University Press, 1978], 201).

CHAPTER 23

Scriptures referenced: Genesis 48:16; Mark 10:7–8; also Bible Dictionary, "Marriage"

Typically, the wedding festivities would last about a week, as indicated in the story of Jacob and Laban in which guests gathered for a feast and further celebration of the "bridal week" (Gen. 29:22–27). A later reference reveals that Samson gave his wedding guests a week, until the end of the bridal feasts, to solve his riddle (see Judg. 14:12). Due to the unusual circumstances surrounding the marriages between Lehi's family and Ishmael's family, I have assumed that the marriage celebrations would be somewhat condensed.

Ancient Hebrews married underneath a *huppah* or canopy, representing the tabernacle where covenants were made with God ("Marriage," *Encyclopedia Americana,* 18:349). The ceremonial ring is only used for the wedding ceremony. A miniature rendition of a house is built on the ring, representing the creation of a new household.

Even in modern times, the bride wears gold ornaments on her wedding day. Jewelry consists of gold necklaces, silver anklets, gold earrings, bracelets, and a nose ring (Samiha al-Katisha, "Changes in Nubian Wedding Ceremonials," *Nubian Ceremonial Life: Studies in Islamic Syncretism and Cultural Change,* John G. Kennedy, ed. [Berkeley: University of California Press [1978], 180). The Old Testament mentions that psalteries or dulcimers—musical instruments with strings—were typical instruments played during this time (Dan. 3:5). Before the wedding ceremony, tradition included a ceremony of washing ("Urs (Wedding)," *Encyclopaedia of Islam,* 1038), which I believe is a possibility during this particular desert wedding. In Matthew 10:6, Jesus teaches the higher law of marriage.

Kiddushin is the marriage ceremony, meaning "sanctification." Drinking wine from the "Cup of Joy" is still done at Jewish weddings today. In modern society, the wine glass is wrapped and crushed, symbolizing the trials the couple will experience and how they will spend their marriage rebuilding the vessel. The prayer shawl represents the symbolic conjugal covering of the groom over the bride, who turns herself over to his protection. The act of blessing the couple with seven blessings is derived from Jewish tradition called *Sheva Berachot* ("Marriage," *Encyclopedia Americana,* 18:349)

Lehi, a descendant of Manasseh, and Ishmael, a descendant of Ephraim, were prophesied to multiply together on the American continent (Gen. 48:16).

Hugh Nibley emphasizes that Laman and Lemuel may have drawn the conclusion that their father was leading them into the wilderness so he could establish his own colony, and that their younger brother, Nephi, would succeed their father (see 1 Ne. 16:38). The act of leading a group of people, forming a colony, and the patriarch naming it after himself is common in the Book of Mormon and also occurred in Greek and Roman history (Hugh Nibley, *An Approach to the Book of Mormon*, The Collected Works of Hugh Nibley 6 [Salt Lake City: Deseret Book, and Provo, UT: FARMS, 1988], 43–44).

CHAPTER 24

Scriptures referenced: 1 Nephi 16:9–10; 13

Although the name *Liahona* is not used until Alma 37:38, the word means "compass" or "director." Therefore, we can assume that is what Lehi and his family may have called it.

The Hiltons describe the chain of wells that dot the Red Sea coast in *Discovering Lehi*. At this point in the journey to Shazer, the wells may have been approximately eighteen to twenty-six miles apart (16). The Hiltons list some of the wild animals in the area in which Nephi and his brothers may have hunted, including wild asses, gazelles, oryx, ibex, reem, pigeons, grouse, partridge, wild cows, and hares (113).

S. Kent Brown explains the possibilities for the location of Shazer in "New Light From Arabia on Lehi's Trail" (*Echoes and Evidences of the Book of Mormon*, 77–79). Hugh Nibley defines *Shazer* as "trees" or "clump of trees" (*Lehi in the Desert*, 78–79).

CHAPTER 25

Scriptures referenced: 1 Nephi 16:14, 18, 23, 25–26

George Potter and Richard Wellington inform us that temperatures along the Frankincense trail would have reached over 120 degrees Fahrenheit by late spring (*Lehi in the Wilderness*, 98). The Hiltons point out that the humidity in the vicinity of Jiddah averages between 60 and 92 percent. With the combination of heat, salt, and sand, even steel will self-destruct (*Discovering Lehi*, 112). Slings woven of goat hair were worn as belts around the waist. They were made of two long straps and connected with a woven pouch about three inches wide (113).

The Atim is an olive tree found in the Asir and Jijaz Mountains. George Potter and Richard Wellington suggest that Atim was probably the type of wood used by Nephi to make his bow. As described by archer H. Walrond in *Lehi in the Wilderness*, characteristics of a good bow include a close-grain wood—free from knots and pins (99–100). The Hiltons indicate that the pomegranate wood is also a likely candidate. It is close-grained, limber, and tough, ideal for a wooden bow (*Discovering Lehi*, 112–13). George Potter and Richard Wellington also suggest that the Bishah oasis was a likely location for the Camp of the Broken Bow (*Lehi in the Wilderness*, 95–98).

Mereesy is dry milk, resembling chalk, and is rubbed in desert water to create a drink. In the Arabian oases, *mereesy* is valued, especially during the summer months when it accompanies the unwholesome diet of dates (Doughty, *Travels in Arabia Deserta*, 1:304).

CHAPTER 26

Scripture referenced: 1 Nephi 16:30

SELECTED BIBLIOGRAPHY

Brown, S. Kent. *From Jerusalem to Zarahemla.* Salt Lake City: Bookcraft, and Provo, UT: Religious Studies Center, Brigham Young University, 1998.

———. *Voices from the Dust: Book of Mormon Insights.* American Fork: Covenant Communications, 2004.

Brown, S. Kent, and Holzapfel, Richard Neitzel. *Between the Testaments: From Malachi to Matthew.* Salt Lake City: Deseret Book, 2002.

Doughty, Charles. *Travels in Arabia Deserta.* 2 vols. New York: Random House, 1936.

Hilton, Lynn M., and Hilton, Hope A. *Discovering Lehi.* Springville, UT: Cedar Fort, 1996.

Nibley, Hugh. *An Approach to the Book of Mormon.* The Collected Works of Hugh Nibley 6. Salt Lake City: Deseret Book, and Provo, UT: FARMS, 1988.

———. *Lehi in the Desert.* The Collected Works of Hugh Nibley 5. Salt Lake City: Deseret Book, and Provo, UT: FARMS, 1988.

Potter, George, and Wellington, Richard. *Lehi in the Wilderness.* Springville, UT: Cedar Fort, 2003.

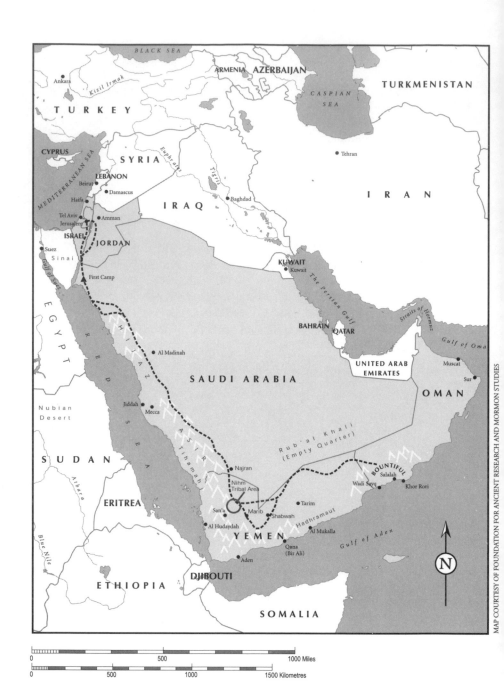

DATE DUE